MW00574220

JAKE: BOOK THREE

JAKE UNDERSTOOD

JAKE: BOOK THREE

NEW YORK TIMES BESTSELLING AUTHOR
PENELOPE WARD

First Edition, March 2015
Copyright © 2015 by
Penelope Ward

This book is a work of fiction. All names, characters, locations, and inci-
dents are products of the author's imagination. Any resemblance to actual
persons, things living or dead, locales, or events is entirely coincidental.

Formatting by Elaine York, Allusion Publishing
www.allusionpublishing.com
Cover by RBA Designs
Cover Photography by PaperbackModel (PBM)

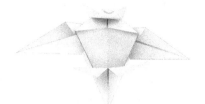

ONE
PRESENT

The sound of the door slamming replayed over and over in my head.

My wife walked out on me.

Seven hours and thirty-five minutes had passed to be exact since she'd left, but it felt like an eternity. She said she'd come back when she cleared her mind but didn't say how long that would take. Nina made two requests before she was gone: not to call her and not to text her.

Not wanting to make things worse, I decided to respect her wishes and spent most of the day staring at the front door from my spot on the couch, hoping that any minute she would walk in and tell me that everything was going to be okay with us.

The truth was I couldn't blame her for leaving. Nina had every right to be pissed at me. We loved each other fiercely and had gotten into our share of fights over the years since getting married, but never had she physically left me. Last night was the straw that broke the camel's back.

This day was a long time coming. In fact, I'd been bracing for it from the moment I first met her. Maybe I was a fool for ever believing that she could handle the situation she'd gotten herself into when she agreed to be with me. It was only a matter of time.

The one bit of good news was that our son, A.J., had been at my mother's when everything went down this morning, so he didn't have to witness it. I had arranged to have him stay there this weekend for a different reason, so it just happened to work out that he wasn't here. I'd told Nina that my mother simply missed her grandson and wanted some bonding time. Ma had picked him up Friday afternoon. Nina had no idea that I'd actually planned a party for her tonight. So, this was suckass timing.

She'd recently finished nursing school after taking several years off to raise our son. I was so damn proud of her and thought it would be nice to surprise her by inviting those closest to us to the apartment for an intimate celebration. Our best friends, Skylar and Mitch, would be driving up to Boston from New Jersey and staying with us for the long weekend. My sister, Allison, and her husband, Cedric, were planning to bring food from Erika's, a dueling piano bar and restaurant on Beacon Hill they'd recently invested in. Tonight was supposed to be one of the most amazing Saturday nights of our lives. It was also why I went to visit Ivy last night—on Friday—instead of my usual Saturday.

That was my first mistake.

A loud knock on the door interrupted my thoughts. My heart began to pound as I leapt up from the couch.

Nina. Baby. You came back.

Nervous excitement transformed into overwhelming disappointment at the sight of Skylar and Mitch standing in the doorway. Apparently, I was so excited to think it might have been Nina, I'd forgotten she would have just used her key instead of knocking. I'd also apparently forgotten to tell them not to bother coming to Boston tonight. There would be no party now. The look of despair on my face must have been instantly obvious.

"Don't look so thrilled to see us, Jake." Skylar stomped the snow off her feet and brushed past me. "We've been in the car for five hours. I have to drop the kids off at the pool stat."

Mitch saw my confused face and clarified, "That means she has to take a piss."

I couldn't help but chuckle at the sight of little Skylar with a baby hanging from a carrier on her chest. Skylar handed their newborn son to Mitch and ran to the bathroom.

I'd known her since she was fifteen, and she'd always been a spitfire. She never held anything back. In that sense, Skylar was like a female version of me, the little sister I never had. It was hard to believe she was all grown up now, but her attitude was the same as always. As much as today had sucked, I was happy not to be alone anymore.

Mitch gave me our usual manly side hug. "How's it going, man? You look like shit."

I patted him intentionally hard on the back. "Thanks, dude. I feel like shit."

Skylar emerged from the bathroom and plopped down on the red couch before taking Mitch Jr. from her husband. "Where's Nina?"

I sat down across from them on the leather recliner and rubbed my tired eyes. "She left...this morning." I swallowed from the discomfort of saying it out loud.

"Where did she go?"

"She wouldn't tell me."

3

Skylar squinted. "What?"

"We got into a fight."

"Hang on." She lifted her shirt and started to undo her bra.

What the fuck?

I instinctively turned my head away. "Uh...do you normally just whip your tit out in the middle of a conversation?"

Mitch laughed. "All the time, actually."

Skylar continued undressing. "Jake, your wife has the biggest knockers on the face of the Earth. I think you can handle some humble side boob while I feed my son."

"A warning would have been nice, that's all."

"I'll keep that in mind." Skylar positioned Mitch Jr. over her right breast, and he seemed to latch on instantly. "Now, spill. What the hell is going on?"

I stared at a picture of Nina hanging on the wall. I'd sketched it when she was pregnant with A.J. Our son was now eight, but it seemed like just yesterday that she was carrying him. We hadn't had any luck getting pregnant again since. First, it was because she was afraid to suffer postpartum depression again, so she wouldn't consider trying for another. Then, after she came around a few years ago, we simply hadn't been able to conceive. My heart felt like it was about to combust as I stared up at the drawing.

I let out a deep breath. "I normally spend Saturday with Ivy. You know that."

"Your ex-wife," Mitch interjected.

I nodded.

I knew he understood the reasoning behind it, but the tone in his voice came off as a little judgmental.

"I needed to free up today and tonight to get stuff ready for Nina's party, so I switched my Ivy visit to yesterday. Because the party was a surprise, I made up a story about Ivy having a problem and my needing to go to the group home last night instead of today. I jinxed myself because when I actually got to Ivy's, they told me she'd been hospitalized. I ended up going to the hospital instead."

"So, why would Nina get that upset? She's used to you seeing Ivy once a week."

"It's never been easy for her, Skylar. You know that. Something was different about her reaction to last night, though. That's what I can't figure out."

"So, what happened with Ivy?"

"The staff at the group home found her trying to climb the roof again and had her admitted. The doctor adjusted her meds and released her this morning. It's the usual routine."

"What happened when you got home last night?"

"That was the problem. I didn't come home until this morning."

Skylar's eyes practically bugged out of her head. "What?"

"I know that looks bad, but there was a storm last night and cars on the road outside of the hospital were spinning out left and right on black ice. They actually ended up closing the road for a while. I called Nina to let her know I'd be spending the night there. Believe me, it was the last thing I wanted to do, and she didn't seem that upset over the phone. I thought she'd understand given the situation."

Skylar pulled the baby off her breast and covered herself. Handing him to Mitch, she got up from the couch and proceeded to smack me lightly upside the head.

"What the fuck, Skylar?"

"I'm sorry. I just had to do that," she said as she sat back down. "Are you insane, Jake? Do you really think there are any circumstances under which it's okay to spend the night with your ex-wife?"

"I told you. They'd closed the road. It was impossible to get home."

"I get it, but you can at least understand that even though you had no choice, Nina still has a right to be pissed about it."

I knew she was right. I had fucked up.

Skylar continued, "Still, though, something doesn't sound right. I could see her being upset, but why would she leave?"

"That's what I'm trying to figure out."

"What did she say when she left?"

"When I walked in the door, she was waiting with her coat on ready to go. She said she needed to get away. I asked if it had to do with the fact that I slept at the hospital, and she came back with 'what do you think?' If I thought for one second she'd feel that way, I would have fucking ice skated home last night. I really didn't think it would bother her like it did."

"Everyone has their limits."

I nodded to myself, feeling like shit for hurting her. It had been almost eight hours, and I missed her so much. I just wanted to hold her and tell her how much I loved her and spend the rest of the night making love to her. But even stronger than that need was the ache in my chest, a deep knowing that there was something more to this than just my staying at the hospital.

Mitch returned from the kitchen with a beer. "Man, forgive me for saying this, but I don't really understand how the hell you do it."

"Do what?"

"Go to see her like you do every week. I honestly don't think Skylar could handle it if it were me."

Skylar rocked the baby to sleep. "It's easy to say that, but people find ways of handling things when they have to. Lord knows, I've handled enough when it comes to us, Mitch." She looked at me. "You didn't ask to be in this situation."

That was why I loved Skylar. She was wise. She understood that I didn't really have a choice. Sure, in life, we're free to do what we want, but when you're trying to do the right thing, there is only one choice. It's not always the easiest choice. Ivy was more like a child to me at this point than an ex-wife. She had no other family and deep down, Nina understood why I couldn't just abandon her, why Ivy needed the continuity of seeing someone who cared about her at least once a week. Nina had always put aside her own needs to allow me to continue to look out for Ivy within reason. That was one of the things I loved about my wife. But I also understood that it would never be easy for her, and I carried a lot of guilt about that. There were rules, though. Visits were only once a week on Saturdays, and if we had a family obligation, that would always come first.

Mitch took a swig of his beer then turned to me. "Did Nina always know about Ivy?"

I bent my head back against the chair, thinking about the days when we first met and the can of worms he just opened up with that question. "No."

Skylar smiled at me. She was one of the only people we were still friends with who also knew us back then. "Jake was still married to Ivy when he met Nina."

Mitch looked shocked. "Say what?"

I chuckled. "You didn't know that?"

"No. I had no idea." He put his feet up on the coffee table. "I'd love to hear this."

"I've heard Nina's version, but I wouldn't mind hearing yours," Skylar said as she walked a sleeping Mitch Jr. over to a portable crib set up in the corner of the room.

I settled back in my seat and crossed my arms. "How much time do you have?"

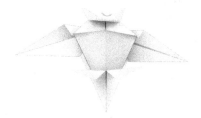

TWO

PAST

The lights of the city illuminated the night sky as I looked out of Ivy's bedroom window. This was always the most peaceful part of the weekend, when she would nap, and I would just watch her sleep before saying good-bye and boarding the late train back to New York City for the week.

Feelings of guilt always crept in right about this time because I'd once again be leaving her alone until the following weekend. There was always too much time to think here when Ivy was either sleeping or in one of her catatonic states. But I'd take these moments anytime over one of her paranoid episodes.

I contemplated what my life had become. It was unconventional to say the least and very hard to explain to anyone. Some days, it felt like there was no one else in the world who could possibly understand. So, very few people in New York knew about these weekends in Boston, knew about my life. You couldn't explain this situation very easily to people in a way that they'd truly get it. The questions alone would make my head spin.

Why do you stay with her, Jake?

How can you fuck other women when you're techni-cally married?

Did you move to New York to get away from her?

The few times I'd opened up to the wrong people about Ivy, I'd regretted it. I didn't need the sympathy or judgment of people who'd never walked in my shoes.

I was practically a kid when I met my wife.

My wife.

I looked down at Ivy's back rising and falling as she slept. We were legally married, but she felt more like a child to me now than a spouse. This wasn't a marriage in the intimate sense or in any way that might make a marriage pleasurable.

Ivy and I met six years ago on Huntington Avenue outside Northeastern University when I was a freshman. She was dancing alone in the rain, and I was instantly captivated. The more I got to know her in the weeks that followed, the more mesmerized I became. She was like no other girl I'd ever met. She played guitar and had some gigs at local venues. As cool as she came off, she didn't have many close friends. I became her entire life. She was impulsive, reckless and had an aura about her that was contagious.

She convinced me to run off to Vegas with her one weekend. Before I knew it, I was eighteen and married by the power vested in Elvis.

Within six months, I knew I'd made a mistake. I truly cared about Ivy, the sex was the best of my life up until that point, and she intrigued me, but I knew that I really wasn't in love with her the way you needed to be in order to spend the rest of your life with someone. Still, I told myself that we could make it work, that I could grow to love her.

Not long into our marriage, things started slowly changing for the worse. Ivy was exhibiting some strange behaviors. At first, it was subtle, like she'd skip classes or not show up for work. Eventually, it catapulted into something beyond my control—something that would change our lives.

Ivy would accuse me of everything under the sun from cheating to plotting to hurt her. She started chain-smoking heavily. She was turning into a different person before my eyes. I didn't understand what was happening, but my better instincts told me she was going to need me even though I was tempted to leave.

Then, on top of everything else, her mother died suddenly. Ivy had no other family except for me. She became more and more dependent, and I became more and more afraid to abandon her in that state. Eventually, it became clear that she needed to be evaluated. I'd put it off, afraid of what the doctors would do to her, but it had gotten to a point where she couldn't even be left alone while I was at work. She'd take off her clothes and roam the street, accuse random strangers of rape, accuse me of rape or devising a plan to murder her. The list of delusions was endless.

I'd heard of schizophrenia but never really understood it. When doctors gave her the formal diagnosis, I read everything I could on it, went to support groups and tried to handle it in the only ways I knew how. Eventually, I had to put her in a group home because I couldn't work and take care of her at the same time.

Some days were better than others. On her best day, a stranger wouldn't be able to tell there was anything wrong. On her worst, I was scared she would take her own life. None of the meds they tried in the early days ever worked, and her illness was considered medically resistant. In the years since, they'd managed to find the right combination to help a little, but it's still not enough. Anything that did work just kept her in a zombie-like state.

I was the one constant in her life. So, while it may have been easy for some people to say I should've left her by now, again, I'd tell them to walk a day in my shoes.

Did I love this woman? Yes. Was I *in love* with her? No. That wasn't reason enough to abandon her, though. She needed my financial and moral support. Staying legally married assured that I could make decisions on her behalf. She needed to feel safe, and I was the only person who could give that to her. So, as her husband, I kept some of my vows. Others weren't so easy.

I had needs.

The sexual relationship with Ivy ended not long after her diagnosis. A few years after she moved into the group home, I began to seek out other women for sex. It was always quick, non-committal, never any strings attached. I'd already resigned myself to the fact that a real relationship based on love wouldn't be possible as long as I was still married to Ivy and caring for her. And that wasn't going to change. No woman would be able to handle it. Ivy wouldn't be able to handle it. So, occasional meaningless sex with women would have to be it.

My thoughts were interrupted when the door creaked open, letting some light in.

"Sorry to disturb you. Is she asleep?" A young Hispanic woman with long black hair down to her ass walked into the room. She looked like she could have been a teenager.

"Yeah, she is. Do you need me to wake her up?"

"No. That's fine. My shift is almost over. I can have Jeri come back in an hour. Someone just needs to give her meds." She held out her hand, and I took it. "I'm Marisol."

"I'm Jake, Ivy's husband. I take it you're new here?"

"Yes. I just started this week. I...uh...didn't realize Ivy was married. I saw your picture on her dresser. I thought maybe you were her brother or something." She looked down at her feet as if she regretted her comment and then glanced back up at me. "Not that she couldn't have...I didn't mean..."

"I know what you meant. It's fine."

I expected her to walk away, but she moved in closer. "Was she always...like this?" This girl was making it obvious that she was new. It wasn't the first time that a staffer hired at this place seemed green. Working in social services, the first rule of thumb: do your job and don't pry into the personal lives of your clients. She'd probably never even worked with the mentally ill before. It was hard to find good staff because the pay was crap considering the responsibilities they had. I guess I couldn't fault her for her curiosity, but it seemed a little inappropriate.

"No. She wasn't always schizophrenic. We met as teenagers. She was..." I hesitated to use the word *normal* and looked over at Ivy's red curls—the one constant—sprawled across the pillow. "She was vibrant, happy then."

Marisol continued to look at me as if she was expecting me to continue, but I didn't. I just kept looking at Ivy sleeping.

"So, when did things change?"

"When she was about nineteen, about six months after we got married. Over the years, she's gotten progressively worse."

"This must be really hard for you."

I really didn't want to be having this conversation with a stranger. Did this chick really think I was going to get into this stuff with her? *Of course, it's been fucking hard for me!* She couldn't begin to understand the road that Ivy and I had been on over the past six years.

"We have our days," I simply said dismissively.

"Well, she's lucky to have you."

I didn't even know how to respond to that, so I didn't.

She continued standing there, clearly unable to read my rigid body language. Then, I could sense her eyes lingering on me and when I looked over at her, she was staring at the tattoos on my arms. She looked up at me with a look I recognized all too well. "I hope you don't mind my asking. Do you have a girlfriend?"

"Why would you ask me that?" I snapped.

"I'm sorry...it's just...you're a very attractive man and clearly a good guy. I just figured...maybe you get lonely. I'm getting off work in fifteen minutes. Would you want to go get something to eat?"

She had to be fucking kidding me.

"No. I have a train to catch."

"A train? Where are you going?"

My responses were getting terser by the second. "New York."

"On a trip?"

"No."

"Wha—"

"With all due respect, aren't you supposed to be working? I'd be willing to bet coming onto a resident's husband is not in your job description."

Marisol walked out without further questioning. I hadn't meant to be that harsh, but she deserved it for treating Ivy like that. Sure, I lived a separate life outside of my marriage and dealt with that guilt. But this girl had no right to make assumptions about the nature of that relationship and to disrespect Ivy right under her nose. Ivy shouldn't have been looked after by people that would take advantage of her so easily.

I felt my heart clench.

Ivy rustled in her sheets as she started to wake up. She leaned up against the headboard and grabbed a cigarette. Her chain smoking had gotten worse over the years. She got up and stood right under the clock on the wall, looking up at it without acknowledging me. She liked to watch the hand go by.

I walked over to her and kissed her gently on the forehead. "Baby girl, I have to leave. I was just waiting for you to wake up so I could say goodbye."

She blew smoke in my face and said, "Don't come back, Sam."

Sometimes, she called me Sam. I had no idea why.

I'll always come back, Ivy…even when you don't know who I am.

On my way out, I demanded to see the house manager to request that Marisol never work with Ivy again. Since I couldn't be here during the week, I needed to be able to trust in the people handling her care.

The blast of cold air outside was a stark contrast to the stagnant air in the group home. I hopped a bus to the Amtrak station and boarded the last train to Manhattan.

During the ride, guilt set in because with every mile closer to my destination, I felt a familiar relief, anticipating the reprieve that the work week always brought. When it came down to it, though, I was trading one place of emptiness for another.

When I approached the entrance to our building on Lincoln Street in Brooklyn, she was staring out the window as she often did late at night. It was like Rapunzel waiting in the wings, except instead of long hair, she wore a scarf tied

15

around her head, and instead of a loving gaze, she gave me the stink eye.

I waved as I always did to mess with her. I knew she wasn't going to wave back, and I knew what was coming.

In her strong Jamaican accent that had become like music to my ears, she said, "Go fuck yourself!"

Right on cue.

I smiled. "Fuck you too, Mrs. Ballsworthy." I meant it in the nicest of ways, and that exchange with my neighbor was always oddly comforting.

Walking up the stairs to my apartment, I shook my head in laughter and repeated to myself, "Fuck you, too."

Yup. I was home.

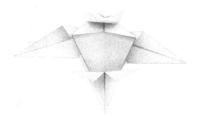

THREE
PAST

Desiree brushed her ass up against me and curled into my pillow. She wanted to cuddle. That meant I needed to get her out of my room as fast as possible.

I immediately got up and disposed of the condom before throwing some pants on. Turning on some music to drown out the guilt in my head, I grabbed a cigarette out of my nightstand and walked over to the window to light it, blowing the smoke outside. Plumes of smoke mixed with my visible breath in the cold air.

I always felt like shit after this, namely fucking someone I didn't care about.

"Jakey, you want to come down to the restaurant for some lunch?"

I turned around to a glimpse of Desiree's bare ass as she rolled off my bed. When she bent down to put on her thong, my eyes caught sight of the purple rose tattoo on her ankle.

Her father owned Eleni's, the Greek restaurant underneath our apartment. I'd gone in there countless times over the past few months, and Desiree always made sure she attended to my small table in the corner. We flirted heavily for a long time, but I resisted making any moves because she gave off a vibe that she was the type of girl who would want more than I could give her (or at least the type that would pretend she didn't and then change her tune).

One afternoon about a week ago, she came right out and told me how attracted to me she was and asked if she could come upstairs with me. She was a beautiful girl with long, dark hair and big brown eyes, and she seemed sweet enough. I hadn't been with anyone sexually in a while, so it was hard to resist a direct offer.

When she started practically attacking me before we even got to my bedroom, I came right out and told her that I couldn't do anything with her if she expected more from me. She assured me that at twenty-one, she felt she was too young for a relationship and just wanted to have some fun. So, I relented.

Twice.

This was our second afternoon rendezvous.

She came over to the window and waved a hand in front of my face. "Earth to Jake."

I looked at her without saying anything and threw my cigarette butt out.

"What's that?" I asked, still lost in my own head.

She wrapped her arms around my torso, and my body stiffened.

"I love your body, Jake. Seriously, it's like a work of art."

I didn't respond, just continued looking at the traffic below. It might have been strange, but I didn't like it when she—or any woman for that matter—touched me outside of sex.

"Did you want to come downstairs for lunch? Are you feeling okay?"

Kind of dead inside, actually. Thanks for asking.

What the hell. I was hungry.

"Yeah. Sure. Let's go downstairs." I put on a shirt and grabbed my keys.

On the way out, I noticed a pink scarf on the floor in the living room that hadn't been there on the way in. It wasn't Desiree's, and my roommate Tarah was at work. Someone else had been in the apartment. Then, it dawned on me that we were supposed to be getting a new roommate today, some chick named Nina from upstate New York. Picking up the scarf, I threw it on the couch and followed Desiree out the door.

I'd gone back into work for the rest of the afternoon after lunch. The shit hit the fan when a major flaw was discovered in one of my designs. The rest of the day was spent trying to save my ass. To make matters worse, Ivy had called me in the middle of it to complain that I hadn't gone to see her the previous weekend when, of course, I'd spent the entire two days with her. My head was spinning.

On the way home, I stopped at the market on the corner and picked out two bunches of bananas. I fucking loved bananas. They were my comfort food. They had to be just right though: yellow with a greenish tip. That meant they'd be sweet, creamy and on the firmer side. An old lady was giving me a dirty look while I made my selection. From her expression, you'd think I was fondling my junk instead of inspecting the fruit. I decided to mess with her, so I took one of the bananas to my mouth, kissed it and winked at her. She clutched her purse, scowled and walked away. That had been the highlight of my day.

When I got to the apartment, I was relieved to find that my roommates weren't home. Given the day I'd had, talking to people was the last thing I felt like doing. I lived with a guy named Ryan and a girl named Tarah. Ryan interned for the district attorney's office and Tarah was a hairdresser for a high-end salon in Manhattan. They were nice enough, but we didn't exactly socialize together. The fact that I took off for Boston every weekend didn't make it any easier to get to know them better. I was pretty sure the two of them were hooking up, actually. I'd be up sketching late at night and would hear him leave his room to go into hers, but I never asked them about it. If I didn't want people getting into my business, I'd stay out of theirs.

I arranged the bananas in the fruit hammock I'd bought a while back then ripped one off the bunch before heading to my room.

Needing to blow off steam, I took out my sketchpad and started drawing yet another variation of my father on his motorcycle. Whenever I felt down, I liked to draw my dad. It made me feel closer to him. My father died in a motorcycle crash when I was five. I'd probably completed hundreds of images of him over the years: riding his motorcycle into the clouds, riding into the sunset. Drawing was my outlet, where darkness spun creativity. It was both a therapy and an expression of sadness at the same time.

I heard the front door slam and then voices in the kitchen. It was Ryan and another girl who wasn't Tarah. *Fuck*. It must have been the new roommate. After my day from hell, it skipped my mind that she was moving in today. I wasn't in the mood to meet her but couldn't exactly stay locked inside my room all night. If I went outside even to grab a drink, I'd have to introduce myself.

I cracked open the door but couldn't get a look at her from where she was standing in the kitchen. All I knew about this girl was that she was a childhood friend of Ryan's and according to him, she looked like one of the Olsen twins. Since I mainly associated the Olsen twins with that show *Full House*, I sort of had this weird vision of a new roommate named Michelle Tanner with puffy cheeks, walking around saying, "you got it, dude."

I smoked a cigarette to gear myself up and was just about to head out to the kitchen when a story she was telling stopped me in my tracks. She giggled as she reminisced with Ryan about an ex-boyfriend in high school who used to write her poems inside of origami birds. Some guy named *Stuart*.

Origami birds? How fucking dumb.

I'm sorry, but I just couldn't help myself. I walked out into the kitchen and laughed. "That is...the STUPIDEST fucking thing I have ever heard."

She jumped a little, seeming startled by my sudden appearance.

I reached out my hand. "Hi, I'm Jake."

She was short, had long, dirty blonde hair and a small pinned-up nose. The only thing about this girl that really resembled the Olsen twins specifically were the gigantic blue eyes now scanning the tattoos covering my arm. Then, she glanced up at me and looked down again quickly when my eyes met hers for a second. You would've thought I was holding a flashlight to her face.

Was I making her uncomfortable?

"You must be Neenee," I joked.

I knew her name was Nina.

"It's Nina, actually." As she took my hand, she finally looked straight into my eyes.

"I know your name. I'm just fucking with you." I smiled.

"Nice to meet you, Jake."

Her hand trembled in mine. I was definitely making her nervous. I just couldn't figure out why.

I decided to break the ice. "So, who is Stuart, why is he making you origami bird poems, and who cut off his balls?"

She laughed. At least she had a sense of humor. And a pretty smile.

A really fucking pretty smile.

"Stuart was my boyfriend freshman year of high school. Ryan decided to bring him up now for no good reason."

"What brings you to Brooklyn?"

"I start nursing school on Monday. Long Island University."

"Isn't that in Long Island?"

I knew where it was.

"No, there's a Brooklyn campus. It's actually not far from the apartment."

"With your fear of subways, that's a good thing," Ryan said.

Wait. What?

"What's this, now?" I asked.

"Thanks, a lot, Ryan," Nina said. Her face was turning redder by the second.

He apologized to her, and she tried to change the subject, but you could tell she was still embarrassed.

I interrupted her because I needed to know. "Are you seriously afraid of the subway or something?"

"She's afraid of everything," Ryan said. "Planes, elevators, heights..."

Nina looked over at me, and whether she realized it or not, the fear in her eyes was apparent.

"I just get a little nervous in crowded, contained places. That's all." She smiled, trying to brush it off.

I nodded in understanding. "It's like a phobia. So, places that make you feel trapped?"

"Yeah, basically."

I got the feeling there was more to this. She might have been trying to downplay it, but her eyes betrayed her, exhibiting a dark honesty that contradicted everything else. Something about the way she looked at me reflected how I felt inside, too. I couldn't explain it, but I experienced a connection with this girl right then. It was like for a moment, she saw through my façade in the same way I could see beneath the fake smile she gave me when defending her phobias. There was a lot more to this, a lot more to her story. And she couldn't begin to know the half of mine.

"Hmn," I said.

She cleared her throat. "So, where do you work?"

She was trying to change the subject. I decided to have a little fun with her.

"I'm an electrical engineer for a company in the city. We design stadium lighting. And at night, I dance...at a male strip club."

The skin on her face pinked up before my eyes. *Bingo*.

"Seriously?"

"Yup." I turned to Ryan. "You didn't tell her she was living with Magic Fuckin' Mike?"

She just stood there speechless. She had this innocence about her that I wasn't used to seeing in girls her age. The effect I seemed to have on her was exhilarating, though. When her face eventually turned from pink to red, I decided to put her out of her misery.

"I'm just fucking with you again."

"You're *not* a stripper?"

"I like you. You're an easy target. It's gonna be fun to have you around."

I walked over to grab a banana and felt her watching me. I bit off the entire first half in an exaggerated way. As much as I loved them, I didn't normally eat them like an orangutan while crossing my eyeballs. I was doing it to get a reaction out of her and enjoyed the suddenly amused look on her face. Her eyes, which were so fearful and sullen moments ago, now seemed to be genuinely smiling back at me.

"I forgot to mention, that's Jake's bushel of bananas over there," Ryan said. "We think he is part human, part monkey."

"You like bananas, huh?" she asked.

"Damn straight, I do," I said. "I fuckin' love 'em. Mmm." Stuffing my face, I inhaled the last half in one big bite.

Nina started laughing as she looked at me like I was crazy. I smiled back with my mouth chock full and started to crack up. I couldn't remember the last time I truly laughed.

When the laughter faded, her eyes lingered on mine, and I felt that strange unspoken connection again that I didn't quite understand. All I knew was that making her laugh was addicting, and I wasn't in such a rush to go back to my room anymore.

I grinned and reached for another banana, my mouth still disgustingly full. I barely got the words out, "Want one?"

"Huh?"

"Want one?" I repeated.

"No, thanks. I'm good."

"I told you Jake was interesting," Ryan said.

Wait. What the fuck was he saying about me to her? Why did I give a shit?

The front door opened, and Nina's attention was abruptly taken away from me when Ryan introduced her to our other roommate, Tarah. Nina and she started talking about girly shit, so I decided to head back to my room.

I tried to get my head back into the drawing I'd been working on, but in between strokes of the kohl pencil, my mind kept drifting back to my new roommate.

How the hell was she going to live in New York City if she had a fear of subways?

I'd draw a little more, and then Nina would pop into my head again.

What the fuck was an origami bird anyway?

I put my sketchbook down, opened up my laptop and typed into Google: *origami birds.*

I chuckled when I saw what they looked like. Then, the nuttiest idea I'd probably ever had in my life popped into my head. I walked over to my desk drawer, searching for construction paper, remembering I'd bought some to make something for my nieces once. The only colors left were yellow and black. I grabbed a few pieces of black and some scissors and went back over to my laptop on the bed then typed: *origami bat.*

I cut a square and folded it into various triangles according to the directions. It took a few tries, but I finally got one that looked halfway decent.

Now, what the fuck to do with it was the question. I wanted to give it to her as a joke, but what would I write in it? I couldn't write a poem to save my life.

What could you write to someone you didn't know? All I knew was that she had phobias and a pretty smile. I knew she was starting nursing school.

I knew she made me feel something.

Then, I thought about the Olsen twins. I didn't really think she looked like them, but I could mess with her about the *Full House* thing. According to Ryan, he'd teased her about it all the time growing up, so she'd get the joke.

I grabbed a silver gel ink pen.

What the fuck were their names again? I typed into my laptop: *Olsen twins.*

Mary-Kate and Ashley.

Okay.

I sat there staring at the paper bat in my hand and couldn't help but laugh at myself. It was official: I had lost my damn mind over a girl.

Scribbling on a notepad, I jotted down different phrases and finally came up with a message.

> *Welcome to the House, Mary Kate!*
> —*Your Stripper Roommate*

That was kind of dumb.

Maybe I would keep it simple. I opened the flap to one of the bat wings and wrote, *Welcome to the "House"* inside.

My door was opened a crack, and I saw her walk down the hall to the bathroom, and soon after, the shower turned on. It was the perfect time to sneak the bat into her room. I started to second guess the generic message. It would seem too serious if I didn't write something funny. So, I grabbed the pen and added something onto the other wing then examined the final note.

Welcome to the "House". ---Jake
How's Uncle Jesse?

Her room smelled like vanilla. The walls were bare and aside from the pink suitcase in the corner, it was relatively empty. A picture of her and some guy sat atop the dresser and made me wonder if it was her boyfriend.

I placed the origami bat on her nightstand and quietly slipped out of the room.

An old Nirvana song played on my iPod. My door was intentionally left open while I lay on my bed. A glimpse of her wet hair caught my eye as she hurried back to her room, and a smile spread across my face at the thought of her finding the bat. It dawned on me for the second time, that up until today, I hadn't genuinely smiled or laughed in ages. At the same time, I knew I was playing a losing game in seeking attention from someone who wouldn't even know who I really was.

I decided to take a shower to try to get my mind off her. Once I entered the bathroom, it became apparent that forgetting about Nina wasn't going to be possible. The leftover steam from her shower filled the room. As I ran the hot water and tried to relax, Nina was everywhere. A strand of her blonde hair stuck to the tile wall. The smell of her coconut lime shampoo saturated the air.

Then, after I stepped out of the tub, a pair of flowery panties lying on the floor caught my eye.

Fuck.

I wasn't sure whether to leave them there or pick them up. A thought crossed my mind that I didn't want Ryan to find them. I didn't know where this was coming from. All I knew was that the thought of him touching her underwear irked me.

Really irked me.

So, I picked them up and took them to my room.

Throwing on some black sweatpants, I decided to bring her the underwear. I knocked on the door, and when she opened, the look on her face proved she wasn't exactly expecting me.

Her eyes trailed the length of my bare chest, and my abs tightened in response. She glanced down for a few seconds at my stomach, which was particularly ripped since I started working out a year ago on my lunch breaks at the office gym. The way her lips parted proved all of my hard work was worth it.

She finally looked up at me. "Ha...hi...what's up?"

A tight tank top clung to her enormous breasts, her nipples protruding through the fabric.

Fuck. Me.

Wearing that, she was definitely not expecting me to knock on her door, and I was definitely not expecting to forget how to breathe. I couldn't even remember why I'd come to her room.

Oh, yeah.

I reached into my pocket. "I found these on the bathroom floor...thought you might want them."

She took them from me, looking adorably embarrassed. Glancing over to the corner of the room, I noticed the bat still sitting in the same spot on the nightstand and assumed she hadn't seen it yet.

As if suddenly realizing that my eyes were making plans for the future with her beautiful tits, she crossed her arms over her chest.

Damn.

"Thanks," she said.

Her face returned to the same shade of pink I recognized from earlier. I smiled in an attempt to downplay the now obvious tension between us. When I felt my dick twitch, that was my cue to step back into the hallway and return to my room. God, I needed to stay away from this girl, or I was gonna be in big trouble.

That night, I tossed and turned as one thought ran through my head like a broken record.

You can never have her.

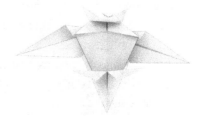

FOUR
PRESENT

"So, I take it you didn't actually stick to your vow to stay away from her," Mitch joked.

"Ugh...no."

I looked down at my phone when a text from Nina came in.

I'm fine. But I need more time alone.

"Is that Nina?"

"Yeah. I promised not to text her but couldn't help it. I needed to know she was okay. She says she's fine but that she needs more time."

"Time for what exactly?"

I shook my head and gazed out the window. Light snow was beginning to fall outside. "Time to think, I guess...time away from me."

Skylar reentered the room holding a mug. She'd gone to the kitchen to put on some tea and to call and check on their two older kids, Henry and Lara, who were staying with Mitch's mom back in New Jersey. Henry was Mitch's son, and Lara was adopted. So, Mitch Jr. was their first biological child together. His birth was a really big deal because Skylar was told she might not ever be able to have children after cancer treatments for lymphoma in her teens. Thankfully, she was in remission now.

"What did I miss?" she asked.

"Nina just texted. She's fine but says she needs more time to be alone."

"Do you want me to call her?"

"No. I know my wife. That would annoy her even more if she thought I got you involved. She doesn't even know you're here, remember?"

"Okay. Let me know if you change your mind."

"She just needs to blow off steam. It'll be okay. She'll come back tonight."

That was what I kept telling myself at least. Truthfully, her walking out scared me shitless. It made me afraid that even after all this time, Nina had finally figured out that she could have done better and that she deserved better.

Sporting fuzzy socks, Skylar kicked her feet up on Mitch's legs. "So, we need to get back to this story."

"Yeah, Jake," Mitch said. "What happened after she moved in?"

"Oh, this is the best part." Skylar laughed. "This was where the quote end quote *tutoring* started."

"Hey, I took it very seriously." I smirked. "I wanted to help her pass math."

"You wanted to help *yourself* to her Pootang."

Skylar always made me laugh.

I chuckled. "Maybe. But at the time, I never thought I'd have a real chance at that. I was really trying like hell to keep it platonic just so I could be around her."

Skylar turned to Mitch. "They came up with this bet that if she got below an A on her math exams, she would have to let Jake take her out to face one of her irrational fears."

Mitch nodded as he rubbed Skylar's feet. "So that brought you closer."

"You could say that."

FIVE
PAST

Holy shit. It was show time.

Nina had gotten a C+ on her first exam. That was actually way better than I thought she'd do given our tedious first study session.

A few days after she moved in, we shared a beer in the kitchen. I'd been home for lunch when she walked in after her first day of classes. (Alright, so I came home in the hopes that I'd run into her.) I'd been gone all weekend to Boston and hadn't been able to stop thinking about her. Even though she was still acting shy around me, she was really easy to talk to, and I enjoyed her company.

We got to chatting about her troubles in math, a subject she needed to pass as part of her nursing curriculum. Math was so easy for me, so I offered to tutor her. Then, the brilliant idea of a bet popped into my head. She'd have to get an A on every exam or face one of her phobias. Fear, after all, is a master motivator. If she didn't accept the bet, I told her I'd renege my offer. It was a win-win situation: either she excelled in math or started overcoming things that were preventing her from fully experiencing life.

Since she feared several things—heights, subways, planes, enclosed spaces, crowds—it took me a while to figure out where to start. But by the time the grade came in, I was ready.

That's how I ended up in the granola aisle of Trader Joe's.

I wanted to ask the sales clerk what she recommended, but what exactly would I say? *Excuse me. I was wondering if you could recommend some light fare that might complement trapping someone in an elevator and torturing them?*

I second-guessed my choices as I stood in the checkout line, but it was too late to go back since I was already running late.

Prime example: hummus. Nothing like garlic breath in a small, enclosed space.

Genius, Jake.

Unsure of how she was going to react to my plan, my heart was pumping the entire way home. It was really more out of excitement, because it would be the first time we'd hung out together outside of the apartment.

Okay, apparently, I had no clue what I was really getting myself into.

Nina wouldn't even look at me as we walked side by side down Lincoln Street. She was really freaking out about this, and I needed to assure her that everything would be okay. I stopped suddenly while she kept walking ahead of me oblivious. When she noticed I was no longer beside her, she turned around.

"Why did you stop?" she asked.

I walked toward her and placed my hands firmly on her shoulders, causing her to wince. I wasn't sure if it was because she was nervous or because it was the first time I'd ever touched her outside of our initial hand shake. It was colder out than I anticipated, and neither of us were wearing jackets. The wind blew the blonde strands of her hair around wildly. She had some beautiful hair.

I rubbed my hands firmly along her shoulders to warm her. The need to comfort her was enormous, but I'd recently studied up on cognitive behavioral and exposure therapy and knew it was necessary to be firm today so that she wouldn't back out. "Nina, I can tell you're going through all these little scenarios in your head right now. It's not helping. The only thing that is ever happening to you is what is happening in the moment, not all of the disastrous possibilities in your mind. So, cut the shit, okay? I'm not going to let anything happen to you."

When we arrived at the DeKalb Avenue subway station, it took some prodding to get her to descend the stairs. I stood down a few steps into the dark stairwell looking up at her as she stayed on the sidewalk. The fear in her eyes was palpable. My heart began to beat faster, and I wasn't sure if it was because I was nervous for her or because of how heart-stoppingly pretty she was as she looked down at me with the sunlight in her hair.

Lifting my hand toward her, I willed her to come to me. "Nina, come on. I've got you."

I continued to silently urge her forward with my eyes. *I've got you.*

When she slowly moved toward me, the second she was close enough to touch, I took her hand and wrapped her fingers inside mine. I couldn't remember the last time holding someone's hand triggered that kind of reaction in me, a sensation I could feel from my head to my feet and everywhere in between.

My hand squeezed hers tightly as I led her down the stairs. Even though I didn't want to, I had to let her go in order to pay the fare.

The faint smell of urine lingered in the air as we sat down on a bench to wait on the platform. The sounds of a man playing the saxophone echoed through the station. When the approaching train screeched to a halt, I grabbed her hand again and led her into the crowded car.

It was the middle of the evening commute, so there were no seats. Her body started to shake as soon as the train doors slid closed. I wanted to hold her, but that probably wasn't the best idea for multiple reasons. I had to constantly remind myself of the boundaries that needed to be set for my own good. Instead, I simply rested my hands on her shoulders to keep her balanced.

"It's okay to feel nervous, Nina. You're not supposed to be comfortable. Stop trying to fight it and just let those feelings be there."

As the train swayed, I kept my eyes fixed on her face to make sure she wasn't going to hyperventilate or anything. She wouldn't look at me. Her cheeks were flushed, and her body continued to tremble in fear. I could only take so much before I placed my hand on her chin and forced her eyes on mine. "How are you doing?"

"Fine. I just want this to be over."

My stomach sank. She had no clue what was in store for her next. I felt bad but reminded myself it was all for her own good.

"Our stop is next." I smiled, and for the first time since stepping on the train, she returned it.

"Eighth Avenue," the announcer shouted over the loud speaker.

She seemed to calm down a little after that. When the train stopped abruptly, my body accidentally pushed into hers, and I could feel her soft breasts against the hardness of my chest. An unintentional moan escaped from under my breath. She looked up at me, and I smiled down at her.

Leading Nina out of the train, I joked, "You're still with us. Was that so bad?"

"It was about what I expected, but I'm glad it's over. Can we take a cab home now?"

Crap. She really did think that was it; she was going to friggin' hate my guts.

If it were anything but a crowded city, we would have attracted a lot of attention. Nina looked like I'd taken her hostage as she reluctantly let me lead her through the sidewalks of New York to an unknown destination. Picture this: A tall, tatted and pierced dude dragging around a little innocent looking thing who was practically shaking in her boots. It must have been like watching Marilyn Manson and Laura Ingalls heading toward you down the street.

After walking in silence for several blocks through Manhattan, we'd arrived at our destination, a high-rise apartment building that my friend Vinny from work managed part-time. He'd set it up so that we could have full use of one of the elevators for as long as necessary.

After I introduced Nina to Vinny, she probably figured I was taking her on an elevator ride. What she didn't know was that it would be so much more than that.

The second I pushed the up button, her panic set in. "Jake, listen, I don't know if Ryan ever said anything, but this whole thing...all of my problems...they started in an

PENELOPE WARD

elevator. It was where my first panic attack happened. I was in high school and got stuck in one and—"

"All the more reason to get past that. If you get in one right now, you can help undo the damage created by your own mind."

She grabbed me by the arm. "Please...I'll do anything else but this." The fear in her eyes was like nothing I'd ever seen before.

She looked like she was about to cry. *Shit*. I had really picked a doozy of an inaugural exercise.

The bell dinged, signaling that the elevator had arrived to the ground level. The doors opened, and I stuck my arm inside to prevent them from closing.

The first teardrop fell down her cheek.

"Fuck. Nina, don't cry. Come on, I promise you that nothing will happen to you in there."

It was amazing how an irrational fear could take hold of someone's common sense. She needed to overcome this, and I'd be damned if I let her chicken out. But I couldn't force her to do anything. Ultimately, she had to be the one to make the decision to step inside.

The black backpack I'd brought with reinforcements was weighing me down, so I placed it on the ground, figuring I would need all my strength in case she freaked out on me. I stepped inside and reached my hand out to her.

After several minutes, she finally took it and let me pull her in.

Yes.

Her voice was shaky. "Leave the door open."

"Okay. We can take this slow."

I continued to hold the door open but knew she was never going to tell me to close it. "You tell me when you are ready to take a ride."

38

"I won't ever be ready. Don't you understand? I won't ever be ready for that door to close."

"Then, you need to let me decide when, okay? You trust me, Nina?"

She squeezed my hand tighter. For a petite girl, she sure as hell had a lot of strength when she was clinging on for dear life.

Then, something amazing happened. She looked me in the eyes, and there seemed to be a shift in her expression. I knew it was the exact moment she decided to put all of her trust in me. For the second time since our adventure began, I had to squelch the urge to pull her into my chest.

"I probably shouldn't trust you, Jake, but the truth is, I do. I'm just scared."

If it was the last thing I did, I wanted to eradicate every last bit of the fear that lived inside of this girl. I wanted her to be happy and wanted to be the one to make that happen even if I couldn't understand where that need was coming from.

"Nina, I'm going to let the doors close now, okay?"

She nodded.

Good girl.

I released the button, but when the doors closed, Nina started shaking. I kept with the plan and pressed the button for the highest floor. She caught me off guard when she grabbed a hold of me, wrapping her arms around my waist and placing her cheek on my chest. Every muscle in my body tightened to resist the feelings that were rocketing through me. My heart thundered against her cheek. I looked down to find that her eyes were closed. Her nails dug into my sides, and I silently willed her to do it harder. I wanted her pain. I wanted anything she could give me in that moment and relished her touch even if it wasn't meant to be enjoyed. I breathed in the clean scent of her hair to calm my sensory overload. She likely had no clue that my own body was in flux for an entirely different reason than her own.

My mouth lightly touched her ear when I said, "You're doing good." I looked up at the digital numbers. "Look. We're on fifty now."

She refused to move her face which was still buried in my chest. "Don't tell me! I don't want to know how high we are."

As much as I never wanted to let her go, we'd reached the top floor. I reluctantly backed away from her, my body instantly craving the return of her warm breasts against my chest. "You want to walk around up here for a bit or do you wanna go right back down?"

"Go back down. Please."

"You got it."

You got it, dude.

She grabbed a hold of my shirt again as the car descended. While I was tempted to bring her closer into me, it was better that I didn't because in seconds, I was about to become the most hated man in her universe.

Nina, I promise. It's for your own good.

I took a deep breath and pressed the red button.

The elevator came to a grinding halt, and Nina screamed like a banshee.

"Jake! Jake? We're stuck! What's happening? What's happening?"

With one hand on the stop button, I kept my cool and held my index finger to my mouth. "Shh."

The look on her face transformed from fright to rage before my eyes. "Please tell me...you...did not just stop this elevator?"

"Calm down, Nina. Calm dow—"

Ow. Fuck!

She'd used all of her strength to smack me in the chest.

"The fuck, Nina. Stop!"

I grabbed her hands and locked them into mine, and my glare burned into hers. She couldn't move from my grasp. As much as her whack in the chest hurt, she was now realizing how strong I was and that she wouldn't be able to compete.

"You told me you wouldn't force me to do anything I wasn't comfortable with. I am begging you...move this elevator...*now*!"

If any residents heard her say that, they'd call the police.

Holding her hands tighter, I said, "Nina, calm down. It's okay. Don't you see you have to stick this out? You have to pass through the moment of panic. If you can get past that and see that nothing happens, you can do anything."

I'd done a lot of research in the last several days on panic attacks. There was always a peak where the symptoms got to their most unbearable, but if the person stuck with the situation rather than running, things would eventually calm down once they realized they weren't really in true danger. Most people ran before they got to that point. The cure lied in sticking it out until the end.

We continued to argue back and forth until she started to hyperventilate. I wanted her to know that the choice was still hers. I moved in closer and placed my hands on her face. "Look at me." I ran my tongue ring across my bottom lip. As crazy as she was acting, I ached to taste her mouth. I wished it were possible to kiss the fear right out of her. Instead, I simply said, "If you make me push that button, the deal's off."

"Fine...deal's off...do it. Now."

Well, that backfired.

I repositioned myself in front of the panel of buttons to block it and decided to firm up my stance. I crossed my arms. "No."

"Jake...push the button."

"No. You'd be back at square one. You have to get over this, and the only way is to experience it. I'm not letting you give up that easily."

She screamed out in frustration and punched the back wall.

"Fuck me! I can't believe this," she said.

Believe me, I'd give anything to know what it felt like to fuck you, Nina.

I joked, "Well, that's one way we could pass the time, but I don't make a habit of doing that with women in the midst of a hyperventilation episode. It's too confusing... hard to tell what's actually causing the heavy breathing."

"Very funny."

I told her I was kidding just in case she didn't get my sense of humor. She ended up crawling down onto the floor in a fetal position next, and that was when I knew it was time to implement phase two.

Her head was in between her knees, so she didn't see me open the backpack. I figured I'd start this party off with a bang. I reached into the bag and pulled out the bottle of champagne I'd brought and prepared to open it.

Here goes nothing.

When the cork flew into the air, it let out a loud pop. Foam shot out and landed all over my plaid shirt. I couldn't help but crack up when I saw the look on Nina's face.

"Jake! What the hell? What THE hell?"

I lifted the bottle. "We're celebrating!"

"You are sick!"

"We are celebrating your survival, Nina! It's been twelve minutes and thirty-three seconds since this elevator stopped, and you're still alive."

I took out two champagne flutes and a picnic blanket I'd brought, nearly hitting her in the face as I fluffed it out and spread it on the elevator floor.

"What are you doing?"

"What does it look like we're doing? We're having a picnic."

I took out the rest of the delicacies I'd bought from Trader Joe's and placed them on the blanket along with my iPod.

"You are not serious!"

"Dead serious. We need to change your negative connotation of elevators. The last time you were in this situation, you associated it with darkness and misery. Now, the next time you get stuck in one, you'll think of the amazeballs picnic we're gonna have."

I poured the champagne and handed her one. She refused to take it.

"You're being a jackass."

"You can take it, or I can drink it all. Then, you'll just be stuck in this elevator with a *drunk* jackass."

I pretended to enjoy the food a little too much while she looked at me as if I were certifiable. There was no rhyme or reason to the assortment I'd selected: Wasabi peas, chocolate-covered cherries, sesame crackers, children's *animal* crackers, hummus. I'd been just trying to get the hell out of the grocery store, but now, in looking at the random stuff I'd picked, it was almost comical.

After several minutes, to my surprise, she started to sample some of the food and had downed her first glass of champagne.

43

Cute little lush.

My plan to take her mind off her symptoms was working. So, now it was time to implement phase three.

I took my iPod, connected it to a speaker and scrolled down to a very special playlist I'd spent most of the previous night putting together.

The first song was *Free Fallin'* by Tom Petty. You should've seen the look on her face when she realized what I was up to. Then, a tiny miracle happened. For the first time since this excursion began, Nina truly laughed, and I followed suit, so relieved to hear that beautiful sound coming from her mouth.

"Nina Kennedy. Is that a laugh I hear? Are you seriously making light of this dangerous and life-threatening situation we are in? Shame on you!"

Then, she threw a cherry at me.

Fuck yeah.

This was exactly the reaction I was hoping for. She was so caught up in the ridiculousness of this situation, she'd forgotten to obsess about her anxiety, and it was no longer building up.

"Jake, you are nuts, you know that?"

"Oh! Speaking of nuts..." I reached into the bottom of my backpack for something I'd forgotten to put out. "You need to sample *my* nuts, Nina. Try these."

I'd fully intended to embarrass her, and it had worked. God, it was so easy. "Why are you blushing?" I asked.

"I don't want to taste your nuts, thanks." She smiled.

She was playing along. What a rush. Now that I knew she appreciated sexual innuendos, I'd have to make a note to throw some more at her. It would be worth it just to see her cheeks light up into that beautiful shade of pink. I had to shake my dirty mind from wondering what other beautiful shades of pink hid beneath her clothes.

I handed her the container of chocolate-covered nuts, and we continued to just enjoy the music together.

"So, Nina, what's been your favorite part about today so far?"

"Hmm...let's see. There were lots," she said facetiously. "But I think number one goes to...pissing my pants a little when you popped the cork, causing me to actually believe for a moment that the elevator had exploded into a ball of fire. Thanks for that."

"That's what I'm here for, Kodak moments like that."

"I appreciate it."

"Nina?"

"Yeah?"

"Next time, I'll pack some spare underwear in the back pack for you."

Just like that, another chocolate-covered Bing cherry flew at my face.

I was feeling a little buzzed, and it made me want to flirt with her. "You're lucky you're cute when you're losing oxygen."

She didn't respond.

Then, she started to laugh when *Stuck in the Middle with You* by Stealer's Wheel came on.

"You like that, huh?" I asked.

"You're crazy...but you know what? I'm not panicking anymore, so there is something to this."

I winked at her. "Good girl." I realized I'd said it in an overtly sexual way that made her blush again.

We stopped talking for a bit and just lay in silence as the music played. Nina closed her eyes, and I decided to do the same. It hit me how exhausting the day had been. I had no clue what time it even was although it didn't matter, because this was exactly where I wanted to be. I was in no rush to go back to reality.

My eyes opened at one point, and hers were still closed. This time, it wasn't out of fear. She looked almost peaceful, and I gave myself a mental pat on the back. It was the first time I could really stare at her without her knowing. Nina was more naturally beautiful than the handful of women I'd been with in recent years. With smooth, milky skin, she didn't need an ounce of makeup. I had the urge to reach over and tuck a piece of her hair behind her ear.

I shut my eyes, and this time when I opened them, I caught her staring at me. She looked away immediately. I closed my eyes again and opened them ever so slightly, just enough to see her but make her think I couldn't and observed her looking over at me the entire time.

What she really thought of me was a mystery. I felt like she was physically attracted to me, but I wondered if I scared her a little.

I snapped my eyes open suddenly. As anticipated, she whipped her head away from me.

I decided to mess with her. "Have you had your fill?"

"Excuse me?"

"Should I put this stuff away?"

A look of relief washed over her face when she realized I wasn't referring to her ogling me. "Oh...yeah...um... yes."

Just as I was done putting the food away, my own nerves kicked in when a song I'd originally debated not adding to the playlist came on. I'd been specifically looking for songs about elevators last night when a tune called *Stuck in the Elevator* came up in my search. Whereas all the other songs I'd picked were meant to be funny, this one was slow, serious and almost hypnotizing. The words conveyed what I couldn't have known last night but exactly what I was feeling right now: that somehow being here with her in this moment felt meant to be.

With my back against the wall, I shut my eyes again and wondered if she was getting the meaning of the song.

Her soft voice startled me. "Who sings this?"

"It's a song I found online called *Stuck in the Elevator* by Edie Brickell. You like it?"

"Yeah. I do."

"Good."

"You're still insane, though," she said quietly.

I opened my eyes to find her mouth spread into the most beautiful smile she'd given me yet. It should have felt good, but instead, it triggered a feeling of dreadful longing inside my gut.

I had a crush on her—like a fucking kid. I couldn't remember the last time I felt like this. Forced to grow up too fast, my teenage years before Ivy were all a blur. I definitely couldn't recall feeling anything remotely similar before. If I were that teenager, life would be simple and nothing would be holding me back from pursuing her. Instead, I was a twenty-four-year-old legally married man playing a dangerous game with my heart. Getting closer to her, knowing that we couldn't ever really be together was a bad idea.

Two voices in my head seemed to be competing with each other as the song continued to play.

The voice of reason was the loudest: *Don't think for a second this girl could ever accept your marriage to Ivy. After you help Nina through this shit, you need to stay the fuck away from her. You hear me?*

Deep beneath that voice, was a weaker one that I was pretty sure lived in an insane asylum somewhere inside my heart. That one seemed to come out with a single message whenever I would lay eyes on her: *Maybe there's a way.*

~~

After we returned home that night, Nina knocked on my bedroom door which was half-way open.

I straightened my back against the headboard and put aside my laptop. "Come in."

She walked over to the bed and sat at the edge of my feet.

"I just want to thank you again for today. I know I must have seemed like a crazy person for a while there."

I shrugged jokingly. "No...no. Not at *all*."

I winked.

She smiled.

I smiled back.

Our eyes locked for a few tension-filled seconds before she looked away. We sat in silence until she looked up at me again. The expression on her face turned serious.

"No one has ever done anything like that for me, Jake. I mean, you put so much thought into it."

Shaking my head, I said, "It was nothing. If anything, it was fun for me."

She covered her face. "I hit you, for Christ's sake!"

I joked, "Eh. Not the first time a woman has hit me in the heat of the moment. Usually, I'm handcuffed and blindfolded, though."

I winked again.

She smiled again.

I smiled back again.

Nina leaned in a little, causing my pulse to race. "You put yourself through all of that, knowing damn well that I was gonna freak out on you. I mean, what was in it for you?"

You.

You were in it for me.

"What was in it for me?" I sat up and moved closer to where she was sitting on the bed and scratched my chin. "I got to watch you go from living in an imaginary place to living in the present. I was able to share it with you because you trusted me. It's exhilarating for me to know I could show you how to live in the moment...because that's all there ever is, Nina. So much stress could be eliminated if we all learned to do that."

She nodded to herself, taking in my words. "This moment...right now...us sitting here....that's all there is. I have to keep reminding myself of that. It's easier to do when someone who is centered is guiding you through it. No one's ever held my hand through anything like that. Thank you again."

"Don't worry about it."

"You know, everyone at home thinks I'm crazy. They never take my anxieties seriously. My parents, my ex-boyfriend..."

Ex-boyfriend.

I wanted to kick this guy's ass, whoever he was. *Fucker.*

It was the perfect window to ask what I'd been wondering since she moved in.

"Is that the guy in the picture in your room?"

Nina shook her head. "No. No, that's my brother."

My heart started beating faster. "You don't have a boyfriend now?"

"No."

Relief coursed through me even though I had to remind myself that it shouldn't have mattered since I wouldn't be pursuing her.

I felt my dick move as her gaze travelled down my shirtless chest and down lower to my six-pack. My pulse quickened when she reached out her hand and placed it over the dragon tattoo on my left forearm.

"What is that?"

My arm tingled from her touch, which felt electric. At any given moment, I felt seconds away from grabbing her shirt and pulling her into a deep kiss. I wanted that so desperately.

I cleared my throat. "It's a dragon."

"I couldn't tell at first if it was a seahorse or a dragon."

"Definitely not a seahorse." I laughed and looked down at her dainty hand on my arm. "You know, long after I got this, I read something once that the dragon is apparently a symbol of strength and power. It also said that the power of the dragon must be balanced with wisdom. Otherwise, the greed that comes with that power turns him into a ravenous creature with an insatiable appetite."

Little did she know, that was a cryptic description of my exact dilemma when it came to her.

The tension in the room was thick when she said, "Wow. That's pretty intense."

"Yeah." I touched my finger to her neck. "What's this, a sea urchin?"

When she looked down, I slid my hand up and pinched her nose.

She laughed. "You tricked me."

"It wouldn't be the first time today."

She rolled her eyes. "That's for sure."

Several seconds of silence passed. She bit her bottom lip nervously as I imagined sucking on it. You could tell she had something on her mind.

The words finally came out. "You know, I was really scared about moving here, but it was something I knew I had to do for myself."

"Why did you choose New York of all places? That's like jumping right into the fire."

"As much as it scared me, I've always dreamt of living here. I told myself if I got into the nursing program, then that was the sign I needed to make the move. I felt so out of place that first day, though. I really considered just going back home."

"I'm really glad you didn't," I whispered.

"Me, too." She glanced over at the wall and hesitated. "You make me feel safe. I realize I don't know you from Adam, but what I do know is that I feel more secure knowing you're here. Is that strange?"

Pressure built in my chest. Hearing her say that felt so good and so awful at the same time. She was right. She didn't know me from Adam and had no idea how true that statement was.

You should get out of here, Nina. Please.

I swallowed and said, "No. It's not strange. I like how honest you are. One of the first vibes I got from you was that you wear your heart on your sleeve. You're not afraid to make a fool of yourself, either, for the greater good. That says a lot about a person."

"Thanks...I think?" She smiled and lightly punched my arm.

There was so much more I wished I could say to her, but it all stayed inside of me.

Then, Nina looked straight into my eyes with a permeating stare when she said, "I think sometimes people come into our lives at a certain time for a reason."

That was the truth. I'd always believed that I was meant to meet Ivy when I did because she was going to need me. At the same time, it felt like destiny in a different way with Nina. I just couldn't figure out why the man upstairs would lead me to her if he needed me to take care of Ivy.

She stayed for another several minutes, opening up to me about her first panic attack that happened in a dark elevator during a high school field trip. She just kept thanking me again for seeing her through things earlier but said she planned to spend the rest of the night studying. She wanted to make sure to get an A on her next exam to avoid another excursion for a while. I couldn't say I blamed her.

My stomach felt unsettled because tomorrow I'd be leaving for Boston. It was the first time since moving to New York that I almost considered staying back in New York for the weekend. But I couldn't.

I decided to make Nina an origami bat that I'd sneak into her room when she went to take her evening shower.

I jotted down some potential poems in my notebook before writing anything in permanent ink inside of the bat.

Well, what do you know? I was a poet and didn't know it.

What I almost wrote:

Sorry you pissed yourself.
I hope we're still friends.
Remind me next time,
To pack some Depends.

What I wished I could have written:

Don't thank me for helping you through.
I should be thanking you.
Getting lost in your smile,
Made it all worthwhile.

What I actually wrote:

You didn't run...you saw it through.
Mr. Bat is proud of you.

SIX
PAST

Reality has a way of smacking you in the face sometimes. That weekend, my visit with Ivy was one of the worst in recent weeks and definitely served as a wake-up call.

On Saturday morning, she seemed to be in a great mood, so I decided to take her shopping that afternoon for winter clothes downtown. We were inside Macy's when she started having one of her delusions about me.

Ivy was trying on some sweaters in the dressing room. Nearly twenty minutes had gone by, and she still hadn't come out. She'd only taken in a few items with her, so it shouldn't have taken her that long. Even though I was standing right outside the fitting area, I started to worry that something was very wrong.

The attendant had disappeared, and Ivy wasn't responding to me. My shoulder brushed by a bunch of plastic hangers on a rack as I barged my way in and spotted Ivy's striped socks underneath one of the stalls.

I knocked on the door. "Ivy, what's going on? Is everything okay?"

"Who are you, and what do you want from me?"

Great.

"You know who I am. It's Jake."

"Leave me alone." Her lighter clicked, and smoke started to fill the room.

I banged on the door. "Ivy! You can't smoke in here."

She threw a wool sweater over the door, and it hit me in the face. "Get away from me, or I'm calling the police."

My heart was racing because I knew all too well where this was headed. Needing to calm down, I let out a deep breath.

"Ivy, please open the door."

She started screaming at the top of her lungs, "Help me! Someone help me! He's trying to hurt me!"

An attendant rushed in. "Sir, you need to get out of here right now! This is a women's dressing room. And she can't be smoking in here."

No shit. Really?

"He's trying to kill me!" Ivy yelled.

"Lady, you don't understand. My wife is mentally ill. She locked herself in there, and I'm trying to get her out."

Before she could respond, store security came in and began dragging me out of the room.

I protested, "Someone needs to open that door and get her out of there."

"Take him away. He's trying to hurt me!" she screamed from behind the door.

"Why should I believe you over her?" said the burly man still holding my arm.

This could not be happening to me.

"Look, just give me a minute to call her case worker. I'll let you talk to her. She'll explain."

Gina's number was on my speed dial. She picked up. *Thank God.*

"Gina, I'm at Macy's with Ivy, and she's having an episode. She's telling people I'm trying to hurt her. I need you to vouch for me and talk to the security people here, so they can help me get her home."

The man spent about three minutes on the phone with Gina while the attendant unlocked the dressing room door. Ivy was huddled in the corner of the fitting room and wouldn't move.

When the security guard got off the phone, he turned to the female employee. "Keep the dressing room closed to the public until he can talk her out." Then, he looked at me with a sympathetic expression. "I'll let you handle this. Let us know if you need any help."

My voice was low. "Thank you."

Ivy stayed still in the same corner and was no longer saying anything. Experience told me she needed some time to come down from one of these freak outs.

After several minutes, I bent down slowly and reached my hand out even slower. "Baby girl, we need to get you home. Please."

She had tears in her eyes as she looked up at me. "Jake?"

"Yeah. It's me." I smiled. "You're okay."

Ivy took my hand and let me lift her up. I grabbed the two sweaters that were strewn on the floor and hung them up.

She caught me off guard when she wrapped her arms around my neck. "I'm scared."

The only thing worse than Ivy's delusions were the fleeting moments when she'd become aware of her illness. I couldn't begin to imagine the confusion and terror trapped inside her mind. It broke my heart when she'd look at me, her eyes pleading for help, because there was really nothing I could do to take the pain away.

"Don't leave me. Please don't leave me," she pleaded.

I held her tighter. "I won't. I always see *you*, Ivy. I know who you are. Don't worry."

She began to cry harder onto my shoulders, and my own eyes started to sting. This would never get easier. I had no problem assuring her that I would always be there, though. How anyone with a conscience could abandon someone in her situation was incomprehensible to me. Everyone has a cross. Ivy's and mine were one and the same. I was somehow chosen to help her carry it in this life. I'd always believed that.

We took the Orange Line train back to the group home. It was a quiet and uneventful ride. I stayed with her until about ten o'clock when I left to head home to my sister's house. Allison, her husband Cedric and their twin girls, Holly and Hannah, lived in the Brookline suburb of Boston, about thirty minutes from Ivy. They offered me their spare bedroom for my weekend stays.

Before I got to their door, I turned around, deciding to head to the neighborhood bar around the corner for a quick drink to clear my head. After the day I'd had, it would have to be something strong.

Beacon's Tavern was dimly-lit with a few televisions playing different cable sports channels. It was surprisingly empty and quiet aside from a couple of guys with strong Boston accents arguing over one of the games.

"Vodka straight, please, Lenny."

The bartender poured my drink and placed it in front of me on the counter. "Haven't seen you here in a while, Jake."

"Just trying to stay out of trouble, I guess," I said before throwing back the liquid courage. The vodka burned my throat as I downed half of it in one gulp.

Avoiding the bar had actually been quite intentional lately. My days with Ivy were always long ones. Because of my weeklong absences, I tried to make the most of my time with her. After leaving the group home on Saturdays, I usually went back to my sister's for a late dinner of left-overs then slept. But occasionally, I'd hit the bar, and it usually ended up with my drinking too much. Waking up with a hangover on Sunday mornings when I had to return to Ivy's was not ideal.

Lenny placed a second vodka in front of me even though I hadn't asked for one. "A lot of guys would be just fine with your kind of trouble, pretty boy."

He was clearly referring to the last time I was in here a few months ago when I left with an attractive blonde named Debra. She and a friend were the only two females in the bar that night and were being hit on by pretty much every single patron. At one point, this drunk dude was coming on too strongly, and Debra looked really uncom-fortable. I walked over and pretended to know her, hoping to take his attention away. When he finally got the hint, she and I started talking and ended up getting along well. She was about ten years older than me and in the middle of a divorce. Like me, she said she wasn't looking to get into a relationship but confessed that she hadn't had sex with anyone since her marriage ended.

She asked me to have a night cap with her because her two kids were apparently with their father for the weekend. Debra ended up going down on me within the first two minutes after arriving at her apartment, and we had sex three times. She screamed so loudly when she or-gasmed, they probably heard it at Fenway Park.

She kept begging me to fuck her again, saying no one had ever made her come the way I had. After that night,

Debra wouldn't stop calling and texting me. Even though I made it clear I wasn't interested in getting involved with her, she insisted that she needed to see me again, basically doing a total one-eighty. That was the main reason I'd avoided coming back to the bar for so long since she only lived down the street, and I was sure she'd been back to look for me.

Briefly looking behind my shoulder, I shrugged. "Not interested in getting into any more *trouble* if you know what I mean, Lenny."

Of course, the encounter with Debra was before Nina came into the picture. No other woman had entered my sexual consciousness since. Swirling the remainder of my drink around in the glass, my mind drifted to my roommate again as it typically did lately. I stayed lost in my thoughts for the better part of an hour before throwing a twenty down and exiting the bar.

The rest of that weekend was spent reflecting on the reality of my situation as it related to Nina. It was easier to think straight when we weren't under the same roof. Even if I were to let something happen between us, it would all be a lie. She deserved better than a guy who wasn't up front with her and could never fully be there for her. She deserved better than to be pursued by a married man. Despite the fact that she made me feel more alive than I probably ever had, it was becoming more necessary by the day to distance myself. It needed to start immediately. This was for her own good and ultimately, mine.

Demons by Imagine Dragons played on my iPod as the subway approached my stop back in Brooklyn. It was ironic because the lyrics described to a tee how I saw myself. I was hiding demons, sure, but if she looked closely enough at me, I felt like Nina should have been able to see that they were there. I often wondered why she never asked me what I did every weekend in Boston. It was as if she knew the answer was something she might not want to hear.

As I walked down Lincoln toward our apartment, I thought back to the same time one week ago and how excited I was then to be able to see Nina again. But after my rough weekend with Ivy and the epiphany I had, the approach home tonight was downright painful now that I'd made the decision to stay away from my roommate. The tutoring would have to be it, mainly because I didn't know how to explain my way out of it.

To add to my miserable state, it started pouring rain. I just wanted to get home, shut my door, take off my wet clothes, maybe rub one off and have a cigarette.

Nothing about this night felt right. Even Mrs. Ballsworthy wasn't at the window like she normally was at all hours. Being told to go "fuck myself" was something I'd come to rely on.

A weird feeling followed me all the way up the stairs to the apartment.

Even though Nina's door was closed, longing developed at the pit of my stomach as I passed her room. Not even a minute home, and I was wishing I could see her. This was going to be one of the hardest weeks of my life.

When I turned the light on in my room, my heart nearly stopped.

I stood frozen in the doorway, unsure of how to handle the sight that greeted me. Nina lay sprawled across my bed, her golden hair covering my pillow. My sketchbooks were all over the bed.

What. The. Fuck.

This should have made me livid, but mainly, it just confused the hell out of me. The normal thing to do would have been to wake her up and ask her what the hell she was doing snooping through my things. Instead, I threw my backpack down and just stood there taking in the sight of her in my bed.

Nina was in my bed.

Her beautiful ass was facing me as she curled into my mattress. I moved closer to stand over her and just watched her breathing. She must have sensed me because her body stirred, and then she started to wake up. She jumped up so fast you would have thought I'd lit a firecracker under her ass.

"Jake...I can explain," she said in a hoarse voice.

I was mad at her, not for being curious and snooping, though. I was mad because seeing her in my bed undid every fucking bit of resolve I'd built up on the ride home.

"What the fuck, Nina?"

A small stream of water from my wet hair dripped down my forehead. Everything was still except for the sound of the rain pelting my window. The ability to speak totally escaped me as she continued to look up at me in fear. She thought I was angry at her. If she only knew the thoughts that were floating through my sexually frustrated mind, how I wished I could take it out on her hard in a different way than she was probably imagining.

She started to speak. "Um...a few hours ago, I was alone in the house, and your door was open. I had thought I left the math workbook in here, so I came inside. I noticed these sketchbooks. I only meant to peek in at the top one, but when I saw how amazing the first drawing was...I just couldn't stop looking."

I swallowed hard, knowing that she'd been looking at drawings of Ivy, drawings of my father, even though she had no idea about the meaning behind them. I thanked my lucky stars that I'd nixed the idea of sketching *her* one night last week because she would have seen that, too.

A mental war continued to be waged inside my head as to whether I should kick her out or ask her to stay.

She continued, "I must have closed my eyes and fallen asleep." Her voice was shaking. She reminded me of a shivering puppy. "I am really sorry. I should have never thought it was okay to look at your stuff. For the record, they are the most phenomenal drawings I have ever seen."

My chest tightened at the compliment. Trying to buy more time to think, I started to stack the sketchpads on top of each other and returned them to their rightful place.

"Again, I'm sorry."

She threw me off guard when she suddenly got up from the bed. I instinctively grabbed her wrist to stop her. "Where are you going?"

I guess I'd made my decision.

"Back to my room."

I was no longer thinking with the right head when I pushed her down onto the bed slowly. "Just stay."

"Stay? What do you mean?"

"I mean...you were comfortable here. Just stay."

"You're not mad at me?"

"I didn't say that. You shouldn't have been snooping."

"I know. I'm really sorry."

I'm really not.

My emotions were all over the place, and this situation was weakening me. As she relaxed into the bed again, that was all the encouragement I needed. All I wanted in the world was to feel her body next to mine, and I was going to let myself feel that tonight.

Just one night.

I knew I was lying to myself.

I hadn't noticed whether our roommates were even home. I walked over to the door and shut it so that they didn't spot her in here. Feeling protective of her, I didn't want them to get the wrong idea.

Then, I shut off the light before removing my wet jacket and taking off my shirt. Even though my pants were a little damp, they stayed on because, well, stripping down to my underwear would have been pushing it.

Tomorrow, I told myself. Starting tomorrow, I would follow through with my plan to distance myself from her. But tonight...tonight I just wanted to sleep next to her.

"Scoot over," I said.

She turned onto her side instantly at my command without question. My chest pressed into her back, and her body molded into mine. She was so warm and soft, practically melting into me. I couldn't resist locking my arm around her waist. We were spooning, and it felt better than anything I'd ever experienced with the opposite sex up until that point. It was sensually intimate and more comforting than anything I could ever remember feeling before. I hadn't held anyone like that in years. But never had it felt like this—like home—to me.

Unable to control all the feelings that were emerging, my breathing became heavier with each second. She was being fidgety all of a sudden and made me wonder if she wasn't comfortable. "You're moving around a lot. You okay with this, Nina? Would you rather go back to your bed?"

"No. I want to stay."

Thank God. Because I seriously didn't know how I could've let her go right then.

"Good," I said before tightening my grip on her side to reaffirm my own stance.

I pulled her closer to me and tried to relax, burying my nose in her hair and taking a long whiff of what I imagined heaven smelled like. I breathed in and out slowly onto her neck. I wished I could taste her. I wished I could consume every inch of her.

At one point, she pushed her soft ample ass into me, and I had to reposition myself so that her butt was against my leg and not my dick. Still, the brief heat of her against me made my cock swell. There was no way I could have kept this control while sandwiched in the crook of her ass. Forget what I said about home earlier...*that* would have been home.

I was painfully hard. I hadn't been with anyone since the day I laid eyes on Nina. She had me cock-whipped and didn't even know it.

Her sweet voice startled me. "Jake?"

"Yeah."

"I really am sorry for invading your privacy."

"It's okay, Nina."

"Thank you."

"Nina?"

"Yeah?"

"Your underwear drawer might get rearranged this week. That's all I'm sayin."

My lips were pressed against her back, and I could feel her laughter vibrating against my mouth.

I tightened my hold on her once again and over the next several minutes, her breathing slowed until she fell asleep in my arms.

As tired as I was, I couldn't sleep a wink. I kept thinking about how on Earth I was supposed to ever sleep alone again after knowing what this felt like. The thought of never getting to experience this again made my chest hurt, and the thought of having to alienate myself from her made me grab onto her even tighter.

At one point, Nina moved in her sleep, and her ass once again managed to land right on top of my helpless dick, now straining through my pants.

If smelling her hair was heaven, then my engorged cock getting stuck in this predicament was hell. It was a pleasurable form of torture, though, and I didn't want to move this time. This was my last opportunity to feel her like this, and I was going to relish every second.

I softly kissed her back as she slept, a feeling of dread growing with each minute.

When the sun came up, she was still sleeping while I had to get up for work. I had a raging case of blue balls that would need to be taken care of in the shower, but it was all worth it. Everything about sleeping next to her last night was something I'd cherish for the rest of my life.

I caressed her hair one last time before I had to leave. A fleeting thought made me feel sick inside. But it was reality.

Whoever gets you someday is gonna be a lucky man.

SEVEN

PAST

During the first couple of weeks after our little sleepover, I stayed true to my word. Aside from our tutoring sessions, every effort was made to stay away from Nina. We never talked about the night in my bed. It was as if it never happened.

She would try to get closer to me, and my having to push her away broke my heart. Truthfully, I wanted nothing more than to let our connection grow organically and to see what could have been, but I'd resolved to do the right thing.

The low point of that time was when she'd made me a batch of banana pudding one night. Nina started a conversation about her conservative upbringing and how liberated she was starting to feel living in New York despite her fears. She began asking me questions about my childhood and was really trying to get inside my head. Instead of opening up, I just shut down and changed the subject. I filled a small bowl and ate the dessert as quickly as I could then thanked her before escaping to my room. I felt like absolute crap for eating and running but not as badly as I felt once I realized that after that night, Nina had given up on trying.

My message had finally gotten through to her loud and clear. Aside from the tutoring, she seemed to avoid me completely after the pudding encounter.

Then, one Thursday evening, Nina was late for our study session. She knew I'd set certain rules, and number one was showing up on time. Despite my soft spot for her, when it came to the math, I ran a tight ship and took it very seriously, often coming across as a hardass.

I planned to call her out on her tardiness, both because I wanted her to take the tutoring seriously and also because part of me was craving the attention I lost from her even though I'd pushed it away. Creating confrontation was, at least, an acceptable form of interaction for me. So, when she finally appeared at the doorway, I immediately gave her shit. On this particular night, for the first time, she decided to dish it out right back to me.

"Well, look who decided to grace me with her presence," I chided.

Nina stood in the threshold. Her hair was wet as she clutched her books in front of her chest. She always did this thing where she hesitated to come in, like my room was a lion's den or some shit.

She wasn't smiling. "I got stuck in a line at the market. Then, it started pouring rain. I got here as fast as I could."

The damp smell of the rain lingered on her body as she stood in the doorway.

"You can come in, you know."

She stepped inside and sat on the bed. "Thank you."

As always, I sat away from her at my desk. Something was different about her attitude tonight. It seemed like she was pissed.

I tried to lighten the mood. "You always seem to get caught in the rain, Nina. Why is that? It's like you attract it. "

She paused and looked me straight in the eye. "I guess if the rain is attracted to me, what would that make you then...fire or something?"

Shit.

"What's that supposed to mean?"

"Don't worry about it," she muttered under her breath.

I knew what the fuck it meant. For the first time, she was calling me out on my hot and cold behavior toward her, except now she'd come to a conclusion that couldn't have been more far off. She believed I wasn't attracted to her when my problem was exactly the opposite.

Just when things couldn't have possibly gotten more tense, she took off her jacket. Her shirt was damp, allowing me a clearer view of the body beneath. A vision of pulling on that shirt with my teeth and sucking the water dry off of her beautiful tits caused blood to rush to my dick.

"Are you sure you don't want to change before we start?"

I don't think she knew that I could see right through the material.

"No. I'm good."

Well, I'm not fucking good with this.

I took out a shirt from my closet and threw it at her. "Here. Put this on."

"But..."

I gritted my teeth and repeated, "Put it on."

She looked down at herself and blushed, finally realizing why I'd been so adamant about it. She took the shirt without further protest, and I turned away so she could change.

She gave me the go ahead to turn back around. My breathing was rapid and quickened even further when my eyes landed on her breasts stretching against my shirt. It was the closest thing that I'd have to my body wrapped around her. She looked so fucking hot in it.

I cleared my throat. "We should get started. Show me the assignment."

She handed me the textbook and some worksheets. "It's on probability."

I rubbed my chin and wracked my brain for some ideas. I always came up with lessons of my own in addition to what homework Nina was given by her professor. She always seemed to pay better attention when she could relate to the examples.

Doing something to break the tense mood was also going to be necessary.

Grabbing a notepad, I wrote a few things down before flipping it around and showing it to her. "Okay...probability. One of these things has a greater likelihood than the other: Nina farts in her sleep. Nina talks in her sleep. Nina does nothing in her sleep."

"You're lying."

"I guess we'll find out."

That night, I snuck another origami bat into Nina's room.

What I almost wrote:

You're lucky you're cute,
When you sleep and toot.
And lucky I don't mind,

The silent but deadly kind.

What I wished I could have written:

To your rain, you said I was fire.
If only I could show you my desire.
Then, you'd clearly see,
What it is you do to me.

What I actually wrote:

Rest assured, you neither fart nor talk in
your sleep.
But should you decide to start tonight,
Mr. Bat won't utter a peep.

My plan to stay away from her suffered two major setbacks in the days that followed.

The first was when Nina found out that she got her first A on a math exam. It was amazing but didn't come as a total shock because she'd been busting her butt with studying lately.

She was preparing a Bananas Foster dessert to thank me for helping her make the grade. That dessert was like crack to me.

We were in the kitchen alone together. I was trying to help by peeling some of the bananas, but all I really ended up doing was distracting her. She was looking up at me while cutting and sliced her finger.

It caused me actual physical pain to see her blood pouring out and triggered a visceral reaction in me. There was no towel in sight, so I wrapped her finger tightly in my shirt. Red kept seeping through and without thinking, I placed her finger in my mouth and started to suck the blood out.

Okay. So, it wasn't the most sanitary choice—a little insane maybe.

I just wanted to make it better. You should have seen the dazed and confused look on her face. It was like she was outside of her body watching it all unfold.

It wasn't supposed to feel sexual; that wasn't my intention. But without a doubt, it was stimulating because, let's face it, having anything of hers in my mouth was going to have that effect. It wasn't even so much my sucking on her finger as it was the way she was looking at me when I did it, like she wanted more of what I was giving her in that moment.

By the time I slowly slid her finger out of my mouth, I was starting to get aroused, and I was pretty sure she was, too. Her cheeks were flushed as I removed my blood-covered shirt and used it to wrap her finger again as she looked down at my bare chest. Her lips were parted in that way they always were when she ogled me. She didn't realize I noticed it.

When she pointed out that I had some blood on my mouth, instead of wiping it with something, I intentionally licked it off as she watched every movement of my tongue slide across my lip. I swallowed it. I wanted her in a primal way, and I guess this was my way of expressing that, even though I wouldn't consider acting on it in other ways.

Still, I realized that wasn't a normal manner of showing it. It was a complete loss of control, forever referred to in my mind as the "vampire incident."

The second major setback was what began the process of my complete undoing when it came to Nina.

It was a Friday, and as usual, my bag was packed and ready to go with me at work for the weekend trip to Boston.

I normally hopped a train after my shift ended, but that entire day, thoughts of Nina would not stop invading my brain. I started convincing myself that being friends with her would be better than nothing, especially since I couldn't seem to stay away from her.

Maybe we could be friends.

Famous last words.

I wanted so much to stay the weekend and just spend time with her.

That night, as I was walking to the train station, I impulsively turned around and headed back to the apartment, deciding to take an early Saturday morning train instead so that we could hang out. I would ask her if she wanted to go out and eat or rent a movie. Those were harmless things, right?

I loved lying to myself, apparently.

Dropping my travel bag by the apartment door, I made my way down the hall. Nina's bedroom door was open, and she was standing there looking at herself in the full-length mirror attached to her closet.

My jaw dropped, and my heart pounded as I took her in. A tight dress hugged her voluptuous body. Her hair was cascading down her back in beautiful long curls that almost reached the top of her amazing ass.

She was wearing stripper heels. Nina looked like she'd been kidnapped and done up by a tribe of whores.

It was the hottest fucking thing I'd ever seen in my entire life.

She hadn't noticed me just outside the door, so I moved in closer. Her dress was bright purple, and I decided to make a dumb joke about it since telling her what I was really thinking might have gotten me arrested. "Nina, Barney the dinosaur called. He wants his skin back."

She flinched when she saw my reflection in the mirror. "Jake! What are you doing here? You're supposed to be on your way to Boston."

"Nice to see you, too."

"Well, it's just that you usually leave from work and—"

I lied to her. "I missed the 5:15 Amtrak, so I might either catch the last train at 9:30 or just go in the morning."

"Oh."

She seemed absolutely shocked to see me and quite uncomfortable. Then, she turned around.

She turned around.

Fuck.

My eyes unapologetically went where they needed to go. The dress had a plunging neckline that showed way too much of her massive cleavage. While the back view looked hot, the front view was downright indecent. My throat seemed to freeze. I knew I should have said something but couldn't find the words. No other woman had so much as crossed my mind sexually since Nina entered my life. My earlier conclusion that staying friends was a good idea now seemed ludicrous as I stood there taking her in and praying away my erection. I sure *had* been lying to myself. My mouth was watering for fuck's sake. The truth was...I was starving for her. Only her.

The way her chest was heaving as I looked at her, the way she always reacted to me made me feel like she wanted me that way, too.

I forced myself to speak. "Nina...you look—"

"Interesting?" She smiled in an attempt to lighten mood.

My hungry eyes travelled slowly downward, taking in her tits and the way the material of her dress clung to her taut stomach. Her bare legs looked longer in heels. "That's one way of putting it."

Our eyes met again. She could tell where my mind was. Hell, it couldn't have been more obvious.

"Jake!"

I turned around to see our roommate, Tarah, enter the room but quickly returned my gaze back to Nina.

"Tarah!" I said, mimicking her shocked tone of voice. Understandably, everyone seemed so surprised to see me here on a Friday night. It dawned on me that maybe they were getting ready to go out on a girls' night.

Would it have been wrong to invite myself?

I plopped down on Nina's bed and joked, "I didn't know we were going out tonight, Nina."

"We...are not going anywhere," Tarah said. "*She* is going on a date."

It was like my world stopped spinning when she said it.

My head and ears began to throb as jealousy hit me like a ton of bricks.

Get your shit together, Jake.

I couldn't.

It was impossible to pretend that this news wasn't wrecking me. As much as I'd tried to distance myself, as much as I knew Nina could never accept my life if she knew the truth...in my heart, I believed she was mine. *Mine.* It was the first time the realization of that deluded misconception really hit me.

The only words that would come out of my mouth were, "I see." My hands formed into fists to ward off the anger building inside me. "I suppose he's taking you to the Vegas Strip in that outfit?"

Tarah said something, but I didn't even hear it because I was too busy staring at Nina, this time into her eyes. I wanted to carry her in my arms back to my room and cover her with my body. I had no right to feel this way and knew I needed to leave before I made a total fool of myself since I apparently couldn't hide my jealousy. This had honestly never happened to me before. Maybe if I'd had a chance to practice this reaction when I was thirteen, I wouldn't have been acting like a teenager right now.

"Have fun," I said with about as much enthusiasm as sending someone off to a funeral. "And don't forget a jacket. You're bound to catch pneumonia dressed like that." I couldn't help myself. I guess I just had to stick that in to further solidify my role as a jealous idiot.

Slamming the door behind me, I returned to my room and literally punched the wall. *Smart.* Taking it out on an inanimate object was really going to help.

I sat on my bed and nervously bopped my feet up and down. The silence was deafening as I held my head in my hands while my heart continued to pound. I was angry with no one but myself for letting my feelings for her get to this level. She had every right to be wined and dined by someone. She deserved the best that life had to offer, and I had *nothing* to offer her.

My body remained in the same position with my head down until I heard knocking in the distance. It must have been Nina's date. The thought made my stomach turn.

I got up and peeked out the door, only able to make out bits and pieces of the guy.

Blondish-brown hair. Clean white shirt. Khaki pants. Boat shoes.

Boat shoes. Really? Fucking dweeb.

With my piercings and tats, I was the polar opposite of this dude. If this was the type she went for, then maybe my vibes from her have been all wrong.

When I heard Nina's bedroom door open, I backed away from my own door so she wouldn't see me creeping. Once she entered the kitchen, I repositioned my ear to eavesdrop.

I could hear him complimenting her and felt bile rising in my throat.

I opened the door a crack to see them. You should've seen the way he was gawking at her. I wanted to choke him because it was exactly the way I was looking at her earlier.

Dirty bastard.

Ryan asked them where they were going, and the guy started talking about some Italian place he was gonna take her to. I was sure he had lots of plans up his sleeve for later, too. I was onto him and needed to let him know it. So, I stepped out into the living room.

"She's always wanted to go to Top of the Rock."

All heads seem to turn around at once to look in my direction.

"Right, Nina? You love a good view from the top of a skyscraper. I hear the scenery is amazing, and the food is great."

Okay, so that was a dick move.

Nina glared at me and wasted no time in talking her way out of my *suggestion.* "We can save that for another time. I was really looking forward to that Italian place."

I gave him a darkened stare, sizing him up before walking forward and reaching out. "We haven't met. I'm Jake."

He gave me his hand, which felt easily breakable. Maybe that was because I was practically trying to break it. *I wanted to break him.*

"I'm Alistair."

"Ass Hair?"

I heard him the first time.

"No...Ali-stair."

"Ah...sorry, my bad."

Nina was quick to stop this little exchange. "Alistair, I think we should get going."

I wouldn't take my eyes off her as she got her coat and prepared to leave with him. My actions were a fucked up way of showing her that I didn't want her to go.

Then, she turned around one last time before leaving, and we had what could only be explained as a private moment where time seemed to stand still. I expected that maybe she would have looked angry after the way I'd behaved. Instead, she seemed to be urging me with her eyes, urging me to stop whatever it was I was doing, urging me to talk to her, to tell her how I felt. There were so many unsaid words in that one look. I knew she could see through me and what my antics were really all about. Jealousy was a bitch, and mine was transparent. It felt like a piece of my heart was walking out the door as she prepared to leave with him. My eyes were screaming a million conflicting things back at her, all the things I didn't have the courage to tell her.

You're so beautiful.

No one is good enough for you.

Please stay.

Stay...away from me.

"Bye," I whispered, unsure if she even noticed. In the blink of an eye, our moment passed, and she was gone. But the aftermath of my actions tonight was far from over.

I'd returned to my room all of one minute before Ryan walked in without knocking.

"What the fuck was that all about?" he spewed.

"Ryan! Please. Feel free to just barge into my room whenever you like and shout f-bombs at me."

"Answer my question."

"What was that?"

"What kind of a game are you playing with Nina?"

"Game?"

"Yes. You've been spending all this time with her under the guise of tutoring, playing with her mind. Then, you take off every fucking weekend probably up to some shady shit. Now, the one time she actually goes out with a normal person, you try to fuck it all up."

"*Normal* person, huh? What does that make me?"

"You know what I mean."

"No. Why don't you enlighten me before I vacuum my fucking rug with your face?"

"I don't really know a thing about you, Jake, and I don't care. But that girl is like family to me, and I don't want to see her get hurt."

"Why would she be getting hurt by spending time with me?"

"She's not your type, okay? She's a good girl."

"And how would you know my type?"

"For one, I've seen you with Desiree."

Fuck. Touché.

"That was nothing."

He looked down at the floor then sighed. "Look, Nina told Tarah that she's developing feelings for you. I'm not gonna sit back and watch her get destroyed by some womanizing asshole."

His admission seemed to melt the anger inside of me.

She had feelings for me?

Fuck. She really did have feelings for me.

It wasn't all in my head.

"You don't know jack shit about me, Ryan, or how I really feel about that girl," I cracked.

Tarah walked in. "Hey, what's going on in here?"

"Tell your boy toy to stop making assumptions before he gets his ass kicked."

She looked at Ryan. "Do you mind leaving me and Jake alone for a minute please?"

He didn't move until she gestured her head toward the door. Then, he quietly huffed and exited the room.

I needed a cigarette badly. I took one out and walked over to the window to smoke.

"You know, you have a really funny way of showing Nina how you feel about her. Why don't you just tell her?"

The smoke slowly streamed out of my nostrils as I stayed staring out at the midnight blue evening sky. My voice was barely audible. "I can't."

"I see the way you look at her. I don't know what's holding you back, but I suspect it's not something small."

Understatement of the year.

This conversation was bordering on dangerous. In my periphery, I could see Tarah with her head of short black hair tilted and her arms crossed as she waited for me to say something. I threw the cigarette butt out.

Finally, I turned to her. "She really has feelings for me?"

Tarah looked behind her shoulder as if paranoid someone was listening. "She'd kill me, Jake, if she knew I was talking to you about it. But yes...she does. She has really strong feelings for you, but I'm pretty sure she's giving up, okay? There's only so much rejection a girl can take before she has to move on."

Rejection? It was resistance.

I let out a deep sigh and rubbed my temples. "Thank you. I'd like to be alone, okay?"

Tarah quietly slipped out of the room as I sat on the edge of my bed with my phone in my hands. The urge to tell Nina how I felt about her was unbearable. I wanted to text her but didn't know what to say.

My fingers then seemed to have developed a mind of their own as they typed.

Don't give up on me, Nina.

Erase.

Come home. We need to talk.

Erase.

I'm sorry I was an asshole.

Erase.

Nina, I was a jerk to you and your little friend.

Send.

I'm sorry.

Send.

And the Barney joke was stupid.

Send.

Actually, you looked so fucking hot in that dress, it made me a little crazy in the head.

Erase.

Actually, you looked stunning.

Send.

I lay back on the bed and shut my phone off before I could say anything further. Staying here tonight in my current mood wouldn't have been good. I felt very out of control and worried I wouldn't be able to resist *showing* her exactly how I felt when she came home. I could easily see her coming to my room to talk. I could more easily see me taking her against the wall before the words even came out of her mouth.

Over the next few minutes, whenever I looked at my bedroom wall, all I could see was a vision of fucking her against it until all of the rage inside of me exploded into her body.

Fuck. I really needed to go.

If I left now, I'd still make the late train to Boston.

I wanted to leave her something so that at least she knew I was thinking of her.

I took out my construction paper and folded a piece into an origami bat. Every time I'd start to write a message, I'd change my mind and crumple it, having to make another from scratch. I did this a few times but just couldn't decide what to write.

The more time that passed, the more I second guessed leaving. What if she came to talk to me? I'd never know. For some reason, I just had to know whether or not she'd come to my room when she got home.

Then, a brilliant idea came to mind. I made yet another bat and wrote inside: ***Looking for someone?***

Bunching up some blankets, I attempted to make it appear like a body was inside my bed. I stuck the bat in the middle of the pile, covering it with a comforter and strategically placed a Red Sox cap peeking out from the top.

Stepping back, I cracked myself up because it really did look like someone was sleeping in there. I made a note of exactly how everything was configured. If she messed it up even by an inch, it would be obvious that she came to see me. At the very least, the thought of freaking her out was amusing. Seeing the look on her face would have been priceless.

It was now completely dark out, and there was only a small window to get to the train station in time. Desiree was exiting the restaurant when I stepped outside. I tried to pretend I didn't see her.

"Jake! Wait up."

I turned around. "Hey, Desiree."

"Long time no see."

"Yeah. I know. I've been pretty busy."

She grabbed my shirt and tugged at it with her long painted nails. "I just got off work. You want to hang out?"

Hang out. Right.

"I'm actually in a rush. I have to catch the last train to Boston. So..."

She leaned in and whispered in my ear, "I'm wearing that thong...red lace...the one you said you liked."

Her saying it had no effect on me. If this were months ago, I'd have likely gone upstairs and taken that thong right off of her. The thought of that was now repulsive. It made me truly realize how deeply Nina had gotten under my skin, how strong my attraction to her was, both physically and emotionally.

"I'm gonna have to pass. I'm sorry. I hope you have a good weekend."

She looked dumbfounded. I left her standing on the sidewalk as I jogged across the street to catch my train.

The next day, sunlight poured through the window in the guest room at my sister's house. I reached for my phone and noticed that a text from Nina had come in earlier that morning.

> *Your body of blankets was getting pretty lonely last night, so I stuffed my ratty bathrobe in there with him. Hope you don't mind. I think*

*they're getting along. They haven't
come out yet.*

My ribs ached from laughing so hard. I wrote back.

*Jake: That's what you get for sneak-
ing into my room again.*

*Nina: You got me. You must have
gotten to Boston late, huh? What
are your plans for today?*

My stomach sank. Could you imagine what the truth
would sound like?

*I'll be spending the day with my schizophrenic wife,
Ivy, meeting with a doctor about signing off on a new
type of trial medication for her and filling out some insur-
ance forms. Maybe if I'm lucky, Ivy won't have a paranoid episode or subsequently try to beat the shit out of me.
I'll spend the day with her then come home late tonight,
get into bed and fantasize about eating you out while I
jerk off.*

I figured it was best to keep that to myself.

*Jake: At my sister's, family stuff,
running some errands.*

Nina: Sounds exciting.

She was digging for info and would have to be crazy
not to suspect that I was hiding something from her. It always amazed me that she wouldn't pry more than she did.

I toyed with the idea of asking her how the date went but didn't really want to hear it if she had a good time. So, I opted not to bring it up.

>*Jake: What are you up to today?*

>*Nina: Studying and trying out a new recipe I think you're gonna like. You really got me into bananas.*

>*Jake: Don't tease me.*

>*Nina: LOL. When do you come home?*

>*Jake: The usual. Late Sunday night.*

>*Nina: These might be waiting for you when you get here if I don't screw them up.*

A picture began to load. It was a photo of frozen bananas covered in dark Ghirardelli chocolate, encrusted with pistachio nuts. *Oh, man.*

>*Jake: Those look so good. Are you trying to kill me?*

>*Nina: Maybe it's my way of getting back at you for last night.*

It was unclear whether she was referring to how I acted toward her date or my blanket trick.

Jake: Well, it's working. You're making me want to come home right now.

For way more than just the bananas.

Nina: See you when you get home.

Home. It really felt more like home there than it ever used to.

Jake: See you soon, Nina.

My sister's voice vaguely registered. "Jake..."

Still looking down at my phone, I muttered, "Huh?"

"Who were you texting just now? I've been standing here trying to get your attention to see if you want to come to breakfast at the diner with us. You didn't even notice me because you were too busy grinning like a fool for the longest time."

"It was no one."

Allison sat at the edge of my bed. "Look at you. Your face. You're lying! Who was it?" She tied her long dark hair up into a bun and bounced up and down tauntingly. Her green eyes were identical to mine; it was kind of freaky.

"Al, don't do this to me. You know I can't lie to you for shit."

"Uncle Jake said 'shit!'" My seven-year-old niece, Hannah, came running into the room and jumped on the bed to tackle me.

"Oof, girl. You're gettin' big!"

"Hannah, don't repeat that word again," Allison said.

My other niece, Hannah's twin, Holly, ran toward me a few seconds later, and both girls were giggling and crawling all over me as I tickled them.

"Girls, get off your uncle and go put your sneakers on. We're leaving in five minutes to go get pancakes."

The girls hopped off of me in unison and ran out of the room just as fast as they came in. All you had to do was mention food, and that was usually their reaction. I could hear my brother-in-law, Cedric, yelling at them for jumping down the stairs.

I stayed lying on the bed with my arms crossed behind my head as I looked up at the ceiling.

She wasn't going to let me off the hook. "So, answer my question."

"Her name is Nina."

"Nina...that's pretty. Who is she?"

"She's my roommate."

"Is she cute?"

"Why do you need to know?"

"Answer the question."

"Yes, she's pretty." I closed my eyes briefly, picturing her face. "She's...beautiful."

"You like her..."

"Al..."

"What's so bad about that?"

"Don't ask questions you know the answer to."

"Do you know when the last time I saw you smile like that was?"

"No, I don't.

"Neither do I, because I don't think I've *ever* seen you smile like that."

I sat up suddenly to avoid the inquisition. "I've got to get going to Ivy's."

"You can't join us for a quick breakfast?"

"No. I overslept, and I have to meet with this doctor at eleven," I said, looking around for my clothes.

"You deserve to be happy, Jake. You know that, right?"

Ignoring her, I threw on a shirt and put my watch on.

She continued, "This girl...does she like you?"

My tone was curt. "That doesn't matter. She doesn't know about Ivy. If she knew, she would freak the fuck out."

"You don't know that for a fact. She might understand."

"Or she might want nothing to do with me, which is a much more likely scenario." It wasn't my intention to shout. "Plus, I've already lied to her by not mentioning Ivy for so long. That, in itself, makes it even worse."

"Why does she think you take off every weekend?"

I let out a single angry laugh. "Honestly? I can't imagine the scenarios running through her head. Either she knows something is up, or she thinks I'm just this weird guy that can't go a week without seeing his sister."

She stuck her tongue out and threw a pillow at me. "Would that be the worst thing in the world?"

The wind outside howled, shaking the window that Ivy was looking out of when I entered her room. She didn't bother to turn around. "You're late."

"I'm sorry. I called you this morning and told you I was meeting with your doctor at his office before coming here. He came in on a Saturday just to meet with me and thinks there's a new trial drug that might make you feel better. He needed to talk to me about it, okay?"

"What's the point?"

"What do you mean?"

"Nothing ever makes me feel better."

"We're trying to change that."

"The only thing that makes me feel better is you, Jake, and you're late!"

Ivy had a dozen different moods that ranged from coherent to completely out of it. The mood she was in at this moment was one of the hardest to deal with because while agitated, she was very aware of things, which in turn made her depressed and angry.

Ivy patted the bed. "Lie with me."

She moved over to one side, and I got in, kicking my feet up and reaching for the TV remote. We'd been watching *Modern Marvels* on the History Channel for about a half-hour when I felt her hand sliding along my thigh and moving close to my crotch. My body tensed. Very rarely did Ivy try to touch me like that, which was why I didn't think twice about getting in the bed with her. The majority of the time, she didn't like to make contact with anyone or be touched in general because she was always convinced people were trying to hurt her.

But once in a blue moon, she'd get into a certain mood where she'd want sex and come on to me.

Out of every scenario with her, this one killed me the most. I just didn't view Ivy that way anymore, plain and simple. It was hard for me to explain it in a way that wouldn't be devastating to her in her temporarily clear state of mind. Even if I were physically attracted to her, it would have been irresponsible to sleep with someone who was not sane the majority of the time.

Back in the early days, when her symptoms were first starting to develop, she'd sometimes get an episode in the middle of intercourse and start screaming for me to get off of her. It made me shudder just thinking about that now.

When I took her hand and moved it off of my dick, she said, "Please."

"No."

"I just want to feel you inside of me again, Jake."

I immediately got up and rubbed my temples then took a deep breath to compose my thoughts. "You know we don't do that anymore, Ivy."

"Why not?"

"Because a long time ago, when you got sick, we decided it wasn't a good idea. Remember? We've talked about this before." We had...countless times.

"You stopped loving me."

My head was pounding. "That's not true. I just love you in a very different way now."

"If you love me at all, why won't you *make love* to me?"

"Ivy, please..."

She started to cry. It didn't matter how many times we'd had this conversation or how many times she cried in front of me, it never got easier, and it never would. And naturally, a part of me did feel guilty because I was technically her husband. I wouldn't have wished this whole situation on my worst enemy.

After a half-hour of silence, Ivy asked me to go out and get her some takeout. By the time I returned to the group home with Chinese, she was chain-smoking, calling me Sam and falsely accusing me of taking so long because I was lacing the food with cyanide.

At least in her delusional state, she wasn't crying anymore. Sometimes, it was just easier to deal with things when she wasn't as aware. The relief that came from that thought made me feel guilty.

Later that night, my phone chimed as I was throwing away the Styrofoam food containers in the kitchen. It was a picture text from Nina depicting the chocolate-dipped bananas she'd made for me.

Talk about my two worlds colliding.

EIGHT

PRESENT

"Wow, man. That's some fucked up shit."

I held up my beer bottle in a salute. "Welcome to my life, Mitch."

Skylar tried to lighten the mood. "Let me guess. You went home that Sunday night, ate Nina's nutty bananas and thanked her with the dagger?"

"Not exactly. Wait...what did you say? Dagger?"

She covered her face in laughter. "Sorry...Nina sort of named your—you know—years ago. That's what she used to call it."

"The *dagger*? Really?"

"You should take it as a compliment."

Mitch reached for some peanuts on the coffee table. "That's pretty impressive." He nudged her. "What's my nickname?"

The baby started crying. "Saved by the bell." Skylar walked over to the playpen in the corner. "Hang on...be right back. I want to hear the rest of Jake's story."

I checked my phone to see if Nina had texted again then went to the kitchen to grab a couple of beers for Mitch and me. When I returned to the living room, I handed one to him and said, "Hey, Bitch, I thought I heard the girls talking about your cock once, too. What was it again, Skylar? The Slim Reaper?"

"Good one," he said. "Actually, I'm pretty sure it's more like The Bone Ranger."

Skylar cuddled Mitch Jr. in the crook of her arm. His fuzzy brown hair was sticking up in all directions. A gnawing feeling developed inside me as I looked at their beautiful, healthy baby. It reminded me all too well that Nina and I hadn't been able to give A.J. a little brother or sister. The stress of infertility had been taking its toll on us in recent months, too.

Skylar interrupted my thoughts. "So, Jake, continue the story. I want to get to the good parts."

"Okay, well...Nina was still working really hard at studying and ended up getting two more A's. I couldn't believe it. She completely threw off my master plan to take her on a helicopter ride over the city. I'd been dying to take her up there."

"She would have *hated* that."

"I know." I snickered. "It would have been awesome."

"There weren't any more excursions?" she asked.

"Not until later."

"So, things just kept going the way they were..."

"One night, things got pretty intense. Nina finally told me about Jimmy."

Skylar looked at Mitch and whispered, "Her brother that died."

"Yeah," I said under my breath. "I'd always seen the picture of the two of them in her room and assumed he was alive. She never talked about him until she started crying out of the blue during one of our study sessions. I'd rolled some dice for a math lesson, and it reminded her of a game she used to play with him when he was sick. That was all it took."

"What did he have again?" Mitch asked.

"Leukemia," I said.

Skylar and Mitch gave each other a look, knowing this conversation would bring up memories of Skylar's own battle with lymphoma.

I continued, "Nina carried a lot of guilt because she stopped going to see him at the hospital right before he died. She couldn't handle seeing him suffer anymore. After he passed away, she lived with that guilt for years." Looking up again at the picture of pregnant Nina on the wall, I thought back to that night. "So, anyway, that was when I first opened up to her about losing my father when I was five. I showed her some of my drawings of him. We realized that we both suffered tremendous losses at a young age. It was just one more thing that bonded me to her."

Mitch nodded. "Was that the night you first kissed?"

"Unfortunately, no. But that was the night I made a major ass of myself."

"What happened?"

"After that emotional conversation in my room, I decided it would be a good idea if we went out and got shitfaced."

He looked stunned. "You managed to not kiss her even while *shitfaced*? I just can't believe you were able to keep your control like that."

"Oh, believe me. There's not much longer to that side of the story, my friend."

NINE

PAST

I chuckled to myself. Nina could seriously throw down. I watched as she ate every last bit of meat off a Chinese chicken wing. It was like watching one of those hot dog eating contests that were always inevitably won by some skinny dude.

We were at *Kung Pao Karaoke*, a Chinese restaurant and karaoke bar I'd gone to one previous time with some co-workers. We had ordered a Pu Pu Platter that had an assortment of appetizers. There wasn't a morsel left by the time we got done with it.

My mood also couldn't have been better because Nina admitted that her date with Alistair was a dud.

Hell yeah.

A few new discoveries were made about Nina that night. One: she loved to eat. Two: she was a major light-weight when it came to alcohol. Three: Her ex-boyfriend had a name: *Spencer*.

"So...Spencer...was he your last boyfriend?"

"Yeah. We broke up a little over a year ago. In retrospect, it was the best thing that ever happened to me.

Besides the fact that I found out he cheated on me, he did nothing but criticize me."

That was a double whammy. To hear that she'd been cheated on and that he'd treated her like crap made me want to hunt him down. The alcohol from the massive scorpion bowl we'd been sharing was going to my head and intensifying my reaction to every word coming out of her mouth. It was also intensifying my reaction to her mouth itself. I couldn't seem to take my eyes off of it.

"What do you mean *criticize*?" My blood was beginning to boil. "What kinds of things did he say to you?"

She looked down, hesitant to answer me. "Let's see... what *didn't* he say? For one, he had no tolerance at all for my anxiety issues. He would just make fun of me instead of trying to understand the condition. And he criticized my body any chance he got."

Fucking A. This girl had the sexiest body I'd ever seen in real life. On any given day, it was a struggle for me to keep from expressing that to her and to keep from *showing* her how I actually felt about it. How could anyone lead her to believe that there was something wrong with the way she looked?

"He criticized *your* body."

"Yeah...all the time."

"Really..."

"Yes. He told me I wasn't athletic-looking enough, that I could stand to lose ten pounds and that my ass was too big."

Nina didn't see it, and it was too noisy to hear, but I cracked a wooden chopstick under the table. Listening to this bullshit was making me so angry. Her ass was too big? *Her ass was phenomenal.* A thousand symphonies played in my head whenever I looked at that ass for fuck's sake.

How could I explain to her how wrong he was without admitting my true feelings?

"Nina...I hope you don't mind me being blunt."

"I don't mind."

"This...Spencer...needs his eyes checked and his ass kicked. There is nothing wrong with your body...not one thing. I hope you didn't listen to him."

When she admitted to believing him in the past, I nearly lost it.

"Nina..." I stopped myself and took a deep breath. I quietly grabbed the last chopstick and cracked that one under the table, too. (I'd need to find something else to destroy if I had to keep holding my thoughts at bay like this.) "Never mind. Just know...that he was wrong, okay?"

"Say what you were gonna say."

"I'm not sure that I should."

"Since when have you become tactful?"

"Since this conversation moved to tits and ass."

She looked amused. So nice that she found it funny, because I was dead serious. It was taking everything in me not to tell her how I felt, that she was the most beautiful woman in the world to me.

"Seriously, whatever you were going to say, I won't be offended."

Offended? Shit! She had it all wrong. I needed to rectify this. Everything came pouring out of me at that point like projectile vomit.

"Okay...in that case, Nina, not just as your friend, but as a man, I am telling you straight up that you have an amazing body. It's perfect. And your nimrod ex-boyfriend was right about one thing: you do kind of have a big ass."

Okay. So that didn't come out exactly right. I was buzzed.

"Excuse me?"

My heart was pounding as I reached across the table to touch her arm. "Let me finish. You kind of have a big ass...but it's the most spectacular ass I've ever seen. You have an hourglass shape, and any man with a pulse knows that's the hottest kind there is. You're beautiful, and what makes you even more attractive, is that you have absolutely no fucking idea just how beautiful you really are."

I let out a slow, deep breath. It was the most honest thing I'd ever said to her, and every word was the truth. She just looked at me with the slightest bashful smile on her face and seemed like she really wanted to say something. She took a long sip of the drink then finally said, "Thank you."

"You're welcome."

You have no idea.

We silently watched a couple of the karaoke acts. Just as some guy named Larry, who looked like he was on psychedelic drugs, started belting out *Jessie's Girl* by Rick Springfield, Nina got up to go to the bathroom. I watched her every move as she walked away. She turned around briefly, and I laughed to myself, realizing she was probably paranoid I was checking out her ass, which I absolutely was until it was completely out of sight.

There was a break in performances, and the stage was empty for the first time all night. An idea popped into my head, and I made my way over to the DJ booth.

Rump Shaker by Wreckx-N-Effect started playing in my head, and I wondered if Nina would get the joke if I got up and sang it. I just wanted to show her how dumb her ex was, and singing a song about big asses seemed to be the most fitting idea at the moment. At least, my drunk brain thought so.

PENELOPE WARD

I didn't think I could pull *Rump Shaker* off, though.

"What songs do you have about big asses?"

"*These Humps* by Black Eyed Peas?" he suggested.

"What else?"

"*Honky Tonk Badonkadonk* by Trace Adkins?"

"Ugh...anything else?"

"What about *Fat Bottomed Girls* by Queen?"

Yes. Effing brilliant. Perfect, in fact.

"Let's go with that one."

"Wanna go next? There's no one in line."

Shit. Did I really want to do this? Hell yes, I did. Making her laugh was way more important than making a fool out of myself.

I waited with the microphone in hand until I saw Nina return to our booth. She looked confused and started looking around for me.

I cleared my throat.

"What's your name?" the DJ asked.

I spoke into the mic, "Spencer."

Nina's jaw dropped when she noticed me on stage, and she covered her mouth with her hand.

"What are you singing, Spencer?"

I whispered to him to lower my volume a little because it was obnoxiously loud.

"This is a special song for Nina. Please forgive me for being such an ass goblin."

She looked around in embarrassment. The look on her face was priceless as her mouth eventually curved into a huge smile.

Once the music started, I really got into it, moving my head to the beat and tapping my feet. My eyes alternated between the words on the teleprompter and Nina's face. She was wiping tears from her eyes. *They were happy tears*. My plan was working.

I vaguely noticed a bunch of women in the front row whistling at me and shouting some vulgar shit as my hips swayed. My mind was too focused on Nina's beautiful smile to care. When you're on stage, the bright lights make everything out in the audience look dark. For some reason, Nina just glowed in the midst of it all. Her hair, her eyes, her smile were all I could see, all I wanted to see.

The people in the crowd were really getting into my rendition of *Fat Bottomed Girls* and were now clapping in unison. Some ladies were standing up and shaking their asses around. It was a hot mess.

Sweat soaked through the back of my shirt, a result of the hot stage lights. When the song finished, I grabbed a napkin and used it on my forehead. Nina gave me a standing ovation as she wiped her eyes.

A couple of girls stopped me as I was heading back to our booth. I was trying not to be rude but really just wanted to get to Nina. Before I blew them off, one of the girls handed me her phone number, which was a pretty desperate move. I knew Nina saw it because my eyes had been on her the whole time. I was hoping she didn't think I asked for it. I later dumped it into the leftover flames from our Pu Pu Platter to show her just how little I cared about those digits. I had to question my actions, though. What was I trying to prove when I should have been steering her away from me instead of making it obvious that I only had eyes for her?

While our time at the karaoke restaurant was coming to a close, the night was just beginning when it came to fending off my feelings for her. Even the Gods were joking about it on my behalf.

"Aren't you gonna open your fortune? Take the one facing you. That's the one meant for you. I'll go first," Nina said. She cracked one open and discarded the cookie. "When one door closes, another opens."

She seemed to be pondering what that meant. My thinking was...it's a damn cookie. Don't take it seriously.

Until...

"Your turn," she said.

I grabbed my cookie and split it open. Without even reading it, I joked, "Big-butt girl make man smile."

Nina giggled. "No sir!"

"I'm kidding. I'm kidding."

"What does it really say?"

The smile on my face disappeared pretty quickly as the words on the slip of paper registered.

Now is the time to make a move.

If I didn't know better, I would have thought this cookie was busting my balls. There was no doubt that under the circumstances, that message seemed made for me. I just didn't know what to do with it.

Nina kept innocently looking at me waiting for a reply.

I coughed. "Now is the time to make a move."

She nodded slowly for the longest time before saying, "Interesting."

"It is...very interesting."

Her eyes were fixated on my mouth as I scraped my tongue ring against my teeth, something I did a lot when I became anxious. We were both definitely feeling quite *happy* after polishing off the scorpion bowl. I couldn't take my eyes off her and was probably making my attraction way more obvious than normal because of my inebriated state.

The weather outside was ten times colder than it had been earlier in the evening. Nina was only wearing a light jacket. There were no cabs in sight, so we decided to walk until we came across one.

I could see my breath. "So, did you have fun?"

"More than I have in a long time." Her teeth chattered as she spoke.

"Good. I'm glad you took my little performance for what it was, and I hope you know I meant everything I said tonight."

"Thank you." She smiled. "I was so broken up over my brother earlier, and once again, you managed to turn a miserable moment for me into something crazy good."

The look of trust in her eyes cut through me.

I'm going to end up devastating you.

The alcohol had loosened my inhibitions, so when she started to shiver, I didn't think twice about rubbing my hands vigorously along the tops of her arms to warm her as we walked. While we weren't totally sloshed, we were both definitely under the influence, and that made me wary about what might happen when we got home. As much as I'd vowed not to let anything transpire between us, I never fully trusted myself with her. Not to mention, we'd never been almost-wasted together.

Even though it was a cold night, the stars were shining brightly in the sky. She looked up as we were walking. "Look how clear the sky is, how pretty the stars are tonight. It makes you want to just reach up and touch them," she said.

I don't know what possessed me to say, "Some of the most beautiful things are those we can only enjoy from afar. The unattainability makes the attraction more intense."

Yes, I'm talking about you.

"So, if the stars were something we could easily touch, they wouldn't be so fascinating?" she asked.

"I'm not sure about that. What I do know is there are some magnificent things that are beautiful but that also can hurt you if you get too close. The sun is an example. It can burn."

Nothing like talking in code while drunk.

"Like fire..." she said.

Fire.

Me.

She knew what I was getting at.

I barely noticed that we'd stopped walking. I looked straight into her eyes and whispered, "Like fire."

The city moved around us as we stood still facing each other in the middle of the sidewalk.

"Sometimes, if you're willing to withstand a little pain in life, you might discover a pleasure that you never would have otherwise known existed. Remember that saying, Jake? You taught me that," she said as she slowly moved in closer to me, our breath mingling together in the frigid air. "Some things might be worth getting burned for."

She definitely wasn't referring to sun or fire, either. She was trying to send me a message, too, and I heard it loud and clear. She knew I was hiding something but was willing to take a chance. Unfortunately, Nina had no clue how bad the truth really was, and I wasn't quite ready to divulge it and risk losing her altogether just yet.

A cab finally approached us. If I thought getting into that car was going to make things less tense, I couldn't have been more wrong.

We slipped into the backseat, and her leg pressed up against mine. When the cab made a sudden turn, she fell right into me. My entire body froze up because she stayed there, her head on my chest. My tormented heart pounded furiously. Staring blankly out of the window, I tried my best to ignore all of the sensations building inside of me. With her scent and the warmth of her body, it was impossible to fight my arousal. My dick was rock hard, and if she moved at all, she'd feel it. I wished I could have pulled her onto my lap to show her exactly how much I wanted her. At one point, she placed her hand on my chest right over my heart that was beating a mile a minute.

Now, Nina *knew* what she was doing to me. If she didn't, she'd figure it out in my bedroom later that night.

TEN

PAST

I couldn't sleep. My mind wouldn't stop rehashing what happened in that cab with Nina.

Get...your shit...together.

As if no woman's ever touched you before like that? The truth was, no woman had ever made me feel the way she just did in that taxi.

Keeping it in the friend zone was starting to wear on me. Tonight proved that these feelings were beyond my control. It took every ounce of strength I had to hold back, and if the ride were any longer, I would have lost it.

Her mouth had been just inches from mine. Her soft fingertips were caressing my chest, and I could feel her breathing on me...sweet, soft, little breaths. My heart had been beating faster than a rabbit in heat, and she felt that. I wondered if she felt my dick throbbing, too.

I could only imagine what she must have been thinking as I sat there frozen like a fucking mummy while she leaned against me. If I'd let my body relax and do what it wanted to, there would have been no going back. And

I couldn't do that to her. Not until she knew what she'd really be getting herself into with me. She deserved better.

Earlier, when we exited the cab, I had asked her to walk ahead of me, trying to buy some time to talk my dick down. It was practically saluting her when I wished her good night and walked back to my room.

I just needed to get some sleep and move past this. But as I tossed and turned, all I could think about was saying "fuck it all" and busting through her bedroom door.

I wondered what she was wearing.

Go to sleep.

I really had to use the bathroom but had been putting it off because I couldn't even trust myself to go straight there without taking a detour to her room.

When I finally couldn't hold it anymore, I walked out to the hall and noticed that there was no light coming from under her door. A sense of relief came over me because if there had been light, I might have been tempted to knock.

Knock her boots.

Get your mind out the gutter!

After I took a long piss, I was leaving the bathroom when her soft breasts knocked right into my chest.

"Whoa! Are you okay?" I asked, rubbing my thumb over the skin of her forehead.

I made the mistake of looking down and noticed she was wearing a lace tank top so small, it looked like one of those things my grandmother had on her coffee table under the candlesticks. *A doily?* I had to pry my eyes upward.

"Yeah...I'm fine. Sorry, I didn't think to check if you were in here. The light in your room was on, so I assumed you were in there," she said.

I leaned against the sink and crossed my arms. "What are you still doing up?"

"I can't sleep, so I came in here to pee."

She flashed me the cutest smile. I loved her smile. God, she was beautiful. I wanted to kiss her.

Wait...she needed to pee. That was your cue to leave. Move, drunk ass.

"Oh...well, I should probably let you do that," I said, backing away from the sink.

She laughed. "Yeah, probably."

"Right..." I said before walking out and closing the door.

I took my hand to my head, shooting an imaginary pistol at my brain as I walked back to my room.

I intentionally left my door open. It was a bad idea, but a part of me just wanted her to come into my room. Maybe we could try that spooning thing again.

Who the fuck was I kidding?

I grabbed my laptop, so that it would look like I was doing something other than waiting impatiently to get another look at her beautiful tits in that top. Why I wanted to torture myself when I couldn't really have her was beyond me.

When she appeared at the doorway, I closed my laptop. My heart pounded faster with each step Nina took toward me. I breathed a sigh of relief when she stopped and sat at the far end of my bed.

Good. Stay far away from me, Nina.

I sat up straighter. "How was your pee?"

"Fantastic."

I couldn't even recall what I said...something like, "good to hear" as my eyes betrayed my brain's better judgment and wandered down to her chest. I could have sworn her nipples were hardening by the second and now, so was my dick. My mouth was watering. All she had to do was look down and she'd see how much I wanted her.

"What were you looking at?" she asked.

Shit.

Busted.

Speak!

I shook my head. "Huh?"

"On your laptop."

Phew.

"Oh...on my laptop. Right. Just useless surfing."

She grinned. "I see."

Our eyes were locked on each other as we just sat there, and this time, I was transfixed by what lie *above* her neck. Looking into her blue eyes was like gazing at a calm ocean. My stare didn't break until the bed next door starting squeaking.

Friggin' Ryan and Tarah having sex.

Well, that was awkward. Say something to break the ice, Jake. While you're at it, break a piece off and rub it over your dick to cool it down.

I cleared my throat and asked sarcastically, "You think they're having sex?"

Nina's cheeks were rosy as she looked down. She was so stinking adorable. "Should we just pretend it's not happening?"

"Yeah. You wanna do a math lesson?"

"Sure."

"Let's see...we can talk about the probability of sixty-nine," I joked.

She blushed even more. "I would say based on that noise, it's very high."

We both started to laugh, but all I could focus on was the fact that she actually knew what sixty-nine meant.

Sweet, innocent girl...with a dirty mind. And I thought I couldn't want her more than I already did.

The noises from next door stopped, but the silence that followed was even more unbearable.

I looked up at her, and she batted her eyelashes at me. She wanted me, too. That was clear and making this so much harder.

I started picking at the lint on my comforter to distract myself from the need building inside of me. It really wasn't working because my mind started going in a different direction. All I could think about was whether or not she was a virgin. Even though she was probably too old to have not had sex, she gave off a vibe of purity and sexual naivety. Maybe if she were a virgin, it would help convince *little Jake* down there that things couldn't go any further anyway, regardless of my holding back.

It was against my better judgment, but I said it anyway. "I bet that prick ex-boyfriend of yours sucked in bed."

She looked shocked at my assertion. After a few seconds, she said, "Actually, he did...big-time."

Okay. Question answered.

My body went rigid as I sat up straighter. "So, you *have* had sex."

"What's that supposed to mean?" She laughed nervously.

"See, now I've made you blush. I'm sorry. You just strike me as a certain kind of girl."

"What kind of girl is that?"

"It's nothing bad. Just...innocent...maybe a virgin." I looked up at the ceiling. What the fuck did I get myself into with this conversation? Just tell her the truth. "The kind of girl that guys like me are dying to corrupt."

She wasn't saying anything. The mood shifted again and grew even tenser. I backed away against the headboard to keep my distance because my willpower was dwindling fast.

Then, she cleared her throat. "Well, in answer to your question...yes, I have had sex, but it was just with him."

"He was your only, and he sucked in bed? That's unfortunate."

"Yeah. It was unfortunate. I never even actually...you know...with him."

"You never what?" I asked. As I looked at her expression, what she meant suddenly dawned on me. My smile faded. Holy shit. *No.* My voice went low in disbelief. "You never came? You never even had an orgasm?"

She shook her head. "Not from another person."

Whatever reserve I had built up was destroyed in that moment as images of Nina touching herself flooded my brain. All of the blood in my body rushed straight to my dick.

I started attacking the lint on my comforter again as if that were going to help. My dick was completely hard now, and there was nowhere to run and nothing I could do. Either I was looking at her beautiful, wanting eyes, hard nipples or thinking about her getting herself off. It was a blue balls trifecta.

My cock twitched as I imagined her eyes closed, spread eagle, clit glistening, pleasuring herself. What did she think about in that pretty little head of hers when she did it? I wanted it to be me. Why was I torturing myself, asking her these questions? Still, I wanted to hear more. If I couldn't touch her, I damn well wanted material for later. I *needed* to hear more. So, I kept on with it.

"So, you come when you touch yourself..."

"Yeah," she simply said.

Fuck.

I closed my eyes for a moment. It was impossible to believe that no guy had ever made her come. I hoped she knew that wasn't normal. "Sex doesn't count if he didn't make you come, Nina. You're basically still a virgin." I bit down on my lip ring in frustration. "He had sex. You didn't."

What a damn shame that no one had ever pleasured her. It made me angry, but in a twisted way, it invigorated me. I wanted nothing more than to be the first man to ever make her come...with my mouth, with my hands, with my cock buried deep inside of her.

You have no idea what I would do to you, Nina, if it were that simple. What I might do to you anyway if you don't get the fuck out of here soon.

I continued to look at her, imagining all the different ways I would make her come if I could. Her cheeks were flush from this conversation alone, and I wondered what they'd look like if I reached over and kissed her senseless.

My body was experiencing a level of physical need that was completely foreign to me. I'd never wanted to fuck someone so badly.

I realized I was staring at her nipples again and had to do something. And God, I needed a cigarette. Trying to quit, I hadn't smoked one in weeks, but desperate times called for desperate measures. Having nowhere to run with a raging hard on was as desperate as it got for me. It was either move from this spot or pull her onto my lap. A change of position was much needed.

I couldn't help but laugh a little when she flinched as I got up from the bed. She had no idea how close I just came to grabbing her face and kissing her, but instead, in a split decision, I practically ran to the window. As I opened it, the frosty air that blew inside the room calmed me down for like a millisecond. Then, I walked over to the drawer, fumbled for a cigarette and lit it, inhaling deeply. The smoke burned my throat as I sucked in again, hoping it would help me control myself.

"Why are you smoking? I thought you quit."

I shook my head. "I did. But I really needed one, and I need to keep my distance right now."

"Why?" she asked.

She wasn't gonna let it go. She knew I'd been trying to quit. If I was smoking all of a sudden, it was obvious that I was losing my shit. I inhaled again and turned to look at her sweet face. Just wanting to open up to her, my heart clenched.

"You really want to know why I'm smoking?"

She nodded. "Yes."

"Because it's keeping my mouth occupied and stopping me from doing something I shouldn't right now." I took another long drag. "You should probably go back to your room."

It was the right thing to say, the right thing to do. She needed to leave because I could only stand so much more of this. She had no idea what she'd be getting into with me, and it wouldn't be fair to spring it on her tonight. It was late, and we were both still a little drunk. Not the time to be having that discussion.

"You're smoking and telling me to leave because you want to kiss me?"

I couldn't help but laugh. As if I only wanted to "kiss" her. Yeah, that would be a start, but there was no end to the list of things I would to do to her, with her, show her for the first time. I dreamt of what that would be like so often while lying in my bed at night. Just kissing would never be an option with how I was feeling about this girl.

I inhaled deeply again and looked over at her. This time, her chest was heaving in anticipation of my saying something, doing something. She even looked a little scared.

Fuck it. Nina, you want the truth? I can't give you what I want to, but I can give you the truth.

"I wouldn't tell you to leave if I only wanted to kiss you, Nina. I'm telling you to leave because I want to taste you and make you come until you scream in every possible way imaginable. It was all I could think about all night long. It's why I couldn't sleep. But now that you just told me no man has ever done that...fuck. That's why I am smoking if you really want to know."

My heart raced.

What the fuck did I just say?

Her face turned bright red as she just stood there. As shocked as I was at myself for blurting it out, it felt like a tremendous weight had been lifted. I'd been dying to tell her for so long how much I wanted her. Absorbing my words, she stayed frozen at the edge of the bed. I put out my cigarette and stayed staring out the window to keep my distance.

I cleared my throat and repeated, "I really think you should go back to your room."

When it started to feel like Antarctica, I closed the window. Without the distraction of the cigarette, I had no choice but to turn to her and noticed her nipples were harder than before. I could now make out almost exactly what her breasts looked like naked. My eyes were glued, and I licked my lips, desperately wanting to taste them through the thin fabric of her shirt.

JAKE UNDERSTOOD

I didn't dare move when her gaze lowered to my crotch. Any doubt that remained about my need for her was now obsolete because I was fully erect. My breathing quickened as her eyes continued to stare down at me.

My heart nearly pounded through my chest when Nina stood up from the bed and walked slowly toward where I was standing. She smelled like sweet vanilla as she stopped just inches away from me. I wanted to devour her but instead held back and took in a long, deep breath, closing my eyes. My lips trembled because it was almost as if I could taste her as I inhaled. *She was so close.* So close, and there was nothing I could do about it.

Not until she knew the truth.

Her glassy eyes were staring up at me when I opened mine, and my chest tightened. She was so pretty. Her blonde hair was in a messy side ponytail that I wanted to roughly pull toward me. My eyes trailed down the length of her body slowly, stopping at her breasts again then down to her taut stomach and up again. The soft skin at the top of her chest glowed in the moonlight, and I yearned to touch it just for a second, to feel the warmth there.

Without thinking, I reached out and gripped her waist. All the control I had built up was immediately destroyed with the sharp intake of breath she let out the second my hand landed on her. It was a torturous indication of what it would be like to be with her. Her body was so responsive to me, even in those moments when we were just sitting next to each other. I knew without a doubt if given the opportunity, not only would I make her come, but I would make her lose all control. Oh, how I wanted to see Nina lose her mind when she came for me.

The thoughts in my head were driving me wild, and my fingers began to gently caress her waist. The longer my hand lingered, the more I lost focus on reality and when I realized my nails were digging into her, I pulled back and growled through my teeth, "Fuck."

What was I thinking touching her? One more second, and I knew I wasn't going to be able to stop myself from taking what I had no right to.

She was breathing heavily and almost looked scared, like she wanted to say something but was holding back. I couldn't blame her. She was the Little Red Riding Hood in this situation and I was the Big Bad Wolf with a big bad boner.

For fuck's sake, say something, Jake.

Before I had a chance to, Nina blurted out, "I want to know what you do when you go to Boston every weekend."

Shit.

Shit.

Shit.

Should I just tell her the truth?

Think!

I blinked repeatedly to buy myself some time. The truth. Yeah, right. Could you imagine? *"Nina, I'm actually married, but it's okay. There's a good explanation. I'm telling you this right now with a stiff willy because..."*

Fuck no! I couldn't tell her now. Not like this.

So, instead, I just blurted out, "It's complicated, Nina."

I felt like an absolute prick. Imagine what she was thinking about my leading her on, trying to kick her out, touching her and now feeding her this bull.

Nina just stood there and looked at me then glanced out the window, looking lost and defeated. She was going to give up on me, and I couldn't blame her.

Looking utterly disappointed, she shook her head and let out a frustrated sigh. "Good night, Jake."

Game over. Well played, dickhead.

I swallowed as she backed away. Feeling helpless, I let her go, knowing I wouldn't get any sleep tonight. My mind screamed, *"I think I might be falling in love with you."* But I said nothing as she walked away and slammed the door.

No paper bat could fix this shit.

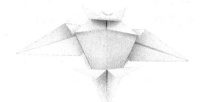

ELEVEN
PRESENT

Skylar stood up from the couch to stretch. "I need a break. This story is giving me lady blue balls."

"Seriously! Even *I'm* getting lady blue balls," Mitch joked as he got up and rubbed her shoulders. "You want to watch the baby, Jake, so Skylar and I can have a few minutes alone to take care of this?"

"Imagine how it was for me, man...living through it."

A loud knock prompted me to jump out of my seat. I flew to the door only to be crushed to find it was my sister and brother-in-law standing there with a bunch of bags.

"Crap. I thought you were Nina. You didn't get my text?"

The smell of marinara sauce wafted in the air as they both pushed past me.

"What message?"

"I texted you that the party's off."

"What? Allison looked down at her phone. "I never got it."

Cedric rolled his eyes. "I'll put the food in the kitchen."

Checking my messages, I scrolled down and noticed I'd mistakenly texted Albert from work instead of Allison. Showing her the screen, I said, "Well, that explains why you never responded."

Allison took off her coat and hung it up. She walked over to hug Skylar and Mitch who were standing to greet her. My sister took the baby in her arms and conversed with them for a bit before walking back over to me.

She pulled me aside. "What the hell is going on?"

Over the next few minutes, I rehashed everything that happened last night from the Ivy visit to Nina walking out this morning.

"Geez...I'm sorry. That really sucks. I hope she comes home soon...for your sanity." She rubbed my arm. "Let me fill Cedric in on what's going on. Be right back."

Allison went into the kitchen then returned and sat next to Skylar who was nursing the baby again on the couch.

Cedric was carrying a bottle of Cabernet and two glasses when he reentered the living room. He grabbed one of the dining room chairs to join us. "All the food's put away. We have enough to feed an army, so if anyone's hungry, it'll just need to be reheated."

He opened the wine, poured two glasses and handed one to my sister. "Can I get anyone else a glass?"

Mitch lifted his Heineken. "I'm good with beer."

Cedric took a sip and looked over at Allison. "Seeing Skylar feeding the baby reminds me of the good old days."

Skylar turned to Allison. "This little guy is attached to my boobs."

Mitch winked. "Now, she's got two Mitch's she has to pry off her tits."

Everyone laughed, and Skylar looked over at my sister. "I don't know how you did it with twins. You nursed them both at once?"

"I did. Those days were crazy but wonderful. It was like having two little coconuts sucking on your boobs all day. They're teenagers now. Can you believe it?"

Cedric pointed to a gray strip of hair at the front of his head that actually looked pretty cool on him. "I have the gray hair to prove it."

Allison looked over at him affectionately. "I think your stripe is sexy."

"I'm glad you do, sweetheart."

My sister lit a few of the candles on the coffee table. My gaze traveled over to the window. The snow outside was now falling more steadily. It was dark out, and that was making me really antsy about Nina coming home.

I quietly texted her as everyone was talking.

Please come home, baby.

A few seconds later, she messaged me back.

I'll call you soon.

Her brief responses today were a bit unsettling, but at least, they confirmed that she was okay. Whether *we* were okay was another matter.

Skylar propped the baby on her shoulder to burp him. "So, before you guys got here, Jake was in the middle of telling us the story of how he met Nina and the days before she found out about Ivy."

I was still looking down at my phone hoping for more from Nina as I mumbled, "Allison's heard the stories before."

"He just told us about the night he practically kicked her out of his room."

My sister nodded and flashed a knowing smile. "*Fat Bottomed Girls*...you mean, that night? Oh, you're getting close to the good parts now."

Mitch laughed. "How could you have possibly recovered from that disaster?"

I took a deep breath and stared into the candlelight. "A strange thing happened after that night. You would have thought I scared her off, right? Well, it was awkward for maybe the first couple of days, but soon after, it was like we started over and really became even better friends in the process. I think she knew deep down that something big was holding me back and that I needed time to be able to work it out. She never pressured me for answers, and well, we stopped putting ourselves in precarious situations with alcohol. She was just there for me and let me have her in the only way I could at that time, which was to give me her heart even if I couldn't have her body. To be honest, those were the weeks when we really fell in love."

TWELVE

PAST

"**C**ocksucker!"
Well, that was new.

It seemed Mrs. Ballsworthy was trying out a new salutation as she welcomed me back from Boston that particular Sunday night.

I waved and shouted up into her window. "I've moved on from fucking myself to sucking cock now? Good one, Balls."

She squinted her eyes at me then slammed the window down.

I swear to God, my life was like a comedy show sometimes.

Since I usually arrived back to Brooklyn pretty late, Nina was normally asleep by the time I got home because she had an early class on Mondays. When I opened the front door on this particular night, it surprised me to find her wide awake, sipping some tea in the living room and flipping through channels. She was curled up in a brown fleece blanket.

I took off my coat. "Hey, you. Whatcha doing up?"

"I was having trouble sleeping."

"Everything okay?"

Nina lowered the volume on the television and sat up. "No. Not really."

I kicked off my shoes and sat down next to her. "Talk to me. What's wrong?"

"Today was a hard day for me. It always is. It's the anniversary of my brother's death. Jimmy would have been going on twenty-five now."

"I'm sorry, Nina."

"It never gets any easier."

"No, and it likely won't."

I wanted desperately to make her feel better but knew that nothing would really help in this situation. I grabbed the mug from her hand and took it to the kitchen to refill it with the kettle water that was still hot on the stove. I poured some into another mug for me, adding fresh teabags and honey to both.

I returned to where she was sitting and handed her the tea. "Here. We're gonna stay up for a little while until you get tired enough to fall asleep."

"You don't have to stay up with me, Jake."

I ignored her and rested my feet on the coffee table as she snuggled into the blanket again for comfort. I couldn't help but wish she'd used me instead.

She took a sip of tea and smiled. "Thank you, though."

"You're welcome."

We were quiet for a few minutes until she said, "Christmas is coming soon. I don't look forward to it anymore because our house is so different now without him. It feels like half our family is gone, you know? It's a lot easier dealing with everything being away from home. I wish I could just stay here."

It would be the first time since she moved in that we would be apart for longer than a couple of days. An uneasy feeling came over me.

"You'll get through it, and if you can't, you can always call me anytime, day or night."

"Thanks. I appreciate that." She stared down into her mug. "I know that he wouldn't want me to be so sad."

"Remember what I was telling you when you first told me about Jimmy? That you need to focus on the happy memories?"

"Yeah."

"Well, just so you know, that's way easier said than done. There are gonna be times when you just find it impossible to do that. And that's okay."

"I know you can relate."

"You were putting yourself through a guilt trip again today, weren't you? Thinking about how you stopped going to see him in the end?"

"Yeah, I was."

"I figured." I slid a little closer to her side of the couch. "Do you know how many times I've sat there and thought about how everything would be different if I had just asked my dad to tell me a bedtime story before he left that final night? Even five minutes might have changed his fate. So, while we should be thinking about happy things, sometimes we torture ourselves by focusing on the hurtful stuff. It's just what we do as humans, I guess."

"I've asked you this before, and you ignored the question. Will you tell me about your childhood?"

After placing the mug on the coffee table, I nestled my back into the couch and looked up at the ceiling. "It was a really good childhood at first, Nina. My parents were crazy in love. My dad had saved my mother after a really rough patch in her life. She'd gotten into drugs and into a lot of trouble before she met him. Anyway, my father just took her under his wing, and she got her shit together. For the first five years of my life, from what little I can remember, it was perfect. We didn't have much money, but there was a lot of love in my house. When my father was killed, my world just imploded. My mother had to work all of the time to keep a roof over our heads. I was alone a lot. Nothing was ever the same again. It pretty much stayed that way. She was really strong, though, and did the best she could. Then, when I was sixteen, I found my sister. My mother had given her up for adoption before I was born. She's actually my half-sister. That's a story for another day, but it was one of the brightest points of my life because all of a sudden, I had this family. She and my nieces, they're everything to me now."

"You're just surrounded by women, huh?"

She didn't know the half of it.

I laughed. "Yeah."

"You'd better have a son someday, then."

The comment made me almost ill, a reminder that kids were likely not in the cards for me.

I quickly changed the subject. "So, what did you and Jimmy like to do growing up?"

"We fought a lot as siblings often do, but we loved each other. It was just the two of us. We led a simple life. You know my dad owned a farm, so we rode around on the tractor a lot. Every Sunday morning, we'd go to the local farmer's market and sell produce. It seemed kind of boring to me then, but of course, I'd give anything to get those days back now."

"Wow, you really *are* a country bumpkin."

"Tried and true. Everything was always homemade and organic, too. You can see why I like to bake you stuff and why I always use fresh ingredients."

"Organic...don't you mean orgasmic? Seriously, no one's ever done stuff like that for me."

"Given you an orgasm?"

Fuck. Don't say stuff like that when I'm trying not to want you.

"Nina Kennedy, get your mind out of the gutter. Nobody's ever *baked* for me. My mother never had the time, and even when she did, God love her, she couldn't cook for shit."

"You know, Jimmy actually never cared for my desserts. He always preferred packaged Hostess cupcakes from the grocery store and used to hoard them in his room. He insisted they were better."

"That's funny."

"Of course, I baked all the time anyway. Baking is to me what drawing is to you. It's therapeutic."

"Yeah. My therapy is much less fattening, though."

"You're really amazingly talented, you know that?"

"Thank you. I've been practicing for a while."

Nina and I sat on that couch talking intimately until one in the morning. Minute by minute, we'd slowly inched closer together until she was leaning her head on my shoulder. I ended up telling her the whole story about how I found my sister. I also told her something that few people knew about, that my mother also had a second daughter born out of wedlock who died as a teenager. Nina was floored that I, too, had lost a sibling even though I never got a chance to know Amanda.

She also opened up to me more about the situation with her loser ex and the circumstances of their breaking up. Spencer had cheated on her with a girl he worked with. Hearing how badly he'd hurt her made me want to hunt him down.

Nina was still wide awake when she asked, "Aren't you tired?"

"Sleep is overrated. I'd rather be up talking to you."

An idea came to mind, and I got up to get my coat.

"Where are you going?"

"I'll be right back. I'll be gone about ten minutes. Don't fall asleep."

Nearly freezing my ass off, I literally ran down the street. It felt like I was high off of her, and I couldn't wait to get back to the warmth of being next to her.

There was a small 24-hour grocery store about two blocks away. The bells on the door chimed as I blew through the entrance.

Weaving through the aisles, I scanned the market for what I was looking for.

I paid the cashier, not bothering to collect the change from my five-dollar bill.

Reentering the apartment, I was out of breath. Nina was still sitting in the same spot.

"Where the heck did you go?"

"Hang on. I'll be there in a minute." I took the paper bag into the kitchen and got out two plates. Removing the Hostess cupcakes from the packaging, I placed a single candle inside each.

Nina covered her mouth in surprise as I set the plates down on the coffee table. With a flick of my lighter, I lit both candles.

"Let's celebrate Jimmy tonight. He'd be disappointed with anything less than these gourmet confections."

Her eyes turned watery. She looked up at the ceiling for a moment and looked like she was sending him a silent message. It was simply beautiful to watch.

"I can't believe you did this. Thank you," she said as she blew out the candle.

I blew mine out too, and we inhaled the cupcakes in silence. Remnants of frosting coated her lips, and I yearned to lick it off.

A few minutes later, Ryan walked into the kitchen for a middle of the night glass of water and dampened the mood. He didn't acknowledge us but gave me the evil eye before walking back to his room.

"What's his problem?" Nina asked.

"He doesn't like you hanging out with me."

"Screw him. I don't care what he thinks. He doesn't know you like I do."

You don't know me like you think you do, baby.

My jaw tightened. "He's said stuff to you about me?"

She put her plate down and hesitated. "He just thinks you're not good for me and has no real basis for it. He's judging you by your looks." She nudged my shirt and chills ran down the length of my body. "I happen to like your looks, and what's inside even more."

I slid away from her, my heart pounding because I was this close to telling her everything. My voice lowered to a whisper. "Did you ever wonder whether Ryan could be right?"

"No," she said defensively. "I may not know everything about you, but I know how you make me feel. Whatever happens...I'm just really glad I met you, Jake."

I feel it too, Nina.

Her statement had an ominous undertone. *Whatever happens.* I'd known for a while that she suspected I was hiding something. The difference now was that our relationship was at a level where it would be impossible to go much longer without telling her. I still needed to figure out when and how.

She repositioned her head on my shoulder. Being close to her like that for a prolonged amount of time was taking its toll on me. At one point, I leaned in closer and breathed in the clean scent of her hair. Then, she turned her face toward me. Our mouths were just inches apart, but I knew if I kissed her like I craved, I wouldn't be able to stop, so I turned my head away. Getting physical with Nina was not an option right now.

When the mood became too tense for our tired minds to handle, out of nowhere she asked, "Have you ever ice skated?"

"That's a random question."

"I've always wanted to go to Rockefeller Center around Christmas time, like I've always seen in the movies. I don't want to go alone, and I know the subway ride and crowds are gonna make me anxious. Would you go with me?"

Was she kidding?

"I've never been on ice skates in my life. I'm positive I'd fall flat on my ass within seconds."

"I'm pretty good, actually. There was a rink near my house growing up, and I'd go there a lot. I could teach you."

"I'd fall on you and crush you."

"No, you wouldn't."

"Nina, you know I'd do anything for you...but that...I just don't think..."

"I'll tell you what...I have two more exams before the end of the semester. These are the hardest ones. You know that. So, the chances are slim that I'll get A's. If I don't, then you know the deal. I have to let you take me on an excursion. If I do, you let me take you ice skating. Come on, it's only fair."

She was right. Those last two exams were going to be killer. The odds were in my favor.

I rubbed my chin and reluctantly said, "Okay, deal."

"Put these on."

Nina returned from the skate rental booth and handed me my size twelves.

I still couldn't believe I'd gotten myself into this. She had received an A minus on her most recent exam. When she first broke the news, I tried to get out of the ice skating by arguing that technically an A minus wasn't an A, but the look of sheer disappointment on her face eventually caused me to cave.

So, the following Tuesday, we found ourselves at the rink at Rockefeller Center. It wasn't as crowded as it might have been on a weekend, so that was a plus. Pretending to be sick, I left work early that day so that Nina and I could venture into the city for my Ice Capades debut.

The weather was clear, cold and sunny. It was an otherwise perfect day except for the fact that I was about to make a complete fool out of myself in front of the girl of my dreams.

Standing up on the skates made me feel about ten feet tall. Nina took my hand as I struggled to balance myself.

"Now, what you have to do first is get used to the feel of the blades on the ice. Gently move your feet back and forth like this." Nina skated in front of me and demonstrated the move. "Back and forth. Back and forth. Back and forth."

I mimicked the movements, but my eyes apparently decided that watching her beautiful ass cheeks move *back and forth* was a lot more fun than paying attention to the foot technique. Nina was wearing fleece leggings that clung to her body, and holy hell it was hot. Needless to say, I ended up falling on my *own* ass as a result.

Two kids barely older than toddler age whizzed by me and laughed.

Great.

To make matters worse, now Nina was helping me up. "You need to dig into the ice, Jake. As soon as you lose that grip, you'll fall."

"I know. I just got a little distracted."

By your fucking beautiful ass.

Gradually, I got my act together, and we practiced the back and forth technique for several minutes until I was able to move on the ice.

"Now, the next thing I'm going to show you is a basic movement called a swizzle."

"A whatchamacallit?"

She giggled. "A swizzle. Watch." Nina's legs opened and closed in slow, gliding motions. "You push your skates apart and let them slowly come back together. Just like this."

If I thought the other stuff earlier was making me crazy, seeing her legs open and close like this made my imagination run wild.

She continued to demonstrate as my eyes stayed transfixed on her body. "Open and close. Open and glide back together, see? That's called a swizzle."

Swizzle.

Me like swizzle.

That was the last thought I had before a heavyset man plowed right into me, knocking me on my ass again.

"Oh my God. Jake!" Nina yelled as she spun around.

"Sorry, man. You alright?" the guy asked as he reached out his hand and helped me up.

I needed to get the hell out of these ice skates before I completely lost every bit of coolness I'd ever built up in Nina's eyes.

"Yeah...yeah, I'm fine," I said.

"Did you not see him coming toward you?"

"I was focusing on your swizzle."

Is that what they're calling it now?

"Okay, take my hand. You need to practice. We'll skate together. You're gonna come forward in a swizzle, and I'm gonna move backwards. Hold onto me." I started moving my feet in the way she'd demonstrated. "That's right," she said. "Apart and together. Apart and together."

We were moving slowly across the ice. "I'm not sure this is a good idea, my holding onto you like this."

"You're doing fine."

Miraculously, I'd finally found a rhythm that worked for me. I was going so slowly that it was nearly impossible to fall. Nina looked gorgeous as she looked up into my eyes while we held hands. She was wearing white earmuffs atop her golden hair that fell in messy waves over her matching white coat. Her cheeks were rosy from the cold air. She reminded me of a sexy ice princess.

She repeated, "You're doing so good."

At one point, she gave me a sweet smile that was so agonizingly beautiful, it made me lose focus and forget to dig into the ice again. I fell, but this time, she went down along with me. As Nina fell back, I landed on top of her.

"Nina! Shit. Are you okay?"

She closed her eyes and for a split second, it seemed like she was crying which caused me to panic. It quickly became apparent that she was actually laughing hysterically. It was just the kind of all-consuming laugh where no sound came out.

My arms were on each side of her. "It's not really funny. I could have crushed you."

She was still laughing. "Well, you didn't. I'm still in one piece."

Her tits were plastered against my chest, and I had to fight my body's reaction; I could feel myself getting hard. But truthfully, I didn't really want to get off of her. It seemed my body much preferred getting off *on* her instead.

Our faces were close when I said, "I'd get up, but I'm not sure how to without falling on my ass again."

She began to laugh even harder at my admission, and now, I was laughing at myself. I could feel her sweet breath on my face. Was I sick for wanting to just stay on the ground with her and never get up?

"You know what? That's good. You needed to fall. Because if you don't fall, you'll never learn how to pick yourself up."

I rolled off of her and sat on the ice.

She got up and kneeled. "Alright, do what I do. Put one foot out in front of you, okay?" I did as she said. "Now transfer all of your weight to your left foot and dig into the ice with your right. Got it?"

I managed to carefully get myself up. We started skating alongside each other when I somehow gained unwanted momentum, slamming into a barrier.

She was laughing as she skated toward me. "That reminds me. I need to teach you how to stop!"

"You think this is funny, huh?"

I teasingly took her earmuffs off her head and put them on mine.

"Hey, lay off my muff!" Her face turned red even though her innuendo was clearly intentional.

God, I loved dirty Nina.

I couldn't help myself. "I prefer to keep your muff closer to my face." Her cheeks turned even redder. "Don't dish it if you can't take it, Kennedy."

She conveniently changed the subject. "I need to seriously teach you how to stop."

"Running my mouth?"

"No...stopping on the ice." She pointed her toes together. "Do this then push your heels out. That's how you stop." She skated around me, starting and stopping several times. I copied the motion, eventually becoming accustomed to it.

She took my hand, and we skated slowly side by side for several minutes. This time, I'd really gotten the hang of it. So caught up in the moment with Nina, I'd barely noticed that the sun had set. The Christmas lights around us looked suddenly magnificent in the darkness.

"It's getting cold. We should probably get going," she said.

I wasn't ready for our date to end. It wasn't an official date, but it somehow felt like the first real date I'd ever been on.

After we returned our skates, I tugged on her coat. "Let's go get some hot chocolate."

"Okay. That sounds good."

We walked to a café around the corner and found a cozy booth that overlooked the giant Christmas tree on the plaza. I watched her as she looked out the window and sipped her drink. Spending this afternoon with her had been one of the best experiences in recent memory for me. All I could think about was how badly I was feeling the need to open up to her. I wanted to share myself with her in any way I could. In that moment, I decided that if she didn't get an A on her next exam, I was going to nix the helicopter idea. It needed to be something bigger and better. We'd go on a plane ride instead, and I'd take her away to Chicago, show her where I grew up. I hadn't been back since I was a teenager, and I wanted to share that experience with her.

"Nina, I love that you're getting A's, but is it wrong that I really hope your last grade sucks?"

"Why is that?"

"There's some place I really want to take you."

A worried look washed across her face. "Now, I'm scared."

"Don't be scared. It'll be amazing."

Inherently, it felt like the end of my hiding the truth was near. It was going to happen after Christmas, which meant that this time of ignorant bliss with Nina would be over soon.

I must have gotten lost in my mind.

"You always do that when you're deep in thought."

"What?"

"Grind your tongue ring against your teeth."

"Does it annoy you?"

"No, not at all."

I wished she'd kept it at that.

Instead, she added, "I think it's sexy."

Her words went straight to my dick, triggering a sweet ache of pleasure and pain. My eyes seared into hers as I nodded slowly. So many possible responses flooded my brain, but I opted not to say anything at all. She couldn't begin to imagine what I wanted to do to her with my tongue.

I crushed the paper cup out of frustration. "We should go."

That night, I was sitting in bed when Nina texted me from her room.

How's my Brian Boitano?

Wait. Who was that? I had to think and then remembered he was an Olympic figure skater.

> *Jake: More like Brian Boita-NO. No, no, no! Never do that again. ;-)*

> *Nina: You were actually pretty good for your first time.*

> *Jake: Yeah...Big Goons on Ice. Don't order me a leotard. Pretty sure it was my first and last time.*

> *Nina: Damn it! I was gonna teach you the Bunny hop jump and half lutz next time.*

> *Jake: Don't you mean half KLUTZ?*

> *Nina: LOL. You make me laugh. Thanks again for coming with me.*

You make me so fucking happy.

Jake: You're welcome.

Later that night, Nina walked down the hall to take her evening shower. I held the paper bat in my hand, waiting to sneak it into her room.

What I almost wrote:

I'd go again fo shizzle,
Just to watch you swizzle.

What I wished I could have written:

I want there to be a million next times.

What I never could have written:

You know what?
I'd give my left nut,
To have my way
With that beautiful butt.

What I actually wrote:

> **Mr. Bat says to hang up my skates...**
> **Because I'm the worst fucking skat-**
> **er in the United States.**

THIRTEEN

PAST

Our very last study session before Nina's final exam rolled around. There would no longer be an official excuse to spend time alone with her on a consistent basis, and it was seriously bumming me out.

Clutching her books in one hand and a plate of muffins in the other, Nina appeared at the doorway. She looked incredibly sexy in a short wool skirt and leather boots.

"I made some banana muffins for our last time."

"Ah! I thought I smelled something baking in the kitchen. Trying to butter up the teacher?" I grabbed one and took a bite. "Mmm...fucking good."

"It doesn't take much, apparently."

I shook my head with a grin. "No, it doesn't."

"Thanks a lot, by the way."

My mouth was full. "For what?"

She handed me the entire plate and sat on the bed. As usual, I stayed at my desk and propped up my feet.

"You know what!" she said.

"Actually, I don't."

"Really? *Baby Got Back*? Ring a bell?"

Oh, snap. I'd actually forgotten about that.

Heh heh.

A few days ago, I programmed a ring tone that played *Baby Got Back* by Sir Mix-A-Lot into Nina's phone.

"You didn't get a single phone call for three days? How are you only realizing it now?"

"You text me all the time, but the only person who really calls my cell is my dad. He rang me in the middle of class. Everyone thinks I'm a freak now."

"A freak who likes big asses."

"According to you, yes. Thank you."

"Hey." I winked. "It takes one to know one."

Even though she was trying to pretend my prank made her mad, she couldn't contain her laughter. One of the things I loved about Nina was that she really got my strange humor even when it was at her own expense. She took everything I threw at her in stride.

I grabbed another muffin and opened up my laptop. "We're sprinting to the finish now, Kennedy. You ready?"

"As ready as I'll ever be."

"I think we need to make this a late one, work overtime. What do you say?"

She handed me some worksheets. "Can we start with probability again? That's the easiest for me. It'll get me warmed up."

As always, I looked over the sample she gave me and changed the variables to names of things Nina could relate to.

"In a group of 200 people, 36 have donkey asses, 52 have asses that are flat as a pancake, and 126 have average-sized butts. Out of all the people, half have muffin tops. If one of these 200 people is to be chosen at random, what is the probability that the person has a donkey ass and a muffin top?"

"How fitting," she said.

About an hour later, we were deep into solving an equation for a different word problem when Ryan walked in.

"This box came for you, Jake." He clumsily threw the package on the bed, and it fell on the ground. Then, before walking out, he gave Nina a look that I didn't appreciate.

"Well, isn't he especially charming tonight," she said.

Picking up the box off the floor, I realized it contained some art supplies I'd ordered. "He's fucking miserable. I don't know how your brother ever got along with him."

"They didn't always get along."

"I thought you said they were best friends."

"Toward the end of Jimmy's life, they were the closest they'd ever been. Ryan was by Jimmy's side when he died, actually." She took a deep breath to compose her thoughts. "Since childhood, our families were close. He and Jimmy had their ups and downs over the years. There were times, though, when my brother and he weren't even on speaking terms."

"Really...well, I can't say that surprises me, considering what an asshole he can be sometimes. What did he do to make Jimmy stop speaking to him?"

Nina pursed her lips and seemed reluctant to answer. Then, she finally said, "Ryan dated his sister."

At first, it didn't register.

His sister.

I felt the banana muffins coming up on me.

Nina was Jimmy's only sister.

Ryan dated Nina?

Fuck.

Nina and Ryan.

I think I finally understood where the term "blinded by jealousy" came from because I could have sworn my vision blurred as my brain processed the shock of hearing those words.

"What? You and Ryan?"

"Yes. Ryan and I briefly dated when I was sixteen."

My stomach sank when she confirmed it. "And you never thought to mention this before?"

"Honestly? No. It was so long ago. I don't see him that way, anymore, Jake. I look at him like a brother. I really always have. It never felt any other way with him. He'd always been around all my life, and we spent enough time around each other that when we got to a certain age, we just started dating. That's kind of how it goes in small towns, I guess."

"But you said...that other guy...Spencer...that he was your first..."

"That's right. I never had sex with Ryan. I was too young."

"You kissed him..."

"Yes."

I knew I was out of line but asked it anyway. "That's all you did?"

"Jake..."

"Answer me," I demanded.

"What do you want me to say?"

"Did he touch you?"

"Yes."

I closed my eyes. "I don't want to know anymore."

"I shouldn't have said anything."

"No, actually, this explains a fuck of a lot, why he won't get off my jock about you. Does Tarah know?"

"I don't think so, unless he's told her without my knowing. Again, it was so long ago. It's almost insignificant. I don't view him like that at all."

My face felt like it was burning up. I felt the need to break something and needed to be alone to let this sink in. "Fair enough." I stood up and handed her the empty muffin plate. "You know what, Nina? I think we've done enough for tonight. It's getting late. I actually have to take a shower. I forgot I have an early meeting tomorrow."

Without saying anything further, I left the room and headed down the hall. Blood was pumping through my ears, and it felt like the hallway was swaying.

I got in the shower and let the water rain down on me. It wasn't helping to lessen the blow of hearing that news. My mind became littered with upsetting thoughts.

The mere idea of him touching her body, sucking on her beautiful tits, going down on her, made me want to vomit. This was only the second time in my life I'd been hit with this level of jealousy, the first being her date with Alistair. This was much worse.

I vowed to stay in the shower until I could calm down. After about thirty minutes, my temper about the situation was starting to wear off. I had no right to feel this possessive toward her, but there was nothing I could do to stop it. I also had no right to fault her for her lie of omission when my own was colossal. Really, the biggest thing that bothered me was that I might never get the chance to experience with her what others had.

While I couldn't help the jealousy, my reaction had been juvenile. I quickly wiped down and threw my pants on. I'd planned to go to her room and apologize but found her sitting on my bed in the same spot where I'd left her.

She got up, and her heels clicked as she walked toward me. "I'm sorry I upset you."

"I'm sorry I reacted that way."

My skin was not completely dry, and a droplet of water ran down my chest. She placed her fingertip over it and swiped it away. The delicate touch was brief but had a lasting effect. My abs tightened in an attempt to control my body's reaction.

"You wanna know something?" she whispered.

My voice was hoarse. "What?" I was barely able to speak. All I wanted was for her to keep touching me. I wanted to push her down on the bed, lift her skirt and make her forget her own name.

"Your jealousy. It feels good."

She traced the tattoos on my right forearm with her finger while my eyes followed the path.

"Well, it doesn't feel good for me."

My body ached for the return of her touch after she stopped and crossed her arms in front of her chest.

"You don't tell me what you're thinking. You don't open up to me, so it's the only thing that shows me how you feel."

"I guess I can't hide everything."

"I want to explain," she said.

"Explain what?"

"What happened with Ryan and me, because I know your imagination is running wild, and you're probably making it out to be something more than it was."

"Fuck, Nina, you don't owe me any explanation. My reaction was uncalled for. It's none of my business, and I really don't want to know. I— "

"We kissed, and he felt me up. That was it. It was nothing below the waist. I never let it get that far."

I let out the breath I'd been holding. It could have been a lot worse. "You really didn't need to tell me that."

"Tell me you weren't going over it in your head just now in the shower."

"Fuck yes, I was."

"I know I don't owe you an explanation, but I care about you, and you were obviously upset by it. I wanted to be honest so that you weren't wasting your time contemplating what I meant."

Guilt was creeping in fast. I'd given her so little honesty in return because of my own fears. I'd taught her to face her fears, and I'd been running from mine to avoid losing her.

"Your honesty is way more than I deserve, Nina."

"Why do you say that?"

"I'm so afraid to hurt you."

"You're scaring me. I don't understand. Please talk to me." She begged, "Please."

I placed my hand on her face and cupped her cheek. "I will. I promise."

After Christmas.

FOURTEEN
PAST

Sixty-Nine.

There's a reason universe rhymes with perverse. The stars aligned, and that number was just a bonus when Nina brought home that exact grade for her final exam. Despite the crappy score, I had prayed so hard that we would get one more excursion together before she had to leave, especially since nothing would be the same once I told her all about Ivy after Christmas.

When she came to my room to break the news about the test, I wasted no time in going online to purchase our tickets.

It was 4:30 a.m. I knew Nina would be freaking out and unable to sleep. I'd purposely left her an origami bat last night with a message that gave away the fact that I'd be taking her to Chicago.

It was just too exciting for me to hold in, but that wasn't the main reason I decided to tell her. These exercises were supposed to be kept secret up until her perceived moment of doom. However, since this would be her very first plane ride, I felt the need to give her a heads up this time.

I knocked on her bedroom door. "Nina, the cab's here. We have to leave."

Her face looked white as a ghost, and she had bags under her eyes. "I don't think I can go through with this."

"I promise it'll be okay. I'll be there every step of the way."

"I've had nightmares about flying ever since I was a kid."

"You do realize how safe air travel is? We're in greater danger driving to the airport."

"Then, I'll seriously wish for an accident to prevent me from having to get on that plane."

"Nina, the cab is waiting. Come. I've got you. Everything is gonna be fine. I can't wait to show you where I grew up."

Her breathing was shaky as she let me take her cold hand.

Traffic was light, and it was still dark out. The ride to the airport was far different than the last time Nina and I were in a cab together. Her body was stiff as a board as she sat away from me and stared straight ahead at the early morning news playing on the small television screen behind the driver's seat. Her body language was no different than if I'd been holding a gun to her head. I was damn proud of her for not refusing to come, though. The choice was always still hers. That proved she trusted me and wanted to overcome her fears. She was a hell of a lot braver than I was in facing my own.

I paid the driver and led a reluctant Nina out of the cab. I'd brought my backpack with some snacks, music and other tricks, but since we wouldn't be staying the night, Nina only had a purse.

As we stood in line at the ticket counter, her body trembled. She was going to need my comfort, both mentally and physically. Just for today, I needed to throw whatever rules I'd had about not touching her out the window. As I rubbed her shoulders to calm her down, she let out a deep sigh upon my touch. As always, she was so responsive to me, which I loved.

I hated how uncomfortable she was and vowed that once we got to our gate, everything in my power would be done to make her feel better. We were early, so there would be a lot of time to kill.

At security, an alarm went off when Nina passed through the detector, so she was pulled aside. Under any other circumstances, watching her being frisked by another woman would have been hot, but it pissed me off because it was putting her further on edge.

We finally got to the seating area with an hour to spare before the flight. I reluctantly left her sitting alone while I bought some things from the shop across the way.

When I returned, I handed her the bag. "Here."

"What's this?"

"Some survival items for you."

She took the candy out first. "Pop Rocks?"

"To counter your ear popping. These cancel it out. Pop some in your mouth. You won't even notice it."

"*I heart New York* underwear?"

I grinned. "In case you pee your pants again."

She wasn't laughing, perhaps because her pissing herself was a likelier scenario than either of us wanted to admit.

Next, she took out a small paperback I bought. It had two guys and a girl on the cover. "*Midnight Ménage?*"

"Just some kinky shit to get your mind off things." I wiggled my eyebrows. "I can read it to you if you want."

She smiled for the first time all morning. "Nina Kennedy, is that a smile? You dirty little minx."

She took out the last item. "A teddy bear?"

"He'll keep you company if I have to get up to use the bathroom."

A hint of another smile spread across her lips. "Jake..."

I took the items. "I'll put everything in my bag for you."

Despite the brief distraction from freaking out, Nina went right back into her own mind soon after. She was staring up at the digital screen that indicated our plane was now at the gate. A boarding announcement rang over the loud speaker.

She gripped my arm. "I don't think I can do this. I'm serious."

"I won't let anything happen to you."

"How can you say that? You don't have any control in this case!"

I placed my hands on her cheeks and looked into her eyes. "We're never a hundred percent in control in life, Nina. We just think we are. Something bigger than us is always in the driver's seat. What we can control is our perception, our reactions to things. We can also control whether we choose to live life or live in fear." I slid my palms off of her face, stood up and held out my hand. "Now, give me your hand. I've got you."

Nina was shaking, but she obliged. I lifted her out of the seat, her delicate arm buckling under the force of my grip. Her soft breasts brushed against my chest as I pulled her into me. I flashed a reassuring smile. "Let's fly."

While my smile went unreturned, she continued to cooperate and dragged her feet all the way to the plane as I rubbed her shoulders.

After we made our way to our seats, an idea came to me. "I'll be right back."

"Don't leave me!" she said as I started to walk down the aisle.

"I'll only be gone a minute."

I walked up to a flight attendant and asked if Nina could visit the cockpit, which was open. The pilots were going over their flight plan.

"I'm sorry, sir, but this is a really packed aircraft. I don't think that's going to be possible."

"My friend has never flown before. She's extremely scared, and I think it would help if she could meet the guys in control."

"I just don't think so."

I glanced worriedly over at Nina. She looked pale, breathing heavily and licking her lips incessantly. "That's her in row nine. Look how petrified she is. People are still boarding. Please? We'll only be a minute."

She must have spotted the terror in Nina's eyes, because she gave in. "Go back to your seat. I'll talk to the pilot and call you up if they allow it."

"Thank you. I really appreciate it."

A few minutes later, she waved her hand at us.

"Come on, Nina. We're gonna go meet the pilots real quick." She took my hand and followed me down the aisle as we squeezed past incoming passengers. I looked behind my shoulders at her and said, "It's not a faceless vessel. You need to see that there are qualified people at the helm."

They wouldn't let me go in with her, so I stayed back just outside the cockpit door. The pilot and co-pilot seemed very friendly, showing Nina all of the controls and touting the years of flight hours they had between the two of them. Both had white hair, so that was a good sign. She was clearly still scared shitless, but I think it helped to re-assure her just a smidge.

I turned to the flight attendant. "Thanks again for your help."

She straightened her navy skirt and licked her lips. "No problem. If you want, you can make it up to me when we land." She smiled. "You're adorable."

Before I could respond, Nina appeared next to me. I nodded once to the attendant, blatantly ignoring her prop-osition and led Nina back to our seats.

Her breathing was becoming erratic. She wouldn't look at me.

"Are you okay?" I asked.

She barely got the word out in between breaths, "No."

"Hold my hand, Nina. Squeeze it as hard as you need to. Breathe."

When the engines turned on, her grip on my hand tightened. She was holding onto me for dear life, her fear more tangible this time than it had been during our ele-vator exercise. The fact that she'd never experienced this before must have made her reaction more intense. When the plane started to move, her breathing became even more uncontrolled, and it sounded like she was wheezing. I'd packed some small brown paper bags in case she hy-perventilated. Taking one out, I handed it to her. "Breathe into this, baby."

So caught up in the moment, I hadn't meant to call her that. It just came out, but honestly, it was doubtful that she even heard it.

The bag didn't seem to be helping her catch her breath, and it was actually freaking me out a little because if she really were in some kind of physical danger, there was no way to get her medical help. I had to think fast in order to get her mind off the impending takeoff somehow. Two ideas came to me: kiss her senseless or tickle her feet.

Since it would make for a sucky memory if she passed out or foamed at the mouth during our first kiss, the second option would have to be it. Nina had told me once that her brother used to torture her by tickling her feet. If I did it on takeoff, she would have no choice but to succumb to laughter. That would make it impossible for her to focus on the scary thoughts that were feeding her panic and causing her to lose her breath.

The plane started picking up speed, and amidst the sound of the roaring engines, I bent down and quickly untied her shoes. Before she could ask me what the fuck I was doing, I started to tickle the bottoms of her feet. She was wiggling, kicking and most importantly, laughing. As the plane tilted upward for takeoff, my ears started to pop, but it didn't slow me down.

"Jake...stop!"

I looked up at her but refused to stop tickling despite her constant begging. Tears of laughter were pouring out of her eyes. The cackle of my own hysterical laughter resonated through the narrow space. When I finally came up for air, we were cruising. The old lady across the aisle was saying a rosary and giving me a dirty look for having interrupted her. We'd disturbed the peace, but it was worth it. Hallelujah.

Nina was still coming down from the laughing fit. Looking annoyed, the flight attendant who'd tried to pick me up earlier came over to us. "Is everything okay over here?"

"Yes. Everything's just perfect."

It was.

We were well into the flight, and Nina had calmed down a bit after listening to some music I'd downloaded for her.

She took off her headphones for a moment. "How much longer?"

"About a half-hour."

"I still can't believe you did that to me."

I raised my brow. "Now, when people ask how you got through takeoff, you can tell them I went down on you."

She punched me lightly in the arm and returned the headphones to her ears.

Nina had been listening to the special playlist I'd put together for the flight. In my typical wise ass fashion, I'd titled the list *Crash and Burn*. The songs in the beginning were meant to make her laugh, but there were a couple that I'd snuck in because they conveyed feelings that were impossible for me to express. At one point, she looked at me, and I knew one of *those* songs had come on.

I took one of her earbuds to hear it and smiled when I realized she was listening to *Come Away with Me* by Norah Jones. That song said it all more than the others. I wished I could just take Nina away some place for a lot longer than a day and not have to deal with inevitably breaking her heart after Christmas. All I wanted was to be with her. For now, this quick jaunt to Chicago would have to do. It wasn't just about getting her over the fear of flying. The trip was also for me, so that I could feel what it was like to take her away just once.

"That's a beautiful song," she said. "I've always loved it. I love it even more now."

Me, too. Because it will always remind me of you.

I yearned to touch her, so when a patch of turbulence came, that was my excuse to grab her hand again. At one point, the plane jolted hard, and she tightened her grip on me. I wanted to hold her, but instead in a silent compromise, took both of her hands inside mine and held them together. "It's almost over, Nina. You did good."

My stomach sank as I absorbed my own words, which I hoped didn't foreshadow the weeks to come.

It's almost over.

It wouldn't be a full excursion without a couple of surprises up my sleeve. Our action-packed morning started with a killer view of the city.

Nina was less than enthused by our stop at the famous Skydeck at Willis Tower. I made her stand with me on the glass ledge that extends out over a thousand feet in the air. We had our picture taken, and I'll always cherish that photo despite the look of terror on her face. That very look in contrast to my wide smile was what made it a classic snapshot that would forever be a keepsake.

The second stop was a visit to the house where I grew up on the South Side. No one was home, so we couldn't go inside. Instead, we sat outside for almost an hour as I told Nina stories about my childhood. I'd gotten the urge to kiss her a dozen times on this trip but never as much as when we were sitting in the backyard of my old house. She'd grabbed my hand and was listening so intently to me reminisce while the breeze blew her hair around. It took every ounce of restraint in me not to reach over, fist that beautiful hair in my hands and pull her toward me.

After we left, the next stop was supposed to be lunch at Bernie's, a retro diner and one of my favorite childhood haunts. On the way there, though, a feeling came over me that I couldn't shake. It wasn't part of the original plan, but I couldn't leave Chicago without making a certain stop.

"How hungry are you?"

"I could take it or leave it," she said. "Why?"

"Do you mind if we take a detour?"

"Not at all."

"Maybe we can pick up something on the way then hit Bernie's for dinner instead of lunch."

I hailed an approaching cab, and we hopped inside.

"Where are we going?" she asked.

My chest hurt just thinking about it. "Naperville."

The cab idled as Nina and I walked up the path of dead, snow-covered grass that led to my sister's plot. Her name, *Amanda Thompson*, was carved into the granite gravestone. Guilt set in because I hadn't been back here since moving to Boston for college. Life happened, then Ivy happened, and the things that were once so important to me here took an unintentional backseat. Dried-up flowers that were half-covered in snow blew in the wind. It made me incredibly sad, but having Nina with me made it a bit easier to face.

I kneeled down at the foot of the headstone. "When you first told me about feeling guilty for not visiting Jimmy during his last days, it reminded me of how I felt after I moved away and couldn't come here anymore. I used to visit her here when I was a teenager a lot. It was out of the way from where we lived. I bought a crap car just to be able to come out here whenever I wanted to keep her company. I only knew her in death, so those visits were all we had, you know? They were what bonded us."

"That was how you met your other sister, right? Here at the gravesite?"

I nodded, still looking down at the stone. On the anniversary of her brother's death when Nina and I had stayed up all night talking, I'd told her all about Amanda. My sister died in a car accident when she was a teenager and was one of two daughters my mother had given up for adoption before I was born and before she'd met my father. I only found out about Amanda when I was sixteen, many years after she died, so I never had a chance to meet her. I met my other sister, Allison, when we ironically showed up at the cemetery at the exact same time one day.

"Even though we'd never met, somehow, I felt closer to Amanda than anyone else in my family. I'd talk to her during my cemetery visits, tell her about my teenage problems, ask her for advice. She almost felt like a spiritual guide to me. And I truly felt she was the one that brought Allison and me together that day."

"That's really powerful. You know she'd be proud of you, Jake."

"It's hard coming here after all the time away. I know it's not the same kind of loss you had, since you actually grew up day to day with your brother."

"But it's just as significant. You don't have the memories I have, which might make it even harder because there are no happy moments to cling to."

"I'd bring flowers every time. I didn't have a pot to piss in back then, but I always scrounged up enough money to buy some. I wanted her to be surrounded by nice things, wanted her to feel loved if she were to look down and see me here. I should've stopped somewhere and gotten some today on the way, actually."

"Don't feel bad. It's really cold. They wouldn't last." Nina kneeled down and put her hand on my shoulder. "In a way, even though she's not around, I bet she's taught you a lot."

"What do you mean?"

"Look at how you are. You're an old soul, so wise. You are who you are because of the losses you've sustained. You've channeled those into a positive attitude about life, while others like me, have let stress manifest into other things. Your sister...her death...have taught you to live in the moment and to not take things for granted."

"Life is too short not to be happy. I've learned that only recently." I turned to her and words that hadn't meant to be spoken aloud escaped me, "I want to be happy again."

After a long silence, she said, "You make me happy."

I rubbed the tip of my finger along her cheek. It felt as if my sister's spirit was giving me strength. Amanda would want me to be happy, to live life to the fullest because she couldn't. That realization gave me the courage to say something I hoped I wouldn't regret. "You make me happy, too, Nina. If nothing else, please always know that."

She gave me only a slight smile, seeming to understand the cryptic undertone in the last part of my admission. "Thank you for bringing me here, for showing me this and other important parts of your life. One step at a time."

"One step at a time," I repeated. That would have to be my mantra over Christmas.

Nina took off her necklace.

"What are you doing?"

"Here's the flower that you didn't bring." The charm on the necklace was a rose inside of a heart. "This one will last forever." She stuck it in the dirt, partially burying it into the ground. "Let it be a gift from me to Amanda, to thank her for helping shape you into the person you are. Without that, I wouldn't be here right now."

I wasn't even going to argue with her because the gesture was so incredibly sweet. "Thank you, Nina."

We stayed for about ten more minutes. In that time, I showed her a photo of Amanda that was tucked away in my wallet. She couldn't believe how much my sister and I resembled each other.

I kissed my hand before placing it on Amanda's stone and whispered, "I'll come back again soon. I promise. I love you, sis."

When we got back into the cab, Nina turned to me. "I'd like to visit her again with you someday."

I smiled. "You mean you'll willingly get on another plane to come here with me?"

She grinned. "You'd probably have to go down on me again."

The remaining hours of the trip were spent talking and eating while nestled inside a booth at Bernie's Diner until the sun set. We were surrounded by nostalgia, from my father's favorite song playing on the mini jukebox (*Crimson and Clover*, which also ironically happened to be a favorite of her brother's) to the milkshakes and burgers I'd grown up on.

By the time we left for the airport, my stomach was full, but it was no comparison to the fullness in my chest. Knowing that Nina was heading home tomorrow to upstate New York for Christmas break and that I was planning to tell her everything after she returned made me wish there were such a thing as a slow motion button in life. Or maybe a pause button.

I'd never been so happy and scared at the same time. Those feelings reached their peak during the plane ride home. Nina and I had an entire middle row of the Boeing 777 to ourselves. It was dark with minimal lighting and eerily quiet. Unlike our earlier flight which was full to capacity, this plane was nearly empty.

Nina's nerves were kicking in but not at the same level as before. Selfishly, I'd looked forward to takeoff because I'd been dying to touch her all afternoon and had been waiting for an excuse to hold her hand again. I had no plans to let go tonight.

As the plane taxied down the runway, our hands were locked together tightly. She was breathing heavily and trembling a little but not hyperventilating this time, probably because the experience wasn't completely unknown to her anymore. When the plane ascended, she closed her eyes and whispered something to herself. Her chest was rapidly rising and falling. Unable to control the need to comfort her, I leaned into her during the takeoff, resting my chin on her shoulder because I knew this was the scariest part of the flight for her.

She calmed down a little once the plane was level again, but her hand was still trembling. Once we were cruising for a while, the flight attendant came by with a drink cart. I placed the order for both of us before Nina had a chance to speak. "Two red wines, please." I whispered in her ear, "It will help you relax."

She quietly nodded as the attendant handed a glass of Merlot to each of us. When I took mine, I said, "I'll hold it, but you're drinking mine, too."

Nina took a long sip. "I don't want to get drunk, Jake. I need to be alert in case something happens."

"No. You're still shaking. What you really need is something to help you chill. I'll be your eyes and ears if anything happens. Keep holding my hand and drink up."

Several minutes after Nina polished off both glasses (which didn't take much prodding), the pilot announced that we may be experiencing some heavy turbulence up ahead. Sure enough, soon after, the aircraft started jerking around almost violently. I hadn't let go of her hand since takeoff. Holding it wasn't going to be enough to get her through this. A distraction was needed.

"We're gonna do something to get your mind off this."

She breathed through her reply, "Okay."

We started playing this game I'd completely made up where we took turns shouting out a word and then had to say the first thing that came to mind.

After a while, the turbulence let up, and our game ended, giving way to her simply asking me a ton of questions. One thing I'd learned about Nina was that alcohol made her chatty and inquisitive.

She turned her body toward me. "If you could travel to any place in the world, where would you go?"

I rubbed my chin pensively. "Probably Italy. My mother has some second cousins who live in Venice. I bet it's beautiful."

"It must be so romantic there. The Gondola rides? The food! Italy is definitely on my list. I would love to go someday."

Maybe someday we will.

"Maybe someday you will," I said.

"If this were a week ago, I would have said that a trip to Europe wouldn't ever be possible because I refuse to fly. But I guess I'm proving right now that I *am* capable of getting on a plane, capable of more than I ever gave myself credit for. If I'm ever brave enough to do this again, so many dreams could become reality for me. Of course, without you to hold my hand, I'm not sure I'd have the courage."

I swallowed the dread creeping up at the implication of my not being there someday to hold her hand. "You'll do just fine with or without me."

Our eyes locked for several seconds.

"I hope it's with you," she said.

I nodded but couldn't bring myself to respond, feeling suffocated by a flurry of emotions. When I didn't say anything, she searched my expression for some semblance of truth. There was no doubt that my behavior was confusing the shit out of her.

She changed the subject. "I never asked you. I know you're spiritual, but are you Catholic? What religion are you?"

"You're just one question after another when you're tipsy, Nina."

"Sorry."

"Don't be sorry. I'll answer your questions all day long if it keeps you distracted." I turned my body toward her to match the positioning of her own body still turned toward mine. "My mother is Catholic, but we never practiced. I don't believe in any one religion. But I do believe in a higher power that some call God. There might be more than one. There might be a whole team in charge, but I don't believe that all of this is just a coincidence without a purpose."

"You believe that everything happens for a reason. You've said that before. I believe that, too. I had a hard time with my faith, though, after Jimmy died."

"I know what you mean. It's a mystery how a good God can also let certain things happen."

"I'm starting to get some of my faith back, though." Her eyes bore into mine. "Since I met you."

Those words made me feel euphoric and like getting punched in the gut at the same time.

"I'm glad you feel that way," I simply said, wishing I could tell her that not only my faith, but my entire outlook on life had changed since she entered my world.

Just when she was getting her faith in life back, though, I was going to drop a bombshell on her that our relationship might never recover from, that would likely break her heart and shatter her faith all over again.

Nina laughed to herself. "Maybe Jimmy met Amanda in heaven and said to her, 'Your brother should meet my crazy sister.' Maybe they conspired to introduce us."

"That's a nice thought." I smiled. "I really like that thought, except Amanda would have said to him, 'Dude, trust me, you haven't met crazy until you've met my brother.'"

Her mouth spread into a wide smile, and I squeezed her hand affectionately.

Our attention then turned to an elderly couple who slowly made their way to the airplane lavatory and entered it together.

I wrinkled my forehead. "You think they're messing around in there?"

She giggled. "That's kind of gross."

"Because I think she's backin' that up. Unless she's helping him wipe his ass, why else would they have gone in there together?"

Nina covered her mouth in laughter with her one free hand. "I guess you could be right."

"I'll tell you something," I said. "I want to be fucking around in an airplane bathroom when I'm eighty-five. That's for damn sure. Why not?"

Her curious stare was penetrating. "Have you ever joined the mile-high club?"

I cringed. Ivy and I had done that years ago on the return trip from Vegas after our elopement. I wanted to be honest about whatever I could with her. "Yes. Once."

She looked embarrassed for having asked and a little disappointed in my answer. "I see."

"It was a long time ago, Nina. I was a teenager."

"I'm not judging. You already know I've never joined. I guess there's a lot I haven't experienced."

"There's plenty of time to rectify that."

"You mean mile-high? But there's only a half-hour left to the flight. That's not enough time."

Her face turned red, and for a split second, a big "what if" crossed my mind. What if I lifted her up and led her down the aisle and into the bathroom right then and there. Would she have let me have her? The answer was honestly a mystery to me. A part of me thought she might slap me, but another part wondered if she'd go along with it, if she'd let me fuck her. My dick hardened at the thought. I'd never know.

Tapping my arm, she said, "Jake, you zoned out. I was totally kidding. I didn't really mean it when I said a half-hour wasn't enough time to...you know."

"Of course, you didn't."

"Half-hour is actually *plenty* of time."

An image of Nina's beautiful bare ass bent over the counter in those tight quarters while I rammed into her from behind came to mind. I had to literally shake my head to rid the thought because my cock was straining against my jeans. It was painfully arousing to imagine. I must have spaced out again.

"Jake...you don't think I was serious. I'm just kidding again."

"I knew that."

I knew it, but my dick is a gullible bastard.

"That's what you get for making me down two glasses of wine. I get fresh," she said.

The sexual tension from that exchange lingered through minutes of silence. Not once had we let go of each other's hands since takeoff.

Deciding to break the ice, I asked, "How are you getting to your parents?"

She bit her bottom lip. "Don't be upset."

"Okay..."

"Ryan was renting a car anyway, so he offered to drive me. It made sense because he's going to the same place. The bus tickets are expensive."

My free hand tensed, forming into a fist. "Uh-huh."

"Are you mad?"

Insanely jealous was more like it, and I didn't want her to see through it. I needed to earn as much of her respect as possible before my telling her everything and also needed to trust her assurance that she wasn't interested in him in that way.

"No, it's fine. I bet he drives like an old man, so I'm glad you'll have a safe way of getting there." I clenched my teeth in envy of his being able to spend several hours in the car with her.

"What will you do for Christmas?"

"I'll be at my sister's. My mother and stepfather will be there, too. They live just outside Boston."

My mother, Vanessa, had remarried a couple of years ago. Her husband, Max, owned the diner where my sister used to work. Allison had introduced them.

"Do you get along with your stepfather?"

"Yeah, he's actually really cool and treats my mother like gold."

"Good. So, everyone on your end will be together for Christmas."

"Yeah. The family all gets together for dinner Christmas Eve, and then we sit by the fireplace and exchange presents. We watch my nieces get spoiled with gifts that I usually end up assembling and putting batteries into."

Of course, I had to omit the part about spending the early part of that evening with Ivy.

"I wanted to get you something but didn't have the chance," Nina said. "I may have to mail you something. What would you want?"

I want you.

I want you not to leave me when you find out.

That was all I wanted. That and to finally be able to show her with my body exactly how I felt about her without having to hold back.

"You don't have to get me anything."

"Are you kidding? After everything you've done for me? I'm definitely getting you something. And if you don't tell me what you want, I'm gonna have to guess, and that could be dangerous. You could end up getting something you hate."

"I'm sure I'd love anything you picked out for me."

"Private ice skating lessons, then?"

"Hmm. Ice *dancing* maybe...with a sequin shirt and spandex. Now, we're talking."

"Be careful what you wish for, Green."

She flashed me the type of smile that was always painful to look at, the sweetest kind that lit up not only her face but her eyes. I looked down at my watch to distract from it and saw there wasn't much time left on this flight. I never wanted it to end, not only the plane ride but the feeling of peace that I was experiencing. Being with her among the clouds like this without the problems that faced me on the ground was something I may never have again. If we kept flying endlessly, that would have been fine by me.

When Nina closed her eyes, my body remained turned toward her. With each passing minute, fear reared more of its ugly face.

My mind drifted into a sea of worry, and it was exactly what I advised Nina against: letting fear of the future overtake the present moment as I imagined the different possible scenarios that could result from my impending confession.

Please understand, Nina.

My thoughts about what might happen after Christmas had consumed me so much that I hadn't even realized I was caressing her hand with my thumb. My body had apparently taken advantage while my brain wasn't paying enough attention to warn against it. It was doing what felt natural. That was my first prolonged physical gesture toward her. We'd held hands several times, innocently spooned and joked around about sexual things. Hell, I'd even told her I wanted to make her come. But aside from briefly grabbing her waist that one drunken night in my room, I'd never actually touched her for any great length of time in a really *sensual* way. While rubbing my thumb against her hand might have seemed like an innocent thing, as soon as she started matching my circular motion with her own thumb, it turned into something altogether different. My strokes became firmer to let her know that I approved of the reciprocation. Just from the way my body was responding, and the way she always reacted to even brief contact from me, I knew that sex with Nina would rock my world. At the moment, I was certain I'd do practically anything to experience being inside of her just once.

I continued to watch her breathing as her eyes remained closed.

We could be so good together. In every way.

I prayed for the chance as her soft tiny thumb circled my big calloused one. She caught me off guard when she suddenly opened her eyes, turning to me and seemed surprised to find me staring at her. My eyes hadn't left her since she'd closed hers. I was caught in the act.

The plane was losing altitude in preparation of the landing, and I became overcome with emotion. The slow descent represented the beginning of a new phase of our relationship, one that would be based on harsh reality, not fantasy.

I had to prepare myself for the likely possibility that I'd lose her and decided that if that were the case, moving out of the apartment would be the only option. To live with her and have to watch her from afar moving on with her life...dating...would be torture. The other side of the coin, if she accepted my life as it was, would bring me everything I'd ever wanted, things I never thought would be possible. What bothered me the most was that I truly had no idea which way it was going to play out.

I finally let go of her hand just long enough to push some of her hair behind her ear. "You better put on your seatbelt. The light just came on."

Trepidation returned to her eyes as she thought about the impending landing. She leaned her head on my shoulder and closed her eyes. I closed mine, too. She'd done it to calm herself down, but I'd done it to cherish the last moments of our flight. Inhaling every sweet breath that escaped her as she exhaled, I attempted to burn the scent into memory, trying to imagine what she tasted like.

After a rough, bouncy landing, the aircraft skidded to a halt. Our hands stayed connected as we exited the plane. We continued to hold hands as we navigated through the crowd at JFK and kept our fingers intertwined during the ride home. It started to snow outside while Christmas music played on the cab radio.

"I wish I didn't have to leave tomorrow," she said, her voice almost pained. "I'm so much happier here than there."

I'm happier when you're here, too.

I tightened my grip on her hand as Josh Groban's rendition of *O, Holy Night* came on. It made me sad that she was dreading Christmas. It was the main reason I was waiting to talk to her about Ivy since I knew the holidays would be hard enough on her. "I really wish you didn't have to go, either."

When the cab dropped us off in front of the apartment, I made no effort to go inside and neither did she. Nina sat on the stoop in front of our building and looked up at the sky while the snow fell on us, forming a powdery layer of white over her hair. Even though it was snowing, the temperature was mild.

She held her hands up to catch the snowflakes. "This is beautiful."

You are.

"It is," I said.

"What time is it?" she asked.

"It's nearly 2 a.m."

She bit her bottom lip. "We should probably go in."

"Do you *want* to go inside?"

"Not really."

"Let's not, then." Determined not to let this day end, I stood up and gave her my hand. "Come on."

"Where are we going?"

"To buy a few things."

We walked the couple of blocks to the all-night grocery store. As we entered the bright lighting of the market, she looked at me inquisitively. "What are we getting?"

"Since we won't be together for Christmas on Sunday, we should have a little party tonight."

Nina was grinning from ear to ear. "I think that's a great idea."

I picked up a carton of eggnog, a small bunch of overly ripe bananas and some holiday sugar cookies. Clutching the paper bag with one hand, I held her hand with the other as we walked back to our apartment.

"Let's stay out in the snow," I said. "I'm just gonna run inside. I'll be right back."

Ryan and Tarah were watching a movie in the living room when I entered the apartment. It surprised me to see them up so late.

"Hey, Jake," Tarah said.

"Hey."

"Where's Nina?"

"She's outside."

Ryan gave me one of his looks but kept quiet as I did my best to ignore him. Grabbing the blender and plugging it in, I dropped some ice, banana and eggnog inside then went over to the liquor cabinet for some rum. I turned on the blender to mix it all together and poured the drink into two large mugs.

When I rejoined Nina out front, a huge smile formed on her face as I handed her one. She took a sip. "Mmm... this is so good. What is it?"

"Iced banana rum eggnog. You like it?"

"I love it."

"Cheers," I said as we clanked our drinks together.

"Cheers."

I nudged her with my shoulder. "This is my kind of Christmas."

"Mine, too."

We munched on the Christmas cookies and drank our spiked nog while the snow continued to fall. We looked up in unison at the sound of a squeaky window opening and knew what would come next.

Mrs. Ballsworthy didn't say anything as she looked down at us. I took a chance when I held up my mug and shouted, "Merry Christmas, Mrs. Ballsworthy!"

We braced ourselves.

Nothing.

Nina and I looked at each other before giving up on a response.

Several seconds later, we heard it.

"Merry Christmas, motherfuckers!"

We fell back in laughter onto the snow-covered stairs.

"Now, *that's* a Christmas miracle." Nina laughed.

Lifting my mug up toward the sky, I chanted, "Merry Christmas to all motherfuckers and to all a motherfucking good night!"

It was practically morning by the time we finally went inside. Nina retreated to the shower, and as always, I snuck into her room. I opted not to leave her a bat that night because I'd been holding onto a pair of plastic gold pilot's wings to congratulate her on making it through her first airplane ride. I left the wings on her nightstand and went back to my room but couldn't sleep.

I'd have to leave for work in the morning and wouldn't see her again before she left since she and Ryan would be hitting the road to beat weekend traffic sometime in the afternoon. It was a Friday, and per usual, I'd be heading to Boston after work.

Before I left the following morning, I snuck a paper bat into her room. It had a hole punched into the top with some fishing line tied into a loop running through it. It was supposed to be a Christmas ornament.

What I almost wrote:

I can't thank you enough for yesterday.
Not just for letting me take you away,
But for seeing it through to the end.
And for being a true friend.

What I wished I could have written:

My Christmas wish this year,
Is to overcome MY fear.
Bet you never knew...
My one fear is losing you.

What I never could have written:

I'd just about die to fuck you in the sky.
So, if you ever want to try mile-high,
Thirty minutes would be more than enough,
To make you come, slow and rough.

What I actually wrote:

Hang this on your tree.
And think of me.

FIFTEEN
PRESENT

My sister reached over to pour more wine. "I'll never forget that Christmas."

"What exactly was so memorable for you?" I asked. "Because I'll tell you what I remember. I remember completely losing my shit."

"You came home a changed person. I could see in your eyes that you had something major on your mind. It was written all over your face. I suspected it had something to do with the same girl you mentioned to me before, but you wouldn't talk to me."

Cedric nodded his head, seeming way too amused. "So, she sent me to do some digging. Remember? I was the one that finally got it out of you. You were lovesick."

Allison slapped her knee. "Lovesick! That's a good way to describe it. My tough, tattooed, hard as nails brother had turned into a lovesick puppy."

Looking utterly entertained, Skylar curled into Mitch and glanced over at me. "So, you couldn't hide it anymore, huh?"

"Being away from her for those two weeks felt like an unbearable eternity. It's funny how being physically apart from someone can intensify the physical need for them. Those days were pivotal because not only did they confirm that I needed to come clean to her the second she came back, but they also made me more determined than ever to find a way to be with her. Losing her wasn't an option anymore because it felt like I needed her to breathe. I convinced myself that I'd find a way to make it work. Toward the end of the vacation, I basically decided to stop hiding the fact that I wanted her, too. I let her clearly know it."

"In what way?" Mitch asked.

"Things started getting sexual between us while we were apart. Maybe it was because of the safety barrier of separation or distance, but I just stopped holding back in that area."

"TMI," Allison shouted.

"Not at all," Skylar said as she crossed her legs and leaned in. "Do tell."

SIXTEEN
PAST

I spit out a piece of stale fruit cake into a red and green Christmas napkin and discreetly dumped it in the garbage, opting for a cookie instead. The buffet choices were limited at the annual Christmas Eve party held at the group home. I'd brought a tray of pigs in a blanket appetizers that people scarfed down within the first ten minutes.

About a dozen family members, residents and social workers packed into the small dining area. It was about four in the afternoon, and most were getting ready to leave.

Sipping hot apple cider, Ivy was in a quiet mood as we sat in the corner.

"Are you going to your sister's house for Christmas stuff tonight?" she asked.

"After I leave here, yes, but I'll stay with you as late as you want."

"Okay," she said, anxiously looking up at the clock.

"I won't leave till you tell me to, Ivy. Alright?"

She didn't respond. During most visits, she typically kicked me out way before I usually planned to leave anyway.

Half of the residents had gone home to their respec-
tive families for the holiday weekend. While Allison and
Cedric told me that Ivy was welcome at the house, bringing her there was something I'd avoided. The one year she
came home with me for Christmas Eve, she had an episode
that scared the living daylights out of my nieces. It wasn't
worth taking the risk again, especially since Ivy wasn't
comfortable there anyway, so there was no point in pushing it.

"Can I give you your present now?" I asked, taking an
envelope out of the inner pocket of my jacket.

She shook her head. "I'm not in the mood."

Shopping for Ivy was tough because she never liked
what I bought for her. Anything of sentimental value, like
jewelry, seemed to make her sad or angry. She hated any
of the clothing I picked out. The one thing I knew she'd
appreciate and actually use (aside from cigarettes, which I
refused to buy her) was a Dunkin Donuts gift card. Ivy took
daily walks there, and I made sure she had enough credit
on the card to last her a year. Their coffee was her favorite,
heavy on the cream and sugar, and I usually picked her up
a hot one before each of my visits.

A few of the residents played instruments, so as was
tradition at this yearly shindig, the slightly off-key Christmas music started to ring out in the opposite corner of the
room. Joe, a middle-aged man, belted out the harmonica
while Charleen, a girl in her twenties, played the electric
keyboard. Junior, a guy in his thirties, who was somewhat
hearing-impaired, played the guitar.

Ivy's eyes focused on Junior's hands as he worked the
strings. Although she was once a talented guitarist, she refused to play anymore, and that made me extremely sad
for her. Her Gibson always sat unused in the corner of her

bedroom as if it were a phantom from a previous life. Anytime I suggested that she try playing, Ivy would become irate.

She continued to quietly watch her housemates perform. Listening to the slow melody, I'd almost nodded off before my eyes wandered downward. Ivy's fingers were starting to move to the rhythm of the music as she stayed transfixed on Junior's guitar. She was playing in the air and positioning her fingers exactly where they would go if she were actually performing along with them. It was the first time she'd ever done anything like that.

A smile spread across my face, and a warmness filled my heart on this otherwise cold and depressing night. It gave me a little bit of hope for her at a time when almost all of it had been depleted. When my eyes started to sting, I got up to throw away my plate as a distraction.

Ivy's social worker, Gina, came up behind me. "Merry Christmas, Jake."

"Same to you, Gina."

Gina was older and had been a licensed social worker for many years. Her black hair was pulled back tightly into a bun, and she was wearing a fugly Christmas sweater with pom poms and tiny bells hanging off of it.

She straightened her glasses. "Miss Ivy girl seems okay tonight."

I looked over at Ivy who was still strumming her fingers in the air. "Yeah. We've had worse Christmases. That's for sure."

A knot formed in my stomach. There had been something I'd wanted to discuss with Gina for a long time, but I wasn't going to bring it up tonight. She must have sensed it by the look on my face when she asked, "Do you have something on your mind?"

I hesitated then said, "There is something weighing on me, actually." I looked around and lowered my voice. "Do you...have a second to talk?"

Gina nodded and followed me into the empty adjacent kitchen.

I didn't quite know where to start. Gina was a kind person and very intuitive, so once I started spilling, she practically spoke for me.

"You know my intention is never to *leave* Ivy, right? I'll never abandon her."

Knowingly, she gave me a sympathetic smile. "You've met someone."

I swallowed, surprised that she knew exactly where this was going. "Yes."

"That was bound to happen, Jake. I understand."

"I never intended it to happen, though. I never wanted this complication, never wanted to hurt Ivy. I've done everything in my power to prevent it over the years, but—"

"It happens, Jake. You don't have to explain it. Does this woman know about your situation?"

A deep breath escaped me. "That's the thing. I'm planning to tell her about Ivy after the New Year, and I don't know how she's going to take it. So, this could be a non-issue if she decides she can't handle it at all. But if she accepts it..."

"If things get serious, you're going to need my help once you communicate everything to Ivy."

"Yes. I mean, not right away, but I need you to help me figure out what my rights are if Ivy and I were ever to..." I choked on the words.

Gina finished my sentence. "Divorce."

"Yeah. It's not something I want if it means losing my ability to care for her, but I just need to know my options legally. I want to make sure I can still make decisions for her. I'm her only family."

Gina placed her hand on my shoulder, and the bells on her sweater jingled. "Don't worry. Let's just take this one step at a time. We'll have to handle it very delicately, of course. But for what it's worth, I've known you for several years now, seen all that you've sacrificed. You're an amazing human being, and you deserve to have love in your life. Don't beat yourself up over this. We'll figure it out. You've been wonderful to Ivy, and she is very lucky to have you."

"Thank you, Gina. Thank you for understanding."

Someone called her attention back to the party, and she looked behind her shoulder. "We'll talk more after the holidays. In the meantime, I'll start researching the paperwork end of things for you." She slipped away before I could thank her again.

Leaning against the counter with my arms crossed, I felt overwhelmed. The reality of the situation was really starting to hit me now that I'd spoken aloud about it with someone. I could see Ivy in the next room, still playing along in her head to the music. This time, the lone teardrop I'd been fighting earlier fell freely down my cheek.

Wrapping paper flew everywhere. I couldn't crumple and discard it fast enough before more was thrown my way. The twins had recently discovered the truth about Santa Claus so were opening all of their gifts on Christmas Eve instead of the following morning.

It was now 9 p.m., and I'd returned from Ivy's a couple of hours earlier. The tree in my sister's living room was nearly as high as the ceiling. The bright multi-colored lights lit up the room as the flames from the fireplace crackled. Pandora radio was playing in the background. My mother and Max were cuddled together on one couch as Allison and Cedric lazily sat sipping their wine on the sofa across from them. I definitely felt like the odd man out, missing Nina something crazy.

Nina and I had been texting back and forth all night. I knew that Christmas Eve was really tough for her because of Jimmy and wanted to keep her spirits up even if we couldn't be together. I might have taken it too far earlier when I sent her a message that I couldn't help thinking about her when *I Touch Myself* by the Divinyls had come on the radio. Even though she didn't confirm it, I wondered if she understood that I was alluding to the night in my room when she admitted that she masturbated. After I'd sent it, it took me nearly an hour to calm the raging hard on that developed just thinking again about her getting herself off. I finally had to retreat to the bathroom to take care of it. (Jingle Bell Jerk Off.)

I'd also told her I missed her. I did, so fucking much even though it had only been a couple of days since our Chicago trip. Maybe it was mental because of the two weeks apart ahead of us.

Hannah interrupted my thoughts. "Uncle Jake, look!" She enthusiastically lifted up what seemed like the hundredth gift opened between her and Holly. This one was a freakish looking doll with gigantic eyes.

"Wow! That's...precious."

Frightening was more like it.

Nina had once confessed that certain dolls scared her when she was little, so I snapped a picture of it with my phone and texted it to her with a message.

Say hello to my little friend. It may be Christmas at your house, but it's Halloween here.

A few seconds later, she responded.

Nina: What the hell is that thing?

Jake: The niece's new doll. You like her?

Nina: No!

Jake: We shall name her Nina.

Nina: Ugh! LOL.

Jake: ;-)

After a few minutes passed, I texted her again.

Jake: I need your address to mail your present. I'm making it next week while you're away.

Nina: I'm intrigued. I'll need to send yours, too. What do you like better, giving or receiving?

Jake: Are we still talking about presents? Either way, I really like both. I love to give actually. LOVE it.

Nina: I was talking about presents, yes. But now I see you're not.

Jake: What do you like?

Nina: If we're talking about actual gifts, I like to give.

Jake: And if we're talking about other gifts?

Nina: It depends.

Jake: On?

Nina: Who I'd be exchanging with and if they're good at giving gifts.

Jake: I'm very gifted.

Nina: I have no doubts that you are.

Jake: Take a picture of your face.

Nina: What? Why?

Jake: Because I'd be willing to bet it's redder than a poinsettia plant.

I typed again.

Jake: And because I miss it.

Nina: My face?

Jake: Yes. I fucking miss your face.

Nina: I miss your face, too.

It was the second time tonight I'd told her I missed her. My ability to hold back was clearly dwindling.

"Jake, can you stop with the phone for one second to come here and open your present?" my mother shouted from across the room.

I put the phone down. "What am I twelve, Ma?"

Actually, with all of the texting back and forth we'd done tonight, I kind of felt like a kid again in the best way. Nina had a knack for making me forget all about my very adult troubles. Every moment spent with her, even when we weren't physically together, made me giddy.

I lifted myself off the ground and scrunched through the piles of giftwrap to join my mother on the couch. She handed me a small box.

"Let me guess...cufflinks?" I joked as I ripped it open. My smile faded, and I froze, staring mesmerized at the stainless steel dog tag chain in my hands. It was heavy, masculine, and the word etched onto the front caused a shiver to run down my spine: *Nomads*. That was the name of the local biker club my father belonged to back in Illinois. I turned it over and engraved onto the flipside were my initials: *J.A.G.*

My voice lowered to a whisper. "Ma...is this..."

She nodded with a haunting intensity in her eyes. "It was his. He was wearing it the night he died."

Suddenly, the metal seemed to weigh heavier in my hands. My fingers tingled as if the piece came alive upon that revelation, as if it were an actual part of my father. He used to always wear this. I'd assumed it was gone from this Earth forever, just like he was. Staring at it in awe, I brushed my thumb along the smooth plate.

"Did you just find this?"

"I've had it all these years, always knew I'd give it to you someday. He'd want you to have it. He'd already had your initials engraved on the back when he wore it. I didn't do that. He did."

My eyes started to feel watery. "You've kept it all this time. Why give it to me now?"

"I was waiting for a special time, maybe your thirtieth birthday, but the truth is, you've just made me so proud over the past few years, seeing everything you've gone through, how you've handled what life's thrown at you. I just didn't want to wait any longer."

I proudly placed it over my head and around my neck. Pressing my hand over my chest, I said, "Thank you. You have no idea how much I needed this right now."

I hugged my mother tightly.

Max patted me on the back. "Wear it in good health, son."

I hadn't opened up to anyone in my family about Nina. The timing of this made me feel like somewhere out there, my dad knew my life was in turmoil, and that I needed this and in turn, needed him. Whether that was unfounded or not, wearing the chain would give me much needed strength.

My attention turned to my sister who was opening one of her presents from Cedric. It was a silver bracelet that had various charms dangling from it. He said he carefully selected ones that represented things that were special to them: a Gemini zodiac symbol, a dollar bill, a butterfly and several others. Allison would not stop gushing about it, and it made me wonder whether Nina would like something like that.

When my sister discarded the box, I discreetly snatched it and memorized the website where you could go online and customize one. While a bracelet might have seemed too personal a gift for someone who wasn't officially my girlfriend, I still had the urge to make her one even if I had to hold onto it for a while or worse, never had the chance to give it to her.

My nieces were busy playing with their new toys upstairs, and the rest of the family had gone into the dining room for some of Allison's chocolate pecan pie. I took the opportunity to sneak into the study and flipped open Cedric's laptop, pulling up the website for the bracelet company. You could drag the charms you wanted onto the virtual silver band for an image of what your finished product would look like. I'd chosen several charms that reminded me of her: a plane, a pair of dice, a little bat. This was seriously the sappiest thing I'd ever done in all of my nearly twenty-five years, though.

The sound of Cedric's deep intentional cough caused me to jump in the swivel chair.

"Well, well, well. What do we have here?"

Shit.

I said nothing as he leaned over my shoulder, his cologne pungent. I wanted to close out of the screen, but damn it, that would have caused me to lose all the work I'd put into the design.

Sap.

"I've been summoned to do some digging to find out whether our suspicions were correct, but you've made my job way too easy, brother."

"Summoned by whom?"

"Your dear sister and mother. They're convinced there's a girl in the picture because of the way you've been acting. Now, clearly, unless you've taken a liking to wearing female jewelry, this proves they were right."

Having Cedric around was like having an older brother. With my dad being gone, I was really grateful that my sister married a cool guy that I didn't mind opening up to.

I let out a deep breath, rolled my eyes and conceded. "I'm so screwed, man."

"Name?"

"Nina."

"Hot?"

"Scorching."

"Nice tits?"

"Legendary."

"Ass?"

"Beyond..."

"Picture?"

I pulled my phone out and scrolled down to the one selfie I'd taken of us during our trip to Chicago. "That's her."

"She's cute." He leaned against the desk and crossed his arms. "It's a lot more than that, though, isn't it?"

"How could you tell?"

"Watching you tonight made me think back to my own lovesick Christmas once. It was the one right after I'd met Allison. You reminded me of how I was that year, the way you were sitting by the fire alone earlier deep in thought, checking your phone constantly, smiling to yourself like a lunatic. You're so wrapped up in a love fog, you don't realize that everyone around you can see it plain as day."

"Damn."

"Yeah." He laughed.

My tone turned serious. "This girl...she makes me feel alive. I don't want to lose this feeling. I'm terrified."

He realized what I was getting at. "She doesn't know about Ivy yet..."

"No. I'm telling her after the New Year."

Cedric nodded in understanding. "You know I was hiding a pretty damn big secret when I met your sister."

"That's an understatement."

"Well...yeah. What our story proves, though, is that love can sustain some pretty fucked up shit. Do you think what you're feeling is love?"

"I haven't labeled what I'm feeling. It's not something I've ever experienced before. How do you *know* exactly?"

"How do you know that it's love?"

"Yeah."

"It's a gut feeling more than anything. But there are a few things that can help you determine if it's real. For one, how do you feel when she's not around?"

"Lost. Sick. Aching. Like I can't breathe."

"Is there any other person in the world you'd rather be with at any given time?"

"No. Not a single one."

He rubbed the scruff on his chin. "Oh. Here's a good one. Does the thought of losing her scare the shit out of you?"

"Hell yes."

"Yeah. You're fucked."

"Thanks."

"It definitely sounds like love."

"That last question really put it into perspective. I'll have to remember that one."

Losing her *did* scare the shit out of me.

That was the moment it hit me.

I did love her.

I was in love with Nina, and I couldn't lose her.

Somehow, I sensed she felt as strongly about me. The fear in her eyes was evident the one time she pleaded with me to open up to her about what I was hiding. Losing me definitely scared her. That might have meant she loved me, too.

"You've got some hurdles to get through, but everything will turn out okay if it's meant to be," he said.

"Thanks for the talk."

Cedric smacked me on the back. "I'll let you get back to being a bracelet-making pussy."

"Says the pussy-whipped guy who gave me the idea."

He chuckled as he walked backwards out of the room. "Come join us for some pie when you're done, fool."

"Alright, man."

Between the realization that I was truly in love for the first time in my life and the fact that I was still reeling from my mother's present, my emotions were all over the place. I retreated upstairs for the night. This Christmas was definitely one that would always stick with me.

Clutching the metal of my father's chain, I looked out the window to clear my head. The moon was almost full and so bright that it lit up my otherwise dark bedroom.

My father's voice was clear as day in my head. *"I love you to the moon."* It was what he used to say before putting me to bed at night when I was a kid. I'd told Nina that story during our long conversation at the diner in Chicago even though I'd never shared it with anyone.

When I was younger, it always fascinated me that you could be across the world from someone and still be looking up at the same moon.

I wanted her to share this moment with me, to see how spectacular the moon was. I picked up my phone.

Did you see the moon tonight?

I waited for a response. Maybe she turned in early, still recovering from our all-night outdoor Christmas party last Thursday night.

Then, it came.

> **Nina: I would have never thought to look out at the moon on Christmas Eve, but I am glad I did. You always have a way of opening up my eyes to things.**

Suddenly, those gigantic blue eyes of hers were all I could see, eyes I never wanted to see go dark ever again, eyes I knew would be filled with sadness and confusion once I broke my news to her.

I would have given anything to have had her with me, to make love to her all night long in this bed with the moonlight shining on us.

> **Jake: There is nothing more I'd rather look at right now, actually.**

> **Nina: The moon is beautiful.**

> **Jake: I was talking about your eyes.**

I kept typing.

Jake: They're the most beautiful eyes I've ever seen. I get lost in them sometimes. They comfort me in a way that nothing else can.

Nina: I love your eyes, too.

I love...you.

My heart was beating out of control as I typed the words:

I l-o-v-e y-o-u.

Fuck.
No.
I immediately erased it.
I couldn't send that.
Not yet.

Jake: I know I've been confusing you. I am sorry. We need to talk when you come home.

There it was. Now that I'd put it out there, there was no going back.

Nina: I think we need to talk, too.

I closed my eyes and shut off my phone, feeling sick to my stomach and gearing up for another sleepless night.

Back in Brooklyn, the emptiness caused by Nina's absence was more profound than it had been in Boston. I ended up not sending her any more messages on Christmas Sunday, though, because I felt like I needed to cool it.

I'd almost texted her that I loved her.

That would have been a big mistake for multiple reasons. For one, it would have been irresponsible to confess such a thing before we had our talk. More so, telling someone you love them for the first time via text message would have been asinine. So, a few days to clear my head were definitely needed.

Even though he'd driven Nina upstate, Ryan had only stayed away for Christmas weekend and had returned to our apartment Monday. Nina was planning on taking a bus back to the city at the end of the two weeks. Tarah had been using every opportunity to get Ryan and me to talk to each other. When she invited me to dinner with them downstairs Tuesday night, I ended up going just to piss him off and came to the conclusion that it was way more fun to kill him with kindness, thereby annoying the fuck out of him.

Nina and I texted on and off, but I mainly focused my time working on a sketch that would be her belated Christmas present. The image came from an idea that popped into my head based on something she said during our Chicago trip. It was finished and framed by mid-week then Fedexed to her parents' house.

When my phone rang Friday afternoon as I was getting ready to leave work, I had a feeling it was her. Having mostly texted while apart, we rarely spoke on the phone, but something just told me she'd call me when she received my package.

I picked up. "Hey, you."

"Jake..."

I closed my eyes at the sound of her sweet voice. I hadn't heard it since she left, and it reawakened the physical need that I'd managed to keep at bay this week.

"Nina..."

I immediately snuck into an empty conference room and shut the door.

"Oh my God. Your present came," she said, sniffling.

"Are you crying?"

"Yes."

"Oh, man, I didn't mean to make you cry."

"It's okay. It's all good." She cleared her throat. "When? When did you do this? *How* did you do it?"

"I used the picture of him in your room. I waited until you went away to start, so you wouldn't notice it gone."

The sketch was of Nina's brother Jimmy and my sister, Amanda. In the drawing, Amanda is whispering something into Jimmy's ear as he laughs with a beaming smile. It was based on Nina's comment that she wondered if they were conspiring in heaven to bring us together. In case she didn't recognize the resemblance, I'd captioned it: *Heaven's Conspirators (Jimmy and Amanda)*. I was pretty confident, though, that my interpretation of both was spot on. Jimmy's eyes came out particularly lifelike.

Sending it was a risk that I hoped didn't backfire. It was an extremely personal gift, not only for her but for me.

"I can't thank you enough for this. Words can never express how precious this is to me. I...love..." she hesitated.

My heart was racing. Was she going to say she loved the portrait...or me?

"I know. I know," I said, not wanting her to say those words because they would completely undo me.

"What did I ever do to deserve this?" she asked.

"Just the fact that you would ask that question is the essence of why I..." Now, I was the one hesitating. *Why I what?* I finished my sentence. "Why I adore you."

It felt like a safer word than *love*, less likely to do irreparable damage if things didn't work out. And it was the damn truth. *I adored her.*

"I adore you, too," she said. "Not only for this, but because you brought me back to life. Thank you."

Long after we hung up, those bittersweet words wouldn't stop repeating in my head all the way to Boston.

If the earlier part of the holiday break represented realizing the depth of my feelings for Nina, the second part marked the unraveling of my sexual control.

It was Saturday night, New Year's Eve. As always, I'd spent the day with Ivy before heading home to Allison's house.

My family's New Year's Eve tradition was to gorge on Chinese food. Every year, Cedric would come home with two large boxes, complaining about how long he had to wait for the takeout. The association between Chinese food and New Year's Eve always baffled me, but it seemed like everyone in Boston had the same idea. This year was no different.

My nieces were begging to stay up until midnight, and per usual, my sister gave in. Cedric and I had just finished up a card game while my mother and Allison watched the Times Square festivities on television.

The fortune cookies left over from our dinner were strewn about on the table. One in particular seemed to be calling to me. I remembered what Nina told me during our Chinese karaoke date. *Take the one facing you.*

Cracking it open, I chuckled because the fortune spoke volumes about my feelings toward her: *It's easier to resist at the beginning than at the end.*

Ain't that the truth.

Even though you could have pretty much applied that message to anything, for me, it related to the intensity of the sexual frustration I was experiencing at the moment.

And the only woman I wanted was hundreds of miles away.

As I stared into the fire and fantasized about her, my phone buzzed with the words that set the tone for the rest of the night.

> **I wish you were here.**

My mouth filled with moisture as my heart raced. I typed.

> **Jake: I was just thinking the same thing about you.**
>
> **Nina: I'm supposed to be going out tonight, but I really don't feel like it.**
>
> **Jake: Why not?**
>
> **Nina: For one, I'm going to be freezing my ass off.**
>
> **Jake: That would not be a good thing. I'd really miss your ass.**

Nina: LOL.

Jake: Where are you going?

Nina: Some friends from high school found out I was in town, contacted me on facebook and invited me to a party. I'm all dressed up, but I'm not sure I'm gonna go.

Jake: Show me what you look like.

Nina: Okay, hang on.

My pulse raced as I held the phone and waited while my dick rose to attention. Was I really so hard up that merely anticipating a picture of her had just given me an erection? I was just so desperate for a look at her again.

The situation in my pants was no better once the image popped up. Nina had taken a selfie in the mirror. She was wearing an emerald green fitted dress. It wasn't low cut, but anything fitted looked indecent on her bountiful rack. Her hair was off her forehead, accentuating the light blue of her eyes that glowed in the bathroom lighting. Her expression reflected a shyness as if she were reluctant to take the picture.

I just kept staring at it. *At her.* I pressed down on the photo and saved it to my camera roll. My phone buzzed.

Nina: No comment?

Jake: I'm still looking at it.

Nina: Oh.

Jake: You look incredible.

Nina: Thank you.

Jake: I almost wish I didn't ask to see it.

Nina: What are you doing tonight?

She changed the subject, causing me to wonder if I'd made her uncomfortable.

Jake: Staying in. My family pigged out on Chinese food earlier. I'll stay up to watch the ball drop then go to bed sometime after.

Nina: You're not going out? With anyone?

Jake: No.

Dread set in as I stared at her question again, realizing that she likely wasn't just referring to tonight. What she probably wanted to know was whether there was another woman in my life. After all this time, I'd never made it crystal clear to her one way or the other. Of course, there *was* someone else but not in the way she might have wondered.

Nina: Does whatever you have to tell me involve someone else?

I was shitting a brick.

The Chinese food seemed like a really bad idea as nausea suddenly consumed me. Refusing to tell her about Ivy over the phone, I froze, not knowing how to address her question. That talk needed to be done delicately and in person so that I could look her in the eyes and assure her of my intentions.

I typed.

Jake: Not in the way you might think.

I closed my eyes, so disappointed in myself for letting this situation go on for as long as it had.

The phone vibrated.

Nina: Do you have a child?

My response was immediate.

Jake: No

Fuck.

Fuck.

Fuck.

The wheels had clearly been turning, probably for months as she played private investigator in her head while trying to figure out my deal. My heartbeat accelerated as I took the phone upstairs, closing the door for privacy then locking it.

I dialed her.

It rang once before she answered right away. "Hello?" Her voice was groggy. It sounded like she was congested.

"Are you crying?" I asked.

"No."

My tone was stern. "Don't lie to me."

"Yes," she said softly.

"Listen to me, Nina. We *do* need to talk, but it's something I was really hoping to discuss with you in person. This is all my fault for being afraid to open up to you for so long. But here's what cannot wait a second longer: You absolutely need to know right now that you are the only person in this world that has my heart, and nothing that I have to tell you will change that."

It was as if what I'd just said went in one ear and out the other when she asked, "Is someone sick or dying?"

"No...no, nothing like that. It's a complex situation, and I'm not sure how you're going to view it. If you insist that I tell you tonight, we'll have the talk now, but I'd really appreciate the opportunity to do it face to face when you come home next week."

"I'm sorry, Jake. I just...it's been so hard. My imagination has been running wild for a long time. I'm scared I'm going to lose you."

She was scared. I remembered Cedric's words and took her fear as a sign that she really did love me.

I love you, too, baby. I just can't say it yet.

"Don't be scared. You won't lose me. I'll always be your friend and more if you'll have me. Please trust that as long as you want me to be around, I will be."

She sniffled. "Okay, I'm going to trust you on this, and you're right. We shouldn't be discussing anything important over the phone."

"Thank you. I'm glad you agree."

"I'd come home early, but my mother arranged for a memorial service for Jimmy at the church the Friday evening before I leave."

"It's only one more week. It'll fly by."

I stared at the ceiling and listened to the faint sounds outside my foggy window. Holiday revelers must have been entering and exiting the trolley that ran down Beacon Street. Many were probably headed to the First Night celebration downtown.

Nina and I remained quiet until I was the first to speak again. "I'm sorry if I ruined your night."

"My night isn't ruined, but I'm definitely not in the mood to go out anymore."

"Good. Don't. Stay on the phone with me. My family is downstairs, but despite that, I was feeling really alone tonight for some reason—until now. You're the only person I want to ring in the New Year with."

"I'd like that."

"You said you're not in the mood to go out. What *are* you in the mood for? Tell me."

"What am I in the mood for? Are you trying to have phone sex with me or something?"

"I wasn't." I snickered. "But if I were, your calling me out on it just now would've ruined it."

"Sorry."

"No apologies needed, because I wasn't *trying* to have phone sex."

"Right."

"By the way, if you change your mind and decide you'd rather go out, just say the word. I wouldn't blame you. You're all dressed up in that pretty little dress with nowhere to go now."

"Not true."

"You're still thinking of going out?"

"No...I mean, I'm not wearing the dress anymore."

A dull ache developed in my groin upon hearing that.

"You're not?"

"No."

"You took it off?"

"Yeah, I was uncomfortable."

My next question sounded almost urgent. "What are you wearing?"

"I'm in my bra and underwear under the covers."

I had to catch my breath.

"Nina?"

"Yeah?"

"Are *you* trying to have phone sex with *me*?"

"You just asked me what I was wearing. Isn't that the universal phone sex lead in? I still maintain *you* were trying to have it with *me*."

"Well, I wasn't considering it until you told me you were practically naked. There's only so much a man can take."

"You do typically exercise a frustrating amount of restraint, though."

"You think I've *wanted* to restrain myself?"

"No. That's the thing. You look at me like you want to devour me, but you act the complete opposite, like you're afraid of breaking me or something. I'm stronger than you think."

"You're partly right. You've become my best friend. I'm very protective. You know that. I've been gentle with you. But that's only one side of me."

"And the other side?"

"You haven't experienced it yet."

"I want to know that side of you, too. I really wonder what that's like."

I was horny as fuck and had no willpower to resist where this was going. I just wanted her. Period. Weaker by the second, the repercussions of letting go just didn't matter to me anymore or at least for the moment.

"I can assure you, there's nothing gentle about the way I want to fuck you. Was that what you were wondering about? I've barely touched you because once I start, I'm not going to be able to stop, and you're not gonna want me to."

"Tell me what you want to do to me."

"You really want me to do that?"

"Yes."

You asked for it.

"There is a difference between having sex and fucking. You've never come. You've never screamed out in pleasure because it felt so amazing that you thought you were losing your mind. You've never been fucked, Nina. I want to show you what that's like in every way. I want to fuck your pussy, your ass, your mouth and make you feel so insanely good that you'll beg me to keep filling you. And by the end, if I haven't ruined you for everyone else, then I haven't done my job."

Those words could never be taken back, but it felt so damn good to let them out. Now, it was clear that we had officially ventured into unchartered territory.

She let out a long, shaky breath. "Wow...okay."

"Was that direct enough for you?"

"Yeah. Actually, it reminded me of what you said to me in your room that one night. I've replayed that one a lot in my head. But you were definitely more specific just now."

"Well, I'm sick of hiding it. And a lot's changed since then in terms of my willpower, and by that, I mean I don't have much of it left. You know what my fortune cookie said tonight? It said, 'It's easier to resist at the beginning than at the end.' I can guarantee you if you were here right now, I would not be holding back. Whether that's right or wrong, I've reached the end." My voice lowered to a whisper. "I need you."

My body buzzed at the sound of her soft voice in my ear. "Do you want to see me?"

"You mean, go there? Come see you? I've considered that, actually."

"No. I meant...my body."

Where was she going with this?

My dick twitched. "You're gonna show me your body?"

"You undress me with your eyes a lot. I love when you do that. But do you want to see what I actually look like?"

Holy shit.

There was only one sane answer to that.

"Fuck yes."

Then, everything just went quiet except for the fact that I felt like I could hear my heart pounding. I could hear things shuffling in the background. What was she doing? Was she taking everything off?

The wait was killing me. Running my hands through my hair in frustration, I had no idea what exactly she'd be sending, whether it would be a video or a photo. My body temperature was rising by the second, so I lifted my shirt over my head and threw it across the room. My cock was so engorged that it felt like it was burning a hole through my pants, which I ended up taking off, too. My legs stiffened as I stretched under my blankets and tried to relax my breathing. I prayed no one in my family knocked on the door and ruined this for me. Just the thought of seeing her naked was putting me over the edge. An out of control excitement ran through me like a teenager watching the opening credits to his first porno. This night was definitely turning into an unexpected surprise. And I was all in.

"Okay..." she said after returning to the phone. "I took a still with my webcam. I'm gonna email it to you, okay?"

"Yeah," I breathed out.

More waiting.

"I've never done anything like this before. I just sent it. Now, I'm nervous."

"Don't be. I don't have to look at it if you don't want me to."

Fuck that. A warning of imminent death upon opening wouldn't have been able to stop me from clicking on that picture.

"I can't believe I just sent that to you."

When my email notification sounded, I swallowed in anticipation, opened my laptop and clicked on the message. It took several seconds for the attachment to open, and my face was burning up with each second that passed.

When the image finally loaded, everything went still as I took in the sight before me. In the photo, Nina was sitting on her bed, leaning slightly to the side with her knees curled in. Her face was also turned sideways as her hair fell over her left breast. Her right one was completely exposed, showcasing a large, flat nipple that was a beautiful shade of light pink. Her breasts looked even bigger than I imagined. Saliva pooled in my mouth from the need to suck on them. Although she wasn't wearing any underwear, you couldn't see her pussy, only the side of her ass. It was a classy pose that reminded me of something I would have sketched. God, she was beautiful.

"You're not saying anything."

Expressing with words what the picture made me feel seemed impossible. My voice was strained. "You're exquisite."

"Was it what you expected?"

I couldn't take my eyes off it. "Far more."

Not only was I so extremely turned on by what the picture did clearly display but also by the cruel tease of what it didn't.

"Will you send me a picture of you?" she asked.

My dick was so hard that my briefs were barely able to contain me.

"If I send you one, you're gonna know what you just did to me."

"I want to see you," she whispered.

"Okay," I whispered even lower.

Positioning the camera over my body, I sucked in as I lay down. My gray boxer briefs were my only article of clothing, but they stayed on. I didn't want to shock her altogether. You could still see the full length of my erect cock, which was resting against my thigh through the material. My abs looked ripped, and I was satisfied with the photo I snapped before hitting send.

"I just sent it."

With my heart pounding, I kept staring at the photo of her while I waited for her to open mine.

Then, she said, "Wow. You're so..."

"Hard."

"Yes. But I was gonna say gorgeous. You're a beautiful man."

"Thank you."

"Your body is amazing, Jake. I've always thought so. And that tattoo on your side...it...does things to me."

Those words. Her photo. I couldn't take it anymore.

Through gritted teeth, I said, "I have a problem."

"What?"

"I can't stop looking at you. I want to touch you. This is torture."

PENELOPE WARD

"What do we do now?"

I let out a single laugh. "You mean, now that we've played 'show me yours, I'll show you mine?'"

"Yes."

"Have you ever thought about me when you touch yourself?" I asked.

"All the time."

"You're *all* I think about when I jerk off, Nina."

"What are you getting at?"

"Our options are limited, but I know what I *really* want."

"Tell me."

It was one of many scenarios that had made its way into my fantasies before.

"I want you to touch yourself while I listen. I want to hear the sounds you make while you're thinking about me until you come."

Her tiny breaths quickened. "Only if you do it with me."

"I would most definitely be joining you. We can come together. Do you want that?"

"Yes."

I didn't hesitate. *I needed this.*

"Lay back. Don't let your mind drift anywhere else but on my voice."

It sounded like she was getting comfortable in her bed. "I love your voice, by the way, always have. It's so deep and raspy. Sexy."

"I'm glad you feel that way because it's all I'm going to be using to make you come. I'm not going to be doing a lot of talking, though, because I want to hear you breathe and the sounds you're making."

"My legs are shaking," she said. "Godammit, Jake. What are you doing to me?"

202

"Are you touching yourself?"

"Yes."

I gripped my shaft. "Good. Me, too. If my cock is this hard and wet from just looking at your picture, I couldn't imagine what it would feel like inside of you."

Her breathing was uneven. My own was even worse. I was starting to lose my ability to speak as my hand slid up and down along my hardness to the sound of her whimpering. We were letting ourselves get completely lost in each other. Intense pleasure fueled by the longing the distance between us caused made it like nothing I'd ever experienced before.

The ongoing vivid image in my head of her legs spread open while she rubbed her fingers along her wet clit was driving me wild as I pumped my slick cock into my hand. The sighs of pleasure coming out of her were bringing me closer to the brink with each second. But mainly, knowing that she was thinking of me, wanting me inside of her as she did it made me crazy.

When her breathing suddenly became ragged, I knew. "You're coming..."

"Yes. Yesss."

Painfully aroused, I'd been struggling to hold my orgasm back from the get go. So, when she told me she was coming, I jerked off faster and within seconds, hot cum shot out onto my stomach, my release so intense I was practically seeing stars.

We both sounded like we'd run a marathon as we breathed together.

The faint sounds of cheering and horns coming from downstairs snapped me out of my stupor. The timing of that briefly freaked me out until I realized the cheers weren't for me. I looked over at the clock, and it made perfect sense.

"It's midnight," Nina said.

"Happy New Year."

"Happy New Year. That was the craziest thing I've ever done," she said, sounding exasperated.

"Yeah...it wasn't a New Year's kiss, but it was pretty fucking awesome."

"If that start was any indication of how the rest will go, it's gonna be a great year."

Her words haunted me as I came down from the euphoria of our first sexual encounter. My heart suddenly started to hurt. This year had the potential to be the best or worst of my life, depending on how things went. I'd find out sooner than I was ready for which way it was going to go. It wouldn't be long before everything came undone.

SEVENTEEN
PAST

The following work week flew by, and before I knew it, my ass was on the train back to Boston for the final time before I'd see Nina again. She'd be arriving in Brooklyn sometime over the weekend while I was gone. We had plans to go out Monday night, and that was when we'd have the talk.

I was on edge the entire ride. I'd never wanted to stay back in New York more than this weekend, but Ivy apparently had a bad week and with Nina possibly not home until Sunday, it didn't make sense to stay behind. I forced myself to make the trip. So anxious to get the talk over with, I wished I could have just waited at the apartment for the moment she walked in, though.

On the train, the sounds around me seemed amplified as my head spun. My feelings alternated between excitement, dread, arousal and nausea.

I'd just arrived to South Station when my phone chimed as I exited the train. It was a text from Tarah.

Nina's birthday is this Sunday. Even though she never told anyone, Ryan just happened to remember. We're throwing her a surprise party downstairs at Eleni's. I think it would be cool if you showed up. 7 pm. Let me know.

I hadn't moved from my spot on the busy Amtrak platform since the message came in. Swarms of people passed by me as my eyes stayed glued to one word: Sunday.

Sunday.

Sunday was January eighth.

My birthday.

Her birthday.

We had the same birthday?

That was friggin wild. She was two years younger than me, so she'd be turning twenty-three. My reaction quickly turned from amazement to disappointment that Ryan knew about her birthday when I didn't. She'd never mentioned it to me. It dawned on me that it probably had something to do with guilt over Jimmy. I understood too well the feeling of not wanting to celebrate a birthday when you lost a sibling who would never have the privilege of marking that milestone again. I'd never told her about mine because I never fussed about my birthday. The eighth of January was historically just another day to me. Not anymore. Now, it would always be Nina's birthday. If for some reason we were not together, I still knew I'd think of nothing but Nina on my birthday for the rest of my life.

Even though I normally left Boston late on Sundays, I wasn't going to miss Nina's party for anything. I'd have to catch a train by three in the afternoon to get there in time.

This development would now change a couple of other things. My family had planned a little get together for me at Allison's since this birthday was my twenty-fifth. They would have to postpone it now. Also, my original plan was to have the Ivy talk with Nina the next time we saw each other. There was no way I was going to ruin her birthday, though. Our birthday.

Now that I'd be seeing her earlier than planned, the extra time we'd be spending together Sunday night before the talk would mean having to exercise a lot of control. The sexual dynamic of our relationship had changed since New Year's Eve, but I still vowed not to touch her until she knew everything. Even though we'd experienced that amazing phone sex, it was hard to believe we still hadn't even kissed.

I returned Tarah's text.

Jake: I'll be there.

Tarah: Great! That's gonna mean a lot to her.

The bracelet I'd ordered her on Christmas Eve was delivered to the apartment yesterday. The plan was to give it to her down the line if things worked out between us. I now knew I wanted to give it to her Sunday for her birthday instead.

Frigid air nearly choked me as I ran down Lincoln Street. I missed the 2:30 train, and that meant arriving at the apartment an hour later than planned. Since Nina didn't know I was coming, I didn't bother to text anyone.

As I passed by the entrance to the restaurant, my pulse raced because I knew she was inside. Still needing to shower and get dressed, I couldn't join the party yet. It would be close to eight by the time I finally got downstairs.

I practically flew through the door to the apartment and took the quickest shower of my life. After slicking my wet hair back, I threw on some jeans and a navy button down shirt, rolling the sleeves up. After a couple of spritzes of cologne and a quick look in the mirror, I had to admit that I looked pretty damn good considering the time it took me to get dressed.

Before heading downstairs, I stopped in the hallway outside Nina's empty room then walked inside. Sitting on her bed, I took a deep breath to calm my nerves, but it had the opposite effect because the air was filled with her vanilla scent, and that just made my body react when I should have been trying to calm my dick. I'd quit smoking weeks ago. Otherwise, this would have been the opportune time for a cigarette. My eyes landed on one of her lace bras that had fallen on the floor, and my body buzzed again with an urgent need to see her. Probably not a good idea to make my entrance downstairs with a hard on. Under the circumstances tonight, the buffer of other people being around us would probably be a good thing.

My feet hurriedly skipped down the steps. The faint sound of Mrs. Ballsworthy's television could be heard on my way down.

The cold air that hit me as I stepped outside was replaced seconds later by the heat of the crowd as I entered the restaurant. Eleni's was packed. A live Greek band played in the corner while a belly dancer stood in the other corner as she prepared to perform. The smell of garlic and barbecued meat filled the air, causing my stomach to rumble in hunger despite my nerves. I hadn't eaten since breakfast.

Squinting my eyes, I looked around for the right table. When I spotted the back of her, my heartbeat accelerated, almost rivaling the drumbeat vibrating through the room.

Her long hair was draped over the back of the chair. She didn't see me.

I heard Ryan shout, "Jake!"

Nina quickly turned around, and all of the action in the room seemed to fade away when our eyes met. Unable to get to her fast enough, my stride got bigger with each step forward.

It had been so fucking long, too long.

"Sorry I'm late. Happy birthday, Nina."

She stood up, revealing a strapless red dress that hugged her body in a way that made me never want to let her out of my sight again. One look at her, and all of my rules about physical contact went straight down the tubes.

Rules? I could barely remember my own fucking name.

Without a second thought, I leaned in and planted a soft kiss on her cheek, my tongue ever so lightly grazing her skin. Two thin braids wrapped around each side of her head as the rest of her hair fell down her shoulders. She looked like a goddess. But she seemed tense.

I had to practically pry my eyes away from her. When I did, I immediately regretted it, because it was then that I realized Nina had been sitting across from someone. My head turned slowly to the left, taking note of Ryan's position across from Tarah. My gaze then moved back to the right, to the spot where a tall redheaded guy was sitting opposite Nina—ogling her.

What in the ever-living fuck.

A primal urge to rip his head off tore through me. My own head was spinning because that seating arrangement looked awfully like a double date, and I was looking awfully like the fifth fucking wheel.

Nina hadn't known I'd be here. Had I walked in on her date?

Rage was building inside of me. I couldn't even look at her anymore. Instead, I stared straight into the eyes of the ginger dude who just became enemy number one.

Before I could get my head on straight to ask what the fuck was going on, Ryan started to introduce me to the guy. "This is our roommate, Jake. Jake, this is Michael Hunt, my co-worker."

Michael Hunt.

Mike.

Mike Hunt.

My cunt.

Douchebag.

I immediately reached out my hand and clenched my teeth. "Mike, is it? Mike Hunt?"

A look of fear was transparent in Nina's eyes. Before anyone could respond to my obvious dig on his name, Desiree walked over to take our drink order. *Desiree.* Great. This night was turning into all sorts of fucked up.

"Jakey...there you are. I thought they said you were in Boston."

"Funny you should point that out, Des. Tarah had told me it was Nina's birthday dinner, so I came home early to surprise her." My stare burned into Nina's. She looked frozen. "Turns out, I was the one surprised." I never took my eyes off Nina as I handed back the menu and said, "I'll take a vodka straight, Des."

My eyes continued to sear into Nina's when Tarah's voice interrupted my trance. "Jake, there is something upstairs I forgot to show you. It's broken, and I don't want to forget to tell you about it. Do you mind...before we order our food?"

She nudged her head repeatedly for me to follow her away from the table.

My chest was rising and falling as we walked out of the dining area through a side door and into the adjacent hallway that also led up to our apartment.

"This isn't what it looks like, Jake."

"You told me to come to this party, and Nina's on a fucking date?"

"It's not a date. She doesn't even know him."

Spit flew out of my mouth when I shouted, "Who the fuck brought him?"

"Ryan did. He thought it would be a bright idea to ambush Nina by inviting this guy from work to the birthday dinner. He's apparently trying to set her up with him."

I grinded my teeth in anger. "Anything to get her away from me."

She nodded. "I think so. I'm actually really pissed at him, too. He never told me he was inviting anyone. It was supposed to be the four of us. I would have never intentionally put you in this situation."

"Why did *she* agree to this?"

"She literally only found out right before we came downstairs. She thought I was in on it and got mad at me. I would have never done that to her. I wanted this night to be special. I was hoping you two would finally get your act together tonight."

"Fuck, Tarah. I don't want her near that guy."

"You don't want *any* guy near her."

"No, I don't."

"You really like her."

"It's so much more than that. You don't know the half of it."

"You two are crazy about each other. You need to tell her how you feel tonight. Whatever it is you're holding back, it needs to end tonight."

"I need to be alone with Nina. Help me make that happen."

"Okay. We'll go back to the table for a bit. Then, at some point, get her alone, and if you guys leave, I'll handle the damage."

"Thank you."

"Come on. Let's go back," she said before leading the way back into the dining room.

When we returned to the table, my shot of vodka was waiting for me. I immediately lifted it to my mouth while Nina watched my every move. The alcohol burned my throat as I downed it all in one gulp, slamming the glass on the table when finished. My eyes darted over to her. She looked like she was expecting me to erupt in anger. Instead, my mouth slowly spread into a wicked grin. A look of relief washed over her face as she returned it with a smile that told me everything I needed to know about where she stood about me.

It was at that moment that I became sure the talk couldn't wait any longer. Deep down, I'd always known this night was going to end in one of two ways: with me inside of her or gone from the apartment. There wasn't going to be a middle ground.

I was done.

Done pretending.

Done waiting.

Done overthinking everything.

Nina belonged to me, and this shit needed to be worked out tonight.

Douchebag Mike was still attempting to talk to her. Nina was in the middle of politely answering one of his questions when I placed my hand on her thigh under the table. I smiled mischievously as she flinched and tripped over her words. Moving my hand slowly upwards, I made my way to her bikini line and brushed my thumb along the seam of her underwear. She had no idea how close she was to getting finger fucked right then and there while in the middle of talking about her molecular biology requirement. Thinking better of it, I slid my hand down the length of her thigh as I squeezed it, sending her a message loud and clear with my hand that she was mine, not his. When she looked over at me, I slid my tongue ring between my teeth, both out of frustration and because it was the one thing I did that she admitted drove her crazy.

I hit my limit. I'd waited enough. Getting up from my seat without excusing myself, I took a deep breath and walked out. Returning to the spot in the empty hallway where Tarah and I had been talking earlier, I took out my phone.

Meet me in the hallway.

My heart was beating faster with each second. I had no clue what I was going to say or do to her. All I knew was that she wouldn't be returning to that seat across from him.

My hands were in my pockets when she appeared.

"Hi," she said.

The skin below her neck was red and a little blotchy. This situation had apparently gotten to her good, too.

"Hi."

"What's going on?"

"That guy was looking at you like he wanted to rip your dress off with his teeth." *I'm the only one that's gonna have the privilege of doing that.* "I had to get out of there before I killed him with my bare hands."

"Why would that bother you?"

She was fucking with me.

"You know why."

I moved in closer to her so that she could feel my words on her face when I spoke. "Why didn't you tell me it was your birthday?"

"I figured you'd be away anyway, so I just never mentioned it." Her admission filled me with regret. Nina clearly felt that she was playing second fiddle to something.

"I would never miss your birthday. Never. You underestimated how important you are to me, Nina."

"I'm sorry."

"You should have told me. Tarah called me Friday when I was already in Boston, so I decided to surprise you tonight."

"You're sneaky."

"You're fucking gorgeous."

I shut my eyes, feeling my composure slipping away. I needed to get her out of here as fast as possible and get the talk over with. Birthday or not, we couldn't go on this way any longer. Seeing her tonight had changed my ability to even wait the twenty-four hours.

"Thank you. You're not so bad yourself," she said. Then, she placed her small fingers on the bottom of my shirt and pulled lightly at the material, causing my dick to harden.

I cleared my throat. "Tarah explained to me about what's his name in there. She didn't know he was going to be here when she invited me. She told me Ryan ambushed you."

"What if I *were* on a date?"

She wouldn't have wanted to hear the true answer to that question because it would have made me sound like a nut.

"I guess if he made you happy, I'd be okay with it."

"I see."

"That was a lie."

"Oh."

"I wouldn't be okay with it. Fuck...I missed you." My hand landed on her tiny waist. When I squeezed it, she closed her eyes instantly as if I'd hit a magic spot. Our first kiss wasn't going to be in this dingy hallway. Still, the need to have my mouth on her was uncontrollable, so I grabbed her hand and kissed it hard.

"I missed you, too," she said.

"Go on a date with me."

"What?"

"Spend the rest of your birthday with me tonight. Let's get out of here right now, go somewhere, anywhere. I just want to be alone with you. I can't say what I want...do what I want...in this hallway."

We devised a plan to make up an excuse and leave. She just needed to use the bathroom first. So, I returned to the table and waited.

Mr. Cunt was busy chatting about work with Ryan. I winked at Tarah and nodded to silently let her know that Nina and I were moving forward with her suggestion that we leave the dinner party.

My stomach was in knots as I used the time that Nina was in the bathroom to plan out the next couple of hours. We'd go to an intimate restaurant for a private dinner. I'd let her in on the secret that today was my birthday, too. We'd return to the apartment, and I would lay everything on the line tonight, hoping and praying that she accepted it.

Never more nervous about anything in my entire life, I grabbed Nina's wine and downed the rest of it. She wouldn't have time to finish it anyway, since my plan was to whisk her away the second she came out of the bathroom. I was going to leave first, call her on her cell pretending to be a family member with an emergency, and then she'd follow soon after. We might have left together, but that would have made things obvious, and Ryan really didn't need to know our business.

My phone vibrated. It was a text from Nina.

You fucked Desiree???

I stood up, staring down at the phone as my heart nearly exploded out of my chest. My stomach churned. What was happening?

Fuck.

Fuck.

Fuck.

When I looked up, Nina was squeezing through cramped tables with mascara running down her cheeks.

My call was urgent, "Nina!"

She wouldn't look at me as she made her way toward the exit. Desiree was watching the whole thing unfold with her arms crossed. It felt like a vein was going to pop out of my neck as I turned to her and screamed, "What the fuck did you say to her?"

She shrugged her shoulders with a smug look on her face.

Fucking whore.

Needing to get to Nina, I didn't even bother to push Desiree for a response. The loud thud of a chair falling caused heads to turn as I knocked into things while running out of the restaurant.

Snowflakes tauntingly danced around my face in the air outside. Mrs. Ballsworthy was in the window.

I held up my hands. "Not tonight, Balls. Fucking not tonight."

I didn't need to be told to fuck myself right now because I was already royally fucked.

EIGHTEEN
PAST

Panting as I skipped over steps to get upstairs as fast as possible, I stopped briefly in front of our apartment door to grab my bearings. My gut told me that nothing was ever going to be the same after I walked in there. And now with this major hiccup, there would be another hurdle to get through before telling Nina about Ivy.

I burst through the door.

Nina was standing in front of me holding a duffel bag. My chest tightened in agony at the vision of her walking out on me. She would leave tonight over my dead body. If either one of us was going to disappear, it was going to be me.

"Nina, please...talk to me. Please."

She placed the large bag in front of her chest. "Stay away from me. I have nothing...nothing...to say to you."

My heart fell to my stomach upon seeing her use the bag as a shield to protect against me. The best course of action was to keep my distance, but there was no fucking way I was going to let her run away. Trying to catch my breath, I stood right in front of the door to prevent her from leaving.

Her hair was disheveled, but she still looked so amazingly beautiful. The blue of her irises was even more striking in contrast to the raccoon eyes caused by her bleeding eye makeup.

"You have to let me explain."

"Explain! You want me to stand here and listen to you explain how you fucked that whore so easily while you put my feelings through the wringer for months, confusing me and sending me mixed messages? You had no problem 'making her come until she screamed'...did you? And believe me, it was a doozy. I heard it for myself."

I blinked repeatedly trying to comprehend it. At first, the words hadn't sunk in.

I heard it for myself.

"Fuck...what? What are you talking about?"

"That's right. The day I moved in. You were fucking her in your room. Remember that day? Well, I was here unpacking. I thought I was alone and didn't realize what was going on until it was too late. I heard everything, Jake...everything." She started to cry.

Flashbacks from the day that Nina moved in played out in my head like a movie on fast forward. Earlier that afternoon marked the final time Desiree and I were together.

The pink scarf on the floor in the living room.

Fuck.

Nina was there.

It felt like I was going to throw up. All this time, she was hanging onto that, probably wondering how the fuck I could be with someone else intimately and not her after all these months. Desiree must have spitefully confronted her in the bathroom, and now, Nina had a face to go along with that memory. It boggled my mind to imagine what it would feel like if the situation were reversed, if I had to endure hearing Nina fucking someone else.

My heart was breaking.

"Oh my God." Walking toward her with pleading eyes, I said, "I am so sorry."

She wouldn't relent. "If you'll excuse me, please get out of my way. I need to find somewhere else to stay tonight."

"You're not going anywhere. Not until you hear me out."

"I told you. I have nothing to say to you."

I placed my hands on her arms that were covered in goosebumps. "I'll leave tonight, but I'm not going anywhere until you let me explain. Do you hear me?" I took my hand to her chin and turned her face toward me. "Look at me." She kept her eyes pointed downward. I repeated, "*Look*...at me."

Never more determined to get a message across, my stare burned into hers until I was sure I owned her full attention.

I tried my best to explain the situation with Desiree, how it was just sex, nothing more. She didn't really seem to be understanding me. When Nina called me a whore, I nearly lost it.

Her bag landed on the floor in a loud thud after I threw it violently on the ground. Taking her hand, I forced her down the hall.

Once in her room, I backed her against the wall and tried once again to get it through her head how big of a mistake Desiree was. I told Nina that my heart hadn't beat the same since the day she moved into the apartment. The next minute or so was a blur as feelings held captive in my heart for months just poured out of me. Eventually, her expression began to soften. My nerves became more shot with each second because I knew I was about to tell her everything.

"You're the first thing I think about in the morning and the last thing I think about at night. And then, you invade my thoughts and dreams in between. I have tried so hard to stop these feelings. I've put up as many barriers as I could stand to, but they are crumbling down. I can't do it anymore." Burying my face in her neck, I spoke onto her skin, "I can't do it anymore...I can't do it anymore." I placed my hands on her hips and covered her mouth with mine. "I've come undone."

Unleashing those three words had set me off. It was like a final button had been pushed. Grabbing her face, I moaned into her mouth as I kissed her deeply with everything in me. The first recognition of her taste made me immediately addicted, needing to not only taste her mouth but every inch of her. Wanting to kiss her deeper, I urged her mouth open as my tongue lashed at hers repeatedly. It wasn't enough. As the kiss became more intense, it was impossible to keep my hands off her body. Her dress ripped as I frantically pulled at the material at her sides.

When Nina grabbed my hair, a groan so deep from the back of my throat vibrated into her mouth. My dick was so excruciatingly hard that when she started to rub up against me, it became necessary to push back before I came. It was *that* bad.

Panting, I placed my hands on her cheeks. "I need to tell you something, Nina. We need to have that talk now."

A look of pure terror washed over her face as several seconds of tense silence passed.

"I don't care about your past or what's going on in Boston. Please...I'm begging you. Let's not do this now. Don't say anything tonight. We'll have the talk tomorrow like we were supposed to. What I need right now more than I have ever needed anything is for you to make love to me, Jake."

My hands shook as they remained cupped around her face. The temptation of taking her up on that offer was simply too strong to resist.

Don't say anything.

Make love to me.

It felt like I might die if I couldn't have her, if I couldn't grant her wishes.

"You have no idea how badly I need to be inside of you right now."

"Please...I don't want to have the talk tonight, okay?"

Getting that taste of her had weakened all of my inhibitions, turning me into a virile beast. In that moment, I could resist Nina no more than a druggie could resist a vial of heroine hanging over his nose.

Wrong or right ceased to exist as I stood before her blinded by an uncontrollable need. I knew I was giving in, because the risk of never having this opportunity again was a significant one, especially after the way she reacted about Desiree. Selfishly, I convinced myself that if given the chance to own her body tonight, I could wreck her for anyone else, make her mine and increase the likelihood that she wouldn't be able to leave me.

I'd made the decision to take what I needed. Knowing already what the answer would be, I made her a proposition to at least help ease my conscience. "Nina, either we have this talk now, or you are going to have to make me a blind promise."

"Okay..."

She was scared. When a teardrop fell down her cheek, I placed my tongue along her skin, licking it away as I whispered against her face, "I need you to promise me... that you won't leave me."

She silently and repeatedly nodded against my forehead.

"Make sure you mean that. Because I can't make love to you the way I want to tonight, only to lose you the next day. It will *fucking* destroy me. I need to know you'll be mine no matter what I throw at you. Promise me."

"I'm yours. I have never belonged to anyone before... but I know that I belong to you."

"Look at me and say it."

"I'm yours. There is nothing that could make me leave you, because I don't think I could live without you."

That was all I needed to hear. Those words meant more to me than anything, and I prayed that she was telling the truth. I searched her eyes for any hints of hesitation; there were none. It didn't take much convincing for my weakened mind and body to agree that it was okay to trust her, okay to give in. Pulling her into me, I knew that this time I wasn't letting go. "Well, that's good, because I wasn't living before you."

I stayed holding her, letting the heat of her body evaporate all remnants of doubt within me.

The words that came out of her next confirmed there was no going back.

"I need you to fuck me, Jake."

We'd started off slow and steady. I'd undressed her down to her underwear, and we just explored each other's mouths for a while. She kept tugging at my lip ring with her teeth while her bare tits rubbed against my shirt. It was driving me insane, and it wasn't long before I'd lose the ability to go easy on her.

She whimpered as I lowered my mouth onto her nipple and sucked hard before switching over to the other side.

"Does that hurt?"

"No...feels good."

I sucked harder, unable to fully believe she'd given me free reign of the beautiful rack I'd spent months worshipping from afar. Her skin was soft, and sweet, and I couldn't wait to mark every inch of her body.

As I continued feasting on her, she placed her hand on my dick, which was bursting through my jeans. She sighed when she got a load of how hard I was.

I clamped down on her nipple gently with my teeth and released it. "Now you know what you do to me. I want to feel what I do to you."

Nudging at her underwear, I slipped my finger inside of her warm opening. She was so incredibly wet that I could hear it as I moved in and out of her repeatedly for minutes. At one point, her pussy was starting to convulse around my hand, so I pulled out before she could come. Unable to resist, I slowly licked every drop of her off of my fingers and moaned, savoring the sweet and salty taste.

"You taste better than I could have imagined."

"I almost came," she said.

"I know. I almost lost it myself because I love how turned on you are. That's why I stopped. But that's not how I want your first time with me to happen. And believe me, Nina, this is gonna be your *real* first time."

According to Nina, she'd never come during sex in her life. Being the first man to make that happen was a challenge I was happy to take on and planned to succeed multiple times tonight. How it was going to happen first was the question.

She needed to lose the panties. I pulled her underwear down and took her in as she stood completely naked before me. A thin landing strip of hair barely covered her beautiful pussy. *My* beautiful pussy now. My mouth watered with a need to devour it. So, I decided that I'd bring her to orgasm with my mouth first.

Feeling like the luckiest man on Earth, I grabbed her face and pulled her into a passionate kiss.

"You're the most beautiful woman in the entire world."

"I want to see you naked too," she said.

I smiled over her mouth and in a low and seductive voice said, "Undress me. I'm yours."

I watched as her tiny fingers worked to undo the buttons of my shirt. She kissed and ran her tongue slowly over the rippling muscles of my chest and abs as if she were worshipping me. She traced lines over my tats with her tongue. My heart was beating a mile a minute from the intensity of feeling her mouth on my body for the first time.

My dick twitched in anticipation as she undid my jeans. When she tried to take my boxer briefs off, I grabbed her wrist to stop her.

"I think we need to keep these on for a little while."

"How come?"

"Because I don't want to lose control and bury myself inside of you before I have the chance to make you come with my mouth. Lay down, beautiful."

I hovered over her and over the next several minutes worked my mouth slowly down her body from one set of lips down to the other.

"Open your legs wide for me, Nina."

She seemed hesitant, giving the impression that no one had ever done this to her.

More insistently, I repeated, "Wider."

I stopped for a few moments to just appreciate the vision of her spread eagle before me. My lips trembled with need as they lowered down onto her. The second the tip of my tongue landed on her pussy, my cock began to painfully throb. My mouth opened and closed over her wet folds, alternating between kissing, licking and sucking her tender clit. Each time the ball of my tongue ring would lap over it, she'd writhe under me, whimpering and kicking her legs.

I'd gone down on women before. The turn on had always been derived from simply knowing that I was giving pleasure to someone else. It was different for me with Nina. Not only was I getting off on pleasuring her, but even more, I couldn't seem to get enough of her taste, of her heat, of her wet arousal on my tongue. I was consuming her greedily like I was starving and couldn't stop. I was torn between never wanting her to come so that I could continue on endlessly and wanting so badly to feel her coming on my face.

Her legs were becoming more fidgety and her breathing irregular. It seemed like she was holding back, trying to prolong it.

"It's okay...let go," I said.

When it seemed like she couldn't take anymore, I decided to stop for a bit to see what would happen. I stuck my fingers inside of her again and rubbed her clit with my thumb.

Her voice was groggy. "Jake..."

"What do you want, Nina? Say it."

"I want you to lick me there again."

"Good, because I want to taste you while you come."

She surrendered the instant my mouth bore down on her pussy again. Her muscles pulsated against my insatiable tongue as she dug her nails into my hair. We screamed out in unison, her hips bucking as I moaned into her, lapping up every last bit of her orgasm.

As she slowly came down from her climax, I rested my head on her stomach, licking the remnants of her sweet come off my lips. I then slowly kissed my way up her body to her mouth, wanting her to taste herself on me.

So painfully hard from what had just taken place, waiting much longer to be inside of her was not an option.

"I want more," she breathed out.

"Now, I want...you."

Nina surprised me when she took the initiative to pull my boxer briefs down. My fully erect cock sprung forward, glistening with precum. She wrapped her tiny hand around my girth and began to stroke me. The euphoric feeling of her touching me was too much to bear, so I got up, kneeling over her. She stared at me in awe, like she was surprised at the sheer size of me. That look of wonder on her face caused more beads of wetness to build at my tip. I enjoyed watching her face as she continued to size me up. When she took my cock in her hand again, I almost lost it.

"Stop," I urged.

I grabbed a condom as fast as I could, ripping it open with my teeth and sheathing myself. I stopped to look down at her, relishing the last moments before she'd be fully and wholly mine. I wanted so badly to tell her that I loved her but didn't have the courage yet. Despite her giving herself to me, I was still terrified of losing her tomorrow, and that fueled the urgent need to be inside of her.

Lowering myself between her legs, I waited before moving in, knowing that I would want to see the look on her face the second I entered her.

"I want you to forget the other sexual experiences you think you had because *this* is your first time. You will always belong to me and unlike your prick ex-boyfriend, *I'm* gonna finish the job."

Her chest was heaving as she looked up at me in anticipation. I ran my nose slowly and teasingly along her neck to take in her smell a final time before claiming her.

Her eyes flew open wide, and she winced as I pushed inside of her in one slow but intense movement. My eyes shut in ecstasy upon feeling her tight, wet pussy wrapped around my dick. For several minutes, a fear of hurting her caused me to move slower than I could stand.

"You're so tight, Nina. So fucking tight. I wasn't expecting it to feel like this at all. It's too good...too hard for me to want to go easy on you."

I knew I needed more, to fuck her harder, rougher, but in discovering how small she was, I wondered if she would even be able to take it.

As if she could read my mind, she said, "Fuck me harder, then."

"You sure you can take it, baby?"

"Yes." She inhaled deeply before exhaling. "Please."

"You don't have to ask me twice."

She screamed out as I rammed into her, "Fuck!"

With each thrust, she seemed to stretch, gradually molding to me. As I moved in and out of her body, I spoke into her ear, "Nothing's ever felt like this. You've ruined me." I whispered even lower, "You've ruined me."

"Oh God...don't stop. Go deeper."

Pumping in and out of her as I lightly bit her shoulder, it was hard to keep myself from coming.

"You're gonna feel this tomorrow," I said into her ear. "You'll still feel me inside of you."

"Good. That's what I want. I want it to hurt."

Shit.

Her words egged me on as I fucked her harder.

"You...belong...to me now, Nina."

She spoke through heavy breaths, "I've belonged to you from the moment you said 'hi, I'm Jake.'"

We laughed against each other's mouths as I continued to pound into her as the bed squeaked over and over. Her sweet words cut deep. I'd always felt that way, too. Somehow, she'd owned me from the beginning even when it didn't make sense to feel that way about a stranger.

When her hands landed on my ass, I let out a growl. That was a serious weak spot for me.

We continued to fuck hard until I sensed she couldn't take it any longer. Her pussy had clenched around me as she closed her eyes tightly.

"Open them. Look at me. I want to look in your eyes when we come together."

I knew no matter what happened that I would never forget that moment. She held my face in her hands, and our eyes locked. When she screamed out in pleasure, every ounce of fear, every emotion I'd ever felt toward her, all of the love exploded out of me as I came in an orgasm so intense, it seemed like it might never end.

As my seed spilled inside of her, I silently mouthed, *I love you. I love you. I love you.*

We'd stayed up for hours fucking to the point of near exhaustion. She wasn't going to be able to walk straight, and it still hadn't been enough for me.

Not only had last night done a number on us physically, but now, almost nothing had been left unsaid.

Nina had nodded off around one in the morning. Watching her sleep had made me restless, and I needed something to get my mind off the day ahead since we'd agreed to have the talk as soon as I came home from work.

I used the opportunity to write her a poem, putting down on paper what I was afraid I'd never be able to articulate in the right way. At the end of it, I finally used the 'L' word.

And as I lay here watching her sleep,
I realize my feelings run deep.
Because they burn and cut like a knife.
I think I love her more than life.

Sleep claimed me shortly after I wrote it. Nina had woken up first around 2 a.m. and had found the poem. The very first thing that came out of her mouth when I woke to find the white piece of paper in her hand was, "I love you, Jake." She'd said it with no hesitation, as if the words were always there at the tip of her tongue waiting to come out.

As beautiful as it was to finally hear them, they also stung in light of this being the day I had to tell her I was married.

Would she still love me?

The clock showed 5:30 a.m. now. She'd finally gone back to sleep around four. My bladder was ready to explode. Even though the thought of leaving her for even a second bothered me, I needed to get up to take a piss.

Lifting myself out of bed as quietly as possible, I stretched then slowly walked down the hall. As I was washing my hands, the sight of Ryan behind me in the mirror caused me to flinch.

His hair was a mess, and his eyes were bloodshot. "Are you happy now?"

The faucet squeaked as I closed it. "Excuse me?"

"Congratulations. You got what you wanted. How did it feel to fuck her?"

"I bet you'd love to know, and I think that's been your problem all along."

"You know what, Jake? When you're long gone, I'm gonna be the one left behind to pick up the pieces of her broken heart."

"You're going to be picking up the pieces of your broken face in a minute if you don't go the fuck back to bed and stay out of our business."

"Nina *is* my business. Always will be. If you hurt her, I'll kill you."

"If you could see beyond your own egotistical jealousy, you'd know that I'd rather die than hurt her. You don't know anything about who I am, Ryan."

"Well, I think it's time we found out."

"Get the fuck away from me."

Intentionally knocking into his shoulder, I walked past him and out of the bathroom. He was lucky that I couldn't afford to fuck up today, otherwise, I would have knocked him out.

Going from dealing with his negativity to the angelic vision of Nina sleeping soundly back in her bedroom was quite the contrast.

As much as I tried not to let them bother me, Ryan's words of warning shook me to my core. It felt like everything was suddenly closing in on me. The sounds of the morning outside were starting to seep through the apartment walls, a reminder that it was going to be time to get ready for work soon. I didn't ever want this day to begin.

The need for reassurance overtook me.

Slowly inhaling the smell of our sex on her body, I nuzzled my nose into her neck. "Get up, baby. I need you."

Nina stirred, pressing her bare ass into my rock hard morning wood. Completely naked against my boxers, she turned around and softly kissed my face.

"Do you have to get up now?" she asked in the cutest raspy voice.

"Not this second. Soon, though."

She must have sensed my stress when she wrapped her hands around my face. "Are you okay?"

"I just...I need to be inside of you again." My voice was strained.

"I want that, too. But we ran out, remember? We don't have anything," she said, alluding to the strip of condoms we tore through last night.

"Shit. I'd forgotten about that." Kissing her nose, I joked, "Do you think it would go off well if I asked Ryan for one?"

She giggled into my face. "That would be hilarious."

Not wanting to ruin our last minutes together, I chose not to tell her about the bathroom altercation between him and me.

She started to lower my boxers then slid her body down so that she was eye level with my crotch.

"What are you doing?" I asked.

"The one thing we didn't try last night."

"You don't have to. You don't..." My ability to speak ceased when she twirled her tongue slowly around my crown. "Ah. God, Nina."

Rubbing her thumb along the tip, she spread my pre cum around as a lubricant and used it to jerk me off. When she slowly licked down my length, my previously tense body had completely surrendered to her.

I barely got the words out, "Fuck...that's good."

She hummed in apparent agreement, and the sound vibrated down my shaft.

"Ahhhh," I moaned as she suddenly took the full length of me down her throat. Gripping the back of her head, I started to fuck her beautiful mouth. I'd imagined those lips wrapped around my cock so many times, but the reality of how amazing it actually felt was mind-blowing.

At one point, she gagged.

"You okay?"

She responded with a nod and proceeded to take me even deeper into her mouth. This couldn't have been her first time sucking cock. She was too damn good at it. I tried like hell to block out that disturbing thought.

My eyes rolled back from the intense pleasure. I could have exploded at any second but was using all the restraint within me to prolong this.

I'd done a good job until she slowly pulled my cock out of her mouth and said, "I want you to come in my mouth."

Even though I wasn't planning on doing that, the open invitation was too tempting. Stroking me faster, she started to suck again and within seconds, hot cum shot straight out of me as she took it all down her throat until it was gone. The orgasm was so powerful, it knocked me on my ass as I lay back, panting and staring at the ceiling.

After twenty minutes of lying together wide awake, I came to the realization that something was seriously wrong with me because my dick was starting to get hard again. I'd never had stamina like this in my entire life.

The time was getting dangerously close to when I'd have to get up for work. I needed to make her come one last time before I left.

"Straddle me," I said. "I want to touch you."

Nina got up and wrapped her legs around me. My head was against the back of the bed as she sat on me and stared into my eyes with a look that was a cross between fear and elation. Her blonde locks were a beautiful mess, covering her chest.

"Move your hair back."

Nina brushed her long tresses behind her back. Her hair was like friggin' spun gold. I placed my hands on her breasts and gently squeezed, massaging them as she continued to look down at me. She had marks all over her body from where I'd sucked and bit on her skin. I couldn't get enough of her last night. We'd both let our guards completely down. There was no holding back our true feelings anymore. Her eyes reflected a level of love for me that, aside from maybe my father, I'd never received from anyone before. I wanted to remember this moment of peace for the rest of my life. I used to think that losing her would devastate me. But after last night, I knew it would kill me.

"I love you so much," I whispered as I moved my hands softly down the sides of her hips. My dick felt ready to explode from the heat of her pussy as she sat over my balls.

What came out of her mouth next really touched a nerve.

"Is love supposed to hurt like this? Why does this hurt?"

I lifted my hand to her face and rubbed my thumb against her cheek. "It wouldn't be real if it didn't. I feel that pain, too. I've never loved anyone like I love you, Nina."

Unable to contain myself, I pulled her down onto my chest and devoured her mouth. The saltiness of my cum lingered on her tongue.

Her wet pussy was grinding back and forth along my dick now. We were completely drowning in each other.

With my departure time approaching, my mind started to go off the rails. It scared me that there was still a chance I might never get to experience this again if things didn't work in my favor.

My hold on her grew tighter. Once again, fear was fueling an intense need to be inside of her. At one point, her body shifted in a way that meant her opening was right over my tip. I couldn't resist slowly pushing inside. I told myself I would stop after just one last quick feel of her. Her warm pussy enveloped my cock, and she began to ride me. We weren't using anything for protection, but the need for her blinded my judgment. When we were physically connected, everything felt safe, like our souls and bodies were finally in alignment. Without any barrier, that feeling was tenfold.

Nothing else registered in that moment, not the time nor the consequences of our actions. When her movements slowed, and I felt her muscles contract, a loud groan escaped me as I emptied inside of her. There was no way our roommates hadn't heard it. It was the most powerful orgasm of my life.

My heart thundered against hers, and we held each other until I had to force myself up.

"Shut your eyes, baby. Go to sleep. It's okay. I'll be back later."

"We're gonna have the talk," she whispered groggily.

I nodded. "Yes."

"I love you."

"I love you, too."

Somberly, I returned to my bedroom to get ready for work. My shower was a reluctant one because I never wanted to

wash the smell of her off me. There would be no time for
one later, though, given our plans for the talk tonight.

After everything we experienced, there was no way I
could leave her empty-handed this morning.

Quickly folding a piece of construction paper into an
origami bat, I knew I'd be late for work as I took my time
pondering a message to leave her with.

What I almost wrote:

*Whoever said Disney was the happiest place on
Earth never knew...*
What it felt like to be inside of you.

What I wished I could have written:

Tonight you're going to feel afraid.
Please don't forget the promise you made.

What I actually wrote:

I am batshit crazy for you. See you tonight.

The heat was blasting in Nina's room when I went to
place the bat by her bedside. It was so warm and cozy, a
safe haven I never wanted to leave.

The blazing morning sun and the cold air outside were a
rude awakening as I pounded the pavement and began the
dreaded day. With my earbuds in, I played *Angel* by Aero-
smith as I walked to the subway station. Thoughts of Nina

set to songs that reminded me of her consumed every second of my commute.

Nothing that transpired after I left the apartment that morning went according to plan. My trust in the belief that everything happens for a reason would be tested in a bigger way than I could have ever imagined.

NINETEEN

PRESENT

had to stop the story. The weeks that followed that morning were some of the hardest of my life. It made me sick to think about them.

Skylar's voice shook me out of my daydream. "Jake, are you alright?"

"No." I stood up. "You know what? I'm really sorry to leave the story undone, but I really don't think I can rehash anything else right now, especially in light of the current state of things."

I walked over to the window and double checked my phone for a text from Nina. *Nothing*. It was getting late. I wasn't going to be able to take much more of this.

Allison and Cedric returned from the kitchen with plates of food they'd warmed in the oven.

"Jake, we're just gonna set up a spread on the table for anyone who's hungry."

"Thanks, sis. You guys eat. I don't have an appetite."

I returned to the leather recliner. Skylar and Mitch stayed on the couch while Allison and Cedric ate in the adjacent dining room. Mitch Jr. was sleeping in the playpen, which we'd moved into the spare bedroom.

Mitch was looking at me like he expected me to continue the story. "I just want to know what happened after you told her."

Scrolling through the text history with Nina from earlier, I scowled. "I didn't get to tell her."

"Huh?"

"Long story short, I got an emergency call from Ivy's group home that afternoon. They'd told me they thought she tried to commit suicide and asked me to rush to Boston. I ended up getting on a plane that day instead of going back to Nina. Ivy ended up being fine, but it was a total mess."

"What did you tell Nina?"

"She wasn't happy, but she somehow continued to trust me when I said it was an emergency related to what I needed to talk to her about. I told her I would explain everything when I returned after a couple of days. It was an absolute nightmare."

Mitch looked horrified. "So, you had the talk as soon as you got back?"

My tired mind couldn't take anymore. "Skylar, Nina's told you the story, right? You want to fill him in?"

"That bastard Ryan had looked up Jake's information in a database at work and found his marriage license. He took home a copy of it that night and showed it to Nina before Jake came back."

"Holy shit. Fuck, man. I'm sorry. She totally thought you were just messing around on your wife, then?"

"She left the apartment and wasn't planning on ever speaking to me again. I came home to Ryan chastising me about it while Nina was nowhere to be found."

Mitch scrunched his forehead in confusion. "Where did she go?"

"She'd somehow become friends with Mrs. Ballsworthy's daughter, Daria. That was strange in itself. Anyway, she moved in with her on the other side of Brooklyn. I had to choke Ryan to get the address out of him. I ended up locating her, and we were finally able to have the talk. But by that time, our relationship had been tarnished."

"How did she take it?"

I grinded my teeth in frustration, not wanting to recall anything about that conversation. "She was shocked, told me she couldn't be with me unless I got divorced. But she did understand my needing to take care of Ivy. Nina had too big of a heart to ever question that."

My sister spoke from behind me. "Those months were horrible for him."

I hadn't realized she was listening in.

She handed me a plate even though I'd said I had no appetite. "It took you a long time to garner the courage to tell Ivy you needed to file for divorce."

"It needed to be done very carefully. Ivy was devastated once I told her I'd fallen in love with someone, mainly because she was sure that meant I'd abandon her. It took some time to hash out all of the legalities. But it was all necessary if I wanted to be with Nina."

"Where did things stand between you and Nina during all that time?" Mitch asked.

So much for not rehashing everything.

I needed to just explain it as simply as possible and then be done with this conversation.

"Bottom line, things were rough for a while. Ryan continued to be an impediment, too. But Nina and I could never really manage to stay away from each other. Case in point, she got pregnant with A.J. during that time. And that surprise was the miracle that saved us. The past nine years haven't gone without challenges, but I feel like our love has only gotten stronger."

I knew Mitch understood where I was coming from because he and Skylar had certainly had their share of drama. They were apart for five years before they finally got their shit straight.

Mitch nodded and scratched his chin. "Has Nina ever met Ivy?"

"No. I don't think that would be healthy for either one of them. Nina never asked to meet her, and Ivy pretends my family doesn't exist. It's the only way she can handle it when she's even aware enough to think about it. It's a coping mechanism."

Mitch Jr. started crying, so Skylar got up to retrieve him from the playpen.

Mitch pointed his finger at me. "By the way, I think we need to tag team, hunt this Ryan down and beat his ass."

"Believe me, he didn't escape my wrath. I ended up beating the shit out of him once when Nina was pregnant. But over the years, he's apologized enough times that I, at least, don't want to kill him anymore. It's hard to avoid him because Nina's parents are still close to his. Ryan and his wife are at a lot of family functions when we go to upstate New York. He married this really cool chick from Australia named Lisa, who clearly has no idea what a dick he can be. She's way too good for him, though. They just had a son they named after Jimmy. They live not far from Nina's parents. He works in law enforcement now for the town."

Skylar was feeding the baby again. "I just can't forgive him for everything he did, especially what happened after A.J. was born. That was just unconscionable."

I straightened in my chair, uncomfortable with where this was going. "After A.J. was born? What are you talking about?"

"When he went to Nina's parents' house during the week she was staying there with the baby...when your work sent you overseas."

My insides were twisting. "Say what?"

"Oh, shit. Nina never said anything to you?"

"Apparently, fucking not."

"I just assumed she did. I'm so sorry, Jake. Crap. I shouldn't have brought it up. I—"

"Skylar! What the fuck happened?" It wasn't my intention to yell, but the fact that she knew about something that I didn't really pissed me off.

"You know how Nina was really depressed, going through all of that post-partum stuff?"

"Of course, I remember. That was exactly why I didn't want her to be alone that week. She was constantly in tears. A.J. was only a few months old. But I'd just started a new job that I really needed, and they made me go to Germany for training, otherwise I wouldn't have been able to take the position. I drove her up to her parents' so they could help take care of her."

"Yeah. Nina called me a lot during that time. No one understood her postpartum depression. Nina's parents thought it meant she was unhappy with you because of the situation with Ivy. Somehow, Ryan got wind of it and showed up there that week, basically professing his love for her, saying that it wasn't too late for them, that he could make her happy, take care of her and the baby."

My body went rigid. I bit down on my bottom lip, nearly drawing blood. I couldn't believe what I was hearing. Immediately taking out my phone, I scrolled down to Ryan's name.

Skylar panicked. "Please don't be mad at Nina. What are you doing?"

"I have that fucker's number. I'm calling him."

No one should have witnessed what I planned to say or do during that call. I walked into our bedroom and slammed the door shut as the phone rang.

The sound of his baby crying in the background was the first thing I heard when the line picked up. Then, came Ryan's voice.

"Hello?"

"Ryan..."

"Jake? What's up? Long time no—"

"The last time I saw you at Sheryl's sixtieth birthday, do you remember what I said to you?"

"Yeah. Uh, you said, 'life is too short to hold a grudge.'"

My hand was squeezing the pillow. I imagined it was Ryan's neck. "Well, forget that. What I meant was, 'life is too short not to smash your head in.' Next time I see you, I'm gonna do just that."

"What? What the hell are you talking about?"

Clenching my jaw, I said, "When I made amends with you, I didn't know that you tried to break up my family after my son was born. All bets are off now."

"I need to explain."

"I'd *love* to hear how you try to explain your way out of this."

Ryan let out a deep sigh that I felt in my ear. "I need to try."

I muttered a myriad of obscenities under my breath.

"Are you listening?" he asked.

"You have one minute."

He was silent. Then, I heard a sniffle.

It sounded like he'd started to cry.

What the fuck?

"Are you crying, you fucking pussy?"

He sniffled again. There was a long delay before he spoke. "I don't know if Nina ever told you that when Jimmy died, I was by his side."

"She did."

"The last thing he said to me before his eyes closed—the very last thing—was 'take care of my sister.'"

He continued to speak. And I let him.

"I never had a problem with you before she moved into the apartment all those years ago. You know that. After she started hanging out with you, she changed. Nina was happy for the first time since Jimmy died. You were able to get her to overcome some of those stupid fears. I hated that you were able to do something that I couldn't. The way I saw it, Jimmy had left me with one responsibility, and I'd failed. I started to really resent you. But more than anything, I was afraid that if you hurt her, she was going to be worse than she was before. You still there?"

"Yes."

"After your marriage to Ivy came out, I became more convinced that I needed to get Nina away from you. Even though the circumstances were unique, I still felt that the whole thing was a recipe for disaster and that she deserved better. When she found out she was pregnant, I truly believed that she was only staying with you because she was afraid to be alone. Soon after that, Tarah moved out and left me when she figured out my obsession with Nina. I confessed to her about some of the things I'd done to try to keep you and Nina apart. So, I had nothing to lose. After your son was born, during the week Nina was staying at her parents' house, I gave it one last college try. My folks had told me that she was really unhappy. I didn't realize it was the postpartum depression. So, I went to her and told her I loved her and that if she wanted to leave you, I'd take care of her. I didn't understand the depth of her feelings for you. Do you know what she told me?"

My voice was barely audible. "What?"

"She told me that even though she felt lost and didn't even really know who she was anymore, the only thing she was sure of in life was how much she loved you. She told me her best hope for me was that I would someday get to experience that kind of soul deep love with someone. Looking back, it's clear to me that I didn't love her that way at all. I'd been trying to win a competition for her. It wasn't until I met Lisa that I understood the kind of love you and Nina have. I know now that I could have never torn you two apart. When you truly love someone, it's indestructible."

"Yeah..."

"So, once again, I need to tell you how sorry I am. I was wrong. Nina and you always belonged together. Jimmy told me to take care of her. But he changed his mind and sent a better man instead."

I closed my eyes. I needed to get my wife home.

"Go back to your baby," I said.

"Are we okay again?"

"I'm not sure. But I probably won't smash your face in."

"I'll take that for now."

"Good night, Ryan."

I hung up before he could respond.

I lay back on the bed to compose my thoughts before dialing Nina. Ryan's words ran through my head. *He sent a better man instead.* It was doubtful that Nina was feeling that way about me right now.

I reached over to the nightstand and lifted a picture of Nina and me taken on a Gondola ride in Venice during our honeymoon. The smile on her face was difficult to take in right now, knowing she was somewhere trying to get away from me, that she was likely thinking about all of the ways I hadn't put her first.

I shuddered.

The sounds of my family and friends talking in the next room seemed miles away.

Forcing myself up, I decided to head to the master bath to splash some water on my face before returning to the living room.

The water cooled my skin but didn't calm me down.

As I wiped my face, a pink box in the small garbage can caught my eye. It was the discarded packaging of a pregnancy test.

I started to feel lightheaded as I bent to pick it up. This was officially my first clue as to what caused Nina to lose it last night. There was no sign of a test stick itself. The box said it included three tests, but the trash came up empty.

I ignored everyone as I bolted through the living room and into the other bathroom where there was nothing in the trash but one of A.J's empty juice boxes. A search of the kitchen garbage also turned up nothing. Not one pregnancy test showed up in the entire house even though the box was empty.

Feeling distraught, I stood in the kitchen, leaning against the granite countertop with my head in my hands. I didn't have to guess what happened. I knew.

We'd taken countless tests together over the past few years, all negative. Each time was more difficult than the last. My fear was that Nina went through that experience alone last night while I was stuck at the hospital, and that fueled her anger toward me.

We'd recently talked about going to see a fertility specialist, but Nina had been scared to go on any drugs. We were supposed to be discussing it again soon now that she'd finished nursing school.

The vibration of the phone in my pocket startled me. Nina's name lit up on the screen. My heartbeat felt like excruciating waves thrashing against the walls of my chest.

"Nina."

"Hi."

"Where are you?"

"I'm at a diner downtown."

"A diner? What are you doing there?"

"I came here to think."

"Have you been there all day?"

"No."

"What have you been doing?"

"At first, I honestly just wandered around aimlessly."

Cedric walked into the kitchen to check on me. "Everything alright?"

Waving him away, I nodded.

"Who was that?"

"That was Cedric. He and Allison are here. You didn't know it, but I'd planned a party for you tonight. That was the whole reason I initially went to Ivy's last night instead of today. Skylar and Mitch are here, too."

"What? Are you kidding?"

"I wish. You made me promise not to call you, so I kept my word. We've just been hanging out here waiting for you, hoping you'd come home."

"Oh my God. I feel horrible. We need to talk, Jake. I was going to come home right now, but I think you need to meet me here if we won't have any privacy."

"No lie, you're freaking me out, baby. But I'll meet you anywhere you want. I'll fucking walk to the ends of the earth if you just tell me we're okay."

Her breathing became uneven, and it sounded like she was crying.

"Nina? You're scaring the living fuck out of me. What's happening?"

"Promise me you won't be mad at me."

A lump formed in my throat. "Mad at you for what? Aren't you supposed to be mad at *me*?"

"Just promise me you won't get upset with what I'm about to tell you."

"Okay. I promise. Whatever it is, I won't get mad. Where were you today?"

A long, uncomfortable silence put me further on edge. What she said next put me *over* the edge.

"I went to see Ivy."

TWENTY

NINA

Everything seemed to be making me cry lately, but it was especially bad that particular Friday afternoon. My eyes were welling up at the drop of a hat. I was so gosh darn emotional. According to my calendar, my period was due, so it made some sense. My hormones always got the best of me around this time of the month but never like this.

When my mother-in-law came to pick up A.J., I'd taken a deep whiff of his hair, not wanting to let him go. Then, a tear fell when saying goodbye to him.

What was wrong with me?

His reaction had made me laugh. *"Mom, you're messing up my Mohawk."*

Recently, he'd convinced us to let him wear his jet black hair longer on the top. Jake shaved the sides so that the top was more prominent. Even though the style looked really cute on him, we wouldn't let him wear it spiked on school days.

A.J. looked nothing like me. With his dark hair, green eyes and dimples, he was all Jake. We used to joke that Jake just shit A.J. out and that I had nothing to do with our son's creation. But of course, my c-section scar and the months of postpartum depression after he was born served as the evidence that I was definitely his mother. I was just the incubator.

A.J. was only going to be forty minutes away in Malden for the weekend, but for some reason, I was going to really miss him. It was rare that he spent the night away from home. At the same time, it would be refreshing for Jake and me to have some time alone. I was really looking forward to having my sexy man all to myself tonight.

The timing was perfect for it. We'd been under a lot of stress lately between my final nursing clinicals before graduation and the ongoing issues with trying for a baby. Just thinking about the past couple of months caused a fresh stream of tears to fall down my cheeks yet again. I needed Jake to come home and knock some sense into me, make me laugh, comfort me, make love to me.

It would be another couple of hours before he returned from work. To pass the time, I decided to take a walk down to the drug store on Harvard Street for some magazines and shampoo.

I stopped by the local café for a to-go coffee and window shopped in Coolidge Corner on my way. The sun was setting, and the streets were bustling with people heading home from work for the weekend.

We lived in the cutest neighborhood. There were lots of eclectic shops and family-owned businesses. Sometimes, I couldn't believe how lucky we were. As I pondered that, my eyes once again filled with moisture. Everything was making me cry.

Snap out of it, Nina.

As I entered the sliding automatic doors at CVS, the bright fluorescent lights helped cool down my emotional state. I took my time browsing each aisle. It was a rarity to be here alone without A.J. begging for sour gummy worms or a cheap toy.

When I stopped in the magazine section, a smiling baby with a cherubic face stared back at me from the front page of a parenting periodical. When my eyes moistened again, a thought crossed my mind.

Could I be pregnant? Is that why my emotions are out of whack?

I hated to ponder it because that would set myself up for disappointment again. I knew better than to get my hopes up. Still, when I passed the reproductive health aisle, I couldn't resist nonchalantly dumping a pregnancy test kit into my basket.

At the register, the attendant smiled at me when she rang up the pink box along with the smiling baby magazine. (I couldn't resist.)

It was completely dark out by the time I ventured back outside. A harsh wind-driven chill in the air prompted me to adjust my scarf over my face. I remembered they were talking about a pretty bad storm that we'd be getting tonight. It made me relieved to know that A.J. was already where he needed to be.

Back at the apartment, I rubbed my hands together, but the friction did little to warm me up. Despite the coziness of our home, the intensity of the cold outside lingered long after I stepped inside. Without A.J. here, it was also eerily quiet.

I'd decided to head to the kitchen to make some tea. The steam from the piping hot water relaxed me as

I steeped the tea bag and debated whether to take the test before or after Jake came home. I hated putting him through the excitement of waiting in vain. The only thing worse than how a negative test made me feel was always the disappointment in his eyes that he tried unsuccessfully to hide. It would be better if I did it alone and kept the negative result to myself.

Guilt often consumed me. Jake had wanted another baby for years, and I wouldn't agree to it. By the time I came around, my body had apparently decided not to cooperate. If I'd given in and allowed myself to get pregnant six years ago, we might have had no problem. Sometimes, it felt like I was being punished for my own selfishness.

Jake was such an amazing father. He deserved to have another child—or two or three. Despite working long hours at his engineering job north of the city, he gave A.J. his full attention from the second he came home until bedtime and even cooked dinner for us much of the time.

We had a great life six out of the seven days of the week.

Except Saturdays.

Saturdays were the black holes of my life because those were the days he'd visit Ivy. He'd leave in the morning, and I'd count the hours until he returned. Sometimes, that would be late afternoon and often times, evening.

I usually cleaned the house or made plans with A.J. to pass the time on those days. We'd always told our son that "daddy goes to help a sick friend." We left it at that.

I had a habit of internalizing my feelings about Jake's relationship with Ivy because it wasn't fair to add more stress to a situation that couldn't be helped. From the moment I learned the truth all those years ago, it was clear that Ivy was like family to Jake. As unfair as it seemed, he'd inherited the responsibility of looking after her. I really did understand his dilemma. But that didn't mean I had to like it or that I wasn't going to get jealous.

I knew with absolute certainty that if I made him choose between us, he'd choose me. He'd even admitted that. But making such a demand wouldn't really remove the situation. I wouldn't be able to live with myself if I had to watch him suffer the guilt of abandoning her. He'd beat himself up over it. You just don't put someone you love in a position like that. The situation with Ivy existed before I ever came into the picture, and it was essentially a part of him. I loved him and had to accept all parts of him—good, bad and ugly.

Most of the time, I was confident enough in his love for me to not let the existence of Ivy get to me. But occasionally, when in a certain mood, I would become angry and resentful that we couldn't just be a normal family without having to live in the shadow of an ex-wife with mental issues.

I never wanted to meet her.

I was terrified she'd be prettier than me or that I'd find out she really wasn't that incapacitated. Most of the time, I was able to compartmentalize all of that insecurity.

Most of the time.

Tonight was not one of those times. My whacky hormones were making me particularly insecure and out of sorts. After dumping the remainder of my tea into the sink, I grabbed the paper CVS bag and took it to the bathroom located off of our bedroom.

It wasn't necessary to read the directions because I'd done this far too many times to count. I took the first test out and peed on it before repositioning the clear cover over the stick as directed.

Five minutes.

The snow was blowing around outside in horizontal bands. Cars that were uncovered on my way inside were now coated in white. Jake was supposed to be home in an hour. I hoped he didn't get stuck on the highway in storm traffic.

Returning to the living room, I covered myself with a knitted throw and tried to focus on the parenting magazine while the early evening weather forecast played in the background.

The phone rang, and Jake's name flashed on the caller i.d.

I picked up. "Please tell me you're not stuck in traffic."

"Hey, baby. I'm off of the highway now, but listen...I have to go to Ivy's tonight."

That news rattled me. "What?"

"I got a call from the group home, and she had some kind of an episode. I told them I'd go check on things tonight. But this means I won't have to go tomorrow, okay? We'll have tomorrow free. A.J. will still be at my mother's. The weather will be better, and we can go out."

I sulked. I was really missing him today. "Alright, I guess."

"Are you okay? I know this sucks ass."

"What time will you be home tonight?"

"As soon as I can. I promise."

"Okay."

"Nina. Be ready for me tonight. I'm horny as hell."

"You're always horny."

"Seriously...you know what I've been thinking about all day? I've had this fantasy running through my head. I almost got hard in the middle of a fucking meeting today."

"Tell me about your fantasy."

"I want to move the couch cushions onto the ground and put them right in front of the electric fireplace. I want you naked and down on all fours in front of the fire with your ass sticking up in the air. Then, I want to fuck you from behind like that with the heat blazing on us while it snows outside. What do you think?"

"I think I want you to come home right now. Just get here as soon as you can after Ivy's."

"I love you, baby. Thank you for understanding."

"I love you, too."

I kept the phone at my ear even though he'd hung up. I was disappointed for sure, but I understood. At least, we'd have a rare Saturday together tomorrow.

The five minutes had long expired, but I was dilly-dallying, pretending to read an article on home schooling. Now that Jake wasn't coming home anytime soon, the thought of being alone, wallowing in the results of another disappointing test seemed dreadful.

After several minutes, I threw the magazine aside, forced myself up and walked into my dark bedroom.

The door to the bathroom creaked as I slowly turned the knob. I took a deep breath and shut my eyelids tightly before looking at the test.

I opened my eyes to two pink lines.

Holding the three positive sticks in my hand, I paced the bedroom unsure of what to do with myself. I'd taken the other tests in the kit just to be sure. I was most definitely pregnant.

Bursting with excitement, I jumped up and down and waved my hands in the air, feeling like a fool. It seemed surreal after all this time. I had seriously given up all hope. Jake and I were very sexually active, so to not get knocked up even once in over seven years made me certain there was a real problem.

I'd heard of this type of thing happening, though. Just when people were ready to start fertility treatments or adopt, they'd miraculously get pregnant.

I had to think of a creative way to tell him. He was going to be ecstatic! My heart felt like it was going to explode just thinking about his reaction.

I decided to place the tests inside an elongated metallic gold jewelry box. After removing the diamond tennis bracelet that Jake had bought me for our one year anniversary, I tucked it away in a drawer and replaced it with the three sticks. I'd pretend it was a present that I'd bought him for supporting me through nursing school. He'd think it was a watch and freak out when he saw what was really inside.

This was going to be so freaking awesome.

I needed to make this a special evening when he came home. I placed the box in my purse and wasted no time venturing into the kitchen. Searching the cupboards, I made sure we had all the ingredients for Bananas Foster.

Bananas, butter, brown sugar, rum...

If ever a night to celebrate with Jake's favorite dessert, tonight was it.

Just as I placed two sticks of butter in the pot, my phone started to ring. It was him.

"Jake?"

"Hey, baby. Listen—"

"Please tell me you're calling to say you're on your way home."

"I'm at the hospital. When I got to the group home, she'd already been admitted."

"Is she alright?"

"Yeah. They found her trying to climb the roof again. What a fucking nightmare. They're going to release her tomorrow."

"Okay...so what does this mean?"

"It was going to mean I'd be running later than I thought. But I just heard they closed the road to all non-emergency vehicles due to black ice. I was looking out the window earlier, and cars were spinning out into each other. It was apocalyptic."

"So, what are you saying?"

"I'm saying I might have to spend the night here unless they open the road. I swear, I feel like I have the worst fucking luck sometimes."

He wasn't coming home.

I was silent, but a tear fell down my cheek. I didn't want him to be able to tell that I was crying.

Deep down, I knew this wasn't his fault, but I couldn't seem to control my reaction.

"Nina? Are you alright?"

"Yes."

"Are you sure?"

"Just be careful," I said.

"I love you."

"I love you, too."

I pressed the red end call button and slid the phone across the counter. I didn't even know where my anger was directed. I just knew I couldn't seem to calm down over this. To make matters worse, the butter I'd been heating for the dessert had completely burned.

"Shit!"

I shut off the flames and angrily threw the hot pot into the sink, splattering the butter everywhere.

The sound of my inner ear ringing amidst the deafening quiet was torturous.

I forced myself to go straight to bed and began to obsess about everything. My fears got the best of me as concern about my emotional state grew. The "what if" monster started to take control of my thoughts.

What if I'm a basket case for the next nine months?

What if I get postpartum depression again?

What if Jake can't handle my issues this time, and it ruins us?

What if Jake is still attracted to Ivy? (That was an oldie but goodie that always seemed to creep in at my worst.)

Then, the "what if" questions turned to "whys."

Why do I have to share my husband?

Why can't we just be a normal family?

Why can't he walk home? (That one made no sense because of the blizzard, and he was on the other side of the city, but I wasn't thinking rationally tonight.)

Why is he with her and not with me?

This self-torture continued through the night. Tossing and turning, I finally fell asleep around four in the morning, only to wake up at six in the same state of mind.

Jake couldn't see me like this. It would ruin what was supposed to be a happy time. I needed to take some time today and calm down before I told him about the baby. My being in this state would tarnish the whole pregnancy announcement.

If I left before he got here, it might freak him out. So, the plan would be to wait until he arrived and then leave for a while to grab my bearings. The only way he'd let me leave was if I was adamant about it.

I received a text about 6:30 a.m.

Road is finally opened. Thank God.
Leaving now. Be home soon.

I got my coat on and threw a hat over my head so that I would be prepared when he came in. I sat in the same spot waiting.

Forty minutes later, the door latched open.

My heart beat faster as I took in the sight of my husband. His flattened hair stuck to the sides of his head. He had bags under his glowing green eyes. He was still the most gorgeous man I'd ever laid eyes on.

Jake ran to me and planted his nose in my neck, releasing a deep breath into me. His skin was cold to the touch. "What a nightmare last night was. They discharged her. She's back at the group home now." He squeezed me tighter. "God, Nina. It feels so fucking good to be home."

Doing everything in my power to fight back tears, I reluctantly pushed back. Even though I was tempted to stay in the safety and warmth of his arms, my mood was out of control, and it would ruin everything. I had to cool it, and that meant leaving.

"Why do you have your coat on?"

"I need to get out for a while. I didn't want you to come home and not find me."

"What? Why? Is it because I spent the night at the hospital?"

That wasn't entirely the issue, but I implied that it was. "What do you think?"

"Baby, I—"

"Listen, last night was just a really rough night. You've never not come home before. Ever. I just...I got upset. It's not only that. I need to clear my mind. I'll be fine. I just need some space."

"Nina, I'm sorry. But I just don't understand."

"Please don't call me and don't text me, okay? I'm serious. I just need to be alone for a while."

The terrified look on his face didn't stop me. I closed the door behind me and never looked back.

The stormy weather of the previous day had given way to a beautiful morning as mounds of white snow reflected the bright rays of the sun.

After a few hours of roaming our neighborhood and two stops into a couple of different restaurants that were open for breakfast, my exact destination was still unclear. Ice crunched beneath my Ugg boots as I continued to stroll along the side streets, still not ready to go home.

When I got to the tracks along Beacon Street, a Green Line trolley approached in the distance. It eventually screeched to a halt in front of me, and the doors opened. I impulsively got inside without paying attention to where it was headed.

I shut my eyes and let the swaying motion of the trolley ride calm me as I thought about the baby growing inside of me. The timing of my first pregnancy couldn't have been worse. It was in the midst of first finding out about Ivy and dealing with all of the changes to Jake's and my relationship that came along with that. The stress leading up to A.J's birth was unprecedented and helped create the perfect storm that led to a really rough time after he was born.

I was determined that this baby would come into the world under different circumstances. Whatever demons or insecurities that remained inside of me needed to be eradicated in the next nine months.

Something written in pen on the back of the seat in front of me caught my eye.

Replace Fear of the Unknown with Curiosity.

I'd had a lot of fears in my lifetime. With Jake's help, I was able to overcome many of them. But when you're a fearful person by nature, often times, old fears are simply replaced with brand new ones. Ivy had been at the root of my anxieties from the moment I first found out about her. Even though Jake never gave me a reason to feel insecure, I couldn't help it. Because I'd never met her, had never even seen what she looked like, she was like this mythical creature that held a small part of my husband's heart. The times I became most insecure were the times that I focused on that one small part I didn't have, rather than the majority I owned.

Replace Fear of the Unknown with Curiosity.

The next stop was Park Street. Vaguely, it registered that Park Street was where I could switch to the Red Line train. The Red Line would take me to Dorchester. Dorchester was where Ivy lived.

I wouldn't admit to myself that I was actually considering going there. If it became truth, I would lose the courage to do something that might be necessary for my own mental health. Maybe I would just peek in the window. Maybe I wouldn't actually say anything to her. But it just suddenly became clear to me that as long as Ivy was a faceless monster in my head, the fear of the unknown would always be there. How could you tackle a fear if you didn't really know what you were dealing with? I took one last look at the words responsible for catapulting an ordinary day into one I hoped I wouldn't regret for the rest of my life.

Replace Fear of the Unknown with Curiosity.

I stood up and clung to a metal pole as the trolley came to a stop.

After dumping change into the open guitar case of a man performing on the platform below, I waited anxiously for the next train—the train that would take me to Ivy's neighborhood. I'd ordered a gift basket for the staff at the group home once as a favor to Jake, so I knew the address. I'd even stalked the house a few times on Google Earth, squinting my eyes to examine every last detail as if I'd get a glimpse of her.

Once on the train, I checked my phone. No text from Jake. Even though I'd told him not to text me, I was surprised but thankful that he listened. I wasn't sure I could have gone through with this if he'd sent a message that made me feel guilty.

The announcement for my stop amped up the adrenaline running through my veins. "Fields Corner!"

As I exited the train, I took out my phone and entered the address into a GPS application.

It would be about a ten minute walk to the group home. As I followed the route, my mouth was parched, and my heart was beating out of control. With each step forward, doubt spread like wildfire. I wasn't sure I could go through with it.

The automated voice stopped me in my tracks. "You have arrived."

I looked up at the giant three-story home. Brown paint was chipping off the siding of the exterior. A wooden plaque with the word *Welcome* carved into it hung on the front door. Wind chimes dangling from the top of the front porch abruptly rang out in the breeze as if to warn me to turn around and leave.

I walked around the side and peeked through a first floor window. Two women were preparing food in the kitchen. The muffled voice of a man singing somewhere inside the house could also be heard.

This was a bad idea. They weren't going to just let me in. What would I even say? I needed to leave, but at the same time, I'd come all the way here and at least, hoped for a look at her.

I returned to the front of the house and stood frozen outside of the door.

Before I could garner the courage to knock, the door flew open.

A heavyset woman with short cropped hair stood before me. "I saw you standing on the porch from the window. The doorbell is broken. You must be Shari."

It felt like all of the saliva had drained from my mouth. "Uh...yeah? Hi."

What was I doing?

She boisterously waved her arm behind her shoulder. "Well, come on in."

"Thanks."

"No. Thank *you* for doing this on short notice. We've had a shortage of volunteers lately. They didn't tell me which day you were coming, just that they'd try to send you whenever you had some time."

She thought I was a volunteer.

"So, I don't know if Valerie told you, but really, it's just basic stuff we need help with...floors, the two bathtubs, most of the deep cleaning that gets neglected. You okay with getting on your hands and knees?"

"Uh...sure."

I followed her down a hallway as she spoke. "I can't tell you how much we appreciate this. With budget cuts, the state only sends a cleaning service out once a month now. And that's just not enough. We have twelve adults in this house. Our priorities are keeping them safe, and that means that the cleaning goes to hell." She reached out her hand. "I'm Nadine, by the way."

I took her hand. "Nice to meet you."

"All the cleaning supplies you should need are in that utility closet. You should start with the floors downstairs then make your way upstairs to the bathrooms. We have one of those fold-out yellow signs that says 'wet floor.' You can place it down in the center of whatever room is wet then move it around as needed as the floors dry. You don't need to do the bedrooms, just the main living area floors downstairs and the bathrooms. Should take you about two hours."

"Okay."

I'd gotten myself into this mess, and now, I would have to literally clean it up.

About a half-hour into scrubbing the floors downstairs, I checked to make sure the kitchen was dry before removing the sign. The plan was to venture upstairs next. I'd assumed Ivy was up there since all of the bathrooms and the residents' bedrooms were located on the second and third floors.

A tall, dark-skinned man donning sunglasses entered the kitchen. He was walking extremely slowly before he sat down.

He caught me off guard when he spoke. "Hey, beautiful."

"Hi."

"Smile. You look gorgeous today, by the way. And you're doing a great job."

"Thank you. That's...uh...nice of you to say."

"It's not that nice."

"What?"

"I don't really know how you look. I'm blind. I'm a ball buster."

"Oh." I laughed. "I see."

"Yes, you do, but I don't."

"Right. Sorry."

"Don't be sorry. It's a beautiful thing sometimes. I get to see everyone for what they really are on the inside without the bullshit on the outside—the masks that people wear."

"That's an interesting way of putting it."

"I can also pretend that every woman looks like Halle Berry. That helps."

"Yes, I suppose it does." I chuckled. "How do you know...um..."

"How do I know what Halle Berry looks like?"

"Yeah."

"I wasn't always blind."

It wasn't any of my business, but I was really curious. I whispered, "What happened to you?"

He pointed to the floor. "You missed a spot."

I flipped around. "Where?"

"Now, how's a blind man gonna see if you missed a spot? I told you. I'm a ball buster."

I smacked my forehead. "What's your name?"

"I'm Leo."

"Hi, Leo. I'm Ni...uh, Shari."

"Niashari. Interesting name. To answer your question, I lost my sight in Iraq. It was a roadside bomb. I'm a soldier."

His admission jarred me into silence. Leaning my mop against the sink, I pulled up a seat across from him. "Wow. I'm sorry. Thank you for your service, Leo."

"Don't look so depressed."

"I thought you couldn't see me."

"That is correct. You're getting better at anticipating my tricks, Niashari."

"Thank you."

"I've never seen you here before," he said.

"Is that another trick?"

"Actually, that one wasn't. But that would've been a good one, too."

"So, how long have you lived here?"

"A couple of years. It's hard to get into one of these state funded homes, so I jumped at the chance. It's not exactly the best fit for me. Most of the people here have behavioral challenges, but I need the assistance with daily living. And believe me, being here definitely helps me realize that there are people with way bigger issues than mine. It's sort of like the opposite of 'the grass is greener.' We all have crosses to bear. They're just different."

"That's funny. My husband says that same exact thing, that everyone has a cross."

"Your husband's a wise man. And probably damn lucky, too."

I could see myself smiling in the reflection of his sunglasses.

"Thank you." The chair skidded against the floor as I got up. "Well, I should get back to work. It was really nice meeting you."

As I started to walk away, his voice stopped me. "Hey, Niashari. Whatever's bothering you, it will be okay, you know."

"How can you tell something's bothering me?"

"I sat on the stairs and listened to you cleaning for a while before I came in here. The way you were breathing seemed off and something about your voice just now...I can tell. The inability to see with my eyes sometimes makes me more in tune to everything else."

"Well, you're very perceptive. But running into you actually helped calm my nerves. So, thanks."

"You could be butt ugly for all I know, Niashari. But you're a ten in my book for taking the time to chat with me. Not many people who walk in here give me the time of day. You're good people."

My eyes began to water. "Thank you, Leo. The pleasure is all mine, believe me."

As I carried the mop and bucket to the second floor, I thought about how sometimes God will place someone in your path at just the right time. Leo demonstrated that no matter the hardship, it's your attitude that will determine the quality of your life. At the same time, he made me realize how fortunate I was. He couldn't have known how much that little interaction meant to me. It was the one thing that gave me the strength to face whatever I'd find at the top of those stairs.

My hands shook as I wrung out the sponge while trying my best not to breathe in the fumes of the chemicals. Using rubber gloves, over the past forty-five minutes, I'd cleaned two toilets, two tile floors and scoured orange crud off of two bathtubs.

Abandoning the cleaning supplies in the corner of the second bathroom, I walked down the hall. My heart pounded as I peeked into whichever bedrooms were open.

In one room, a blonde woman who looked to be in her early twenties stared vacantly at a television. That couldn't have been Ivy. She was too young. And I did know that

Ivy had red hair. That was pretty much all I knew about what she looked like since I never asked Jake to show me a picture.

A middle-aged man watching a football game waved to me from another room.

I was starting to really feel like I was violating the residents' privacy. I'd continue down the hall to the end. If I didn't spot her, maybe I would just take my cleaning supplies downstairs and leave.

When I got to the second to last room on the right, I froze. All life around me seemed to still as a flash of fiery red caught my eye.

The first thing I noticed was her long mop of thick red curls. The woman who looked to be about my age was staring up at a wall clock while bouncing back and forth between the balls and heels of her feet. She hadn't noticed me as I stood there observing her like she held the answers to all of life's mysteries. She *was* the big mystery of my life.

Only the side of her face was somewhat visible. Her hair hid most of her profile.

A television in the corner was on low volume, but she focused all of her attention on the clock.

What was so fascinating?

The smell of cigarette smoke emanating from the room was suffocating and caused me to break out into an unintentional cough. She whipped her head to the left, and her eyes met mine in a penetrating stare.

We were face to face.

Ivy.

We finally meet.

She was beautiful, not in a glamorous way, but in the natural way that even years of abusing your body apparently couldn't destroy. Her skin was fair, and she had small features. A few freckles were splattered across her cheeks. What surprised me the most was how tall she was, probably almost as tall as Jake.

Her incendiary stare continued to burn into me as I took a few steps forward into the room. She surprised me when she turned back toward the wall as if I wasn't even there.

My body inched closer. "Ivy?"

Her attention was still fixed on the clock when she answered, "No."

"You're not Ivy?"

"No."

I cleared my throat. "What's so interesting about the clock?"

She turned her face toward me again and said nothing. A few seconds later, she said, "I'm trying to make it go back, reverse time."

Blinking repeatedly, I tried to make sense of what she'd just said. It was heartbreaking in so many ways.

I walked behind her to a chest of drawers and lifted a frame that held a photo of Jake and Ivy. My husband had his arm around her in the snapshot. My hand began to quiver as Jake's green eyes stared back at me from the frame. It was overwhelming to see him so young in a time before I ever knew him. It was also painful to see him looking so happy with someone else. Ivy had the same long, red hair back then, but her expression was full of life, a stark contrast to the current distant look on her face. Staring at the picture was like venturing into a time machine I never would have willingly boarded.

As I examined it mesmerized, Ivy turned around toward me. I felt like I needed to say something.

"Nice picture. Who is this?"

"That's Sam."

"Sam?"

"He's a bad person."

My heart felt like it dropped. Hearing her say that made me feel sorry for Jake. I couldn't imagine what it must have been like to care for someone who didn't even know who you were some of the time. You had to be a self-less person to deal with this situation.

I gently swiped the glass that covered the image of my husband's face. A thick layer of dust coated my fingertip. Returning the frame back to the top of the bureau, I noticed a note and picked it up, recognizing right away that it was written in Jake's handwriting.

Ivy's Week Ahead:

Sunday: Relax

Monday: Science Museum Outing

Tuesday: Appointment with Dr. Reynolds

Wednesday: Gina Visit

Thursday: Toni is coming to trim your hair.

Friday: Happy Birthday, baby girl. 33!

Saturday: That nuisance Jake comes back.

Overcome with emotion, I swallowed the lump in my throat. While it was heartwarming to see how meticulously he looked out for her, seeing that he used the term baby girl had sparked unwanted jealousy.

In an eerie coincidence, as if he could sense my inner turmoil, a text from Jake came in.

> ***Are you okay? Please talk to me. You have me worried sick.***

I quickly typed a response.

I'm fine. But I need more time alone.

Ivy walked over to the nightstand and took out a box of cigarettes. She lit one, inhaled then startled me when she spoke. "What is your name?"

"Shari." I coughed. "What's yours?"

A cloud of smoke floated toward me as she exhaled. "Aria."

"Aria?"

"What are you doing here, Shari?"

"I'm a volunteer."

"Did Apollo send you?"

"Apollo?"

"The god of music."

Jake had told me a little about Ivy's delusions over the years. It was starting to dawn on me that I'd caught her in the middle of one.

Tilting my head, I asked, "Why would he have sent me?"

"Are you one of his other conquests?"

"No. I can safely say I am not."

"He's going to save me. He loves me even though I'm a mortal. Because I'm a talented musician."

"Well, that's great."

"Did you know that operatic arias are the most beautiful pieces of music? That's where my name comes from. Aria is synonymous with music."

Jake had mentioned that Ivy used to play the guitar. That was one of the few things I knew about her. An amber-colored guitar leaning against the wall in the corner of the room caught my eye.

"So, you're a musician. I see the guitar over there. Do you play?"

Nothing could have prepared me for what happened next. Ivy quickly put her cigarette out and sat down on the bed. She started to rock back and forth. The change was like a light switch had been turned off. She wrapped both of her hands around her head and started pulling her hair. Then, she burst into tears.

A flash of panic hit me. I felt helpless. The bed creaked as I sat down next to her.

"It's okay, Aria. Whatever it is, you'll be okay."

The reality of how far gone Ivy's condition was had never really registered with me before. Seeing it for myself gave me a clearer understanding of what Jake had been dealing with all of these years.

There was a knock at the door.

A woman walked in holding a small Dixie cup. "Ivy girl, I have your medicine." She seemed unphased by Ivy's wailing, which told me it happened a lot.

The worker didn't question me. She simply walked over to Ivy, gave her two pills and watched as she drank every last drop of the water.

"Stick out your tongue," the woman said, apparently needing to make sure Ivy actually swallowed the medicine.

Ivy did as she was told. "Ahh."

I noticed for the first time that her teeth were quite stained.

The woman promptly left, shutting the door behind her.

Outside the window, snowflakes were falling. We sat in silence for several minutes. Thankfully, she'd calmed down. I couldn't help staring at her, taking in every last detail as she towered over me on the bed. Subtle wrinkles were starting to form around her mouth, probably from all the years of smoking. It was hard to imagine that Jake had once been married to her, had made love to her over and over. I shuddered. The knowledge that my husband had been inside of her caused my stomach to turn. I really tried not to let my mind go there, but I couldn't help it.

At one point, she wiped her nose with her sleeve. Her eyes were swollen and red when she slowly turned to me. "I'm Ivy."

"Hi, Ivy."

"Why are you here?"

"I'm not sure," I said honestly.

"Me, neither. I'm not sure why I'm here anymore most days."

The deeper meaning of her statement made me overcome with sadness for her. I didn't know what to say. "I'm sorry."

"No one ever stays. People come in here to give me medicine or check to make sure I'm alive then they leave. I'm usually alone. Just as well. I don't know how to be around people anymore. Well, except Jake." She laughed almost maniacally. "I haven't scared him away yet."

"Jake, huh..."

Ivy stood up, walked over to the bureau and picked up the very picture I'd been holding earlier. She brought it over to me. "That's him."

My poker face was getting harder and harder to maintain. I wasn't going to pry or force her to label what he was to her in order to satisfy my own morbid curiosity. I knew the truth, and I knew it must have been painful for her to think about losing him. It was probably easier if she didn't have to refer to him as anything specific anymore. Or maybe she didn't always realize she'd lost him. It seemed impossible to know what she was really thinking.

She returned the frame to the bureau without saying anything else.

This situation was getting to be too much for me. I knew I really needed to get up and leave but wasn't exactly sure how to approach it. She seemed to want me there, which was surprising and unsettling.

Ivy got up again, walked over to the television and shut it off. Sitting back down on the bed, she closed her eyes and slowly exhaled. She startled me when she grabbed my wrist for support then said, "Go over there and bring me the guitar." When I hesitated, she yelled, "Go!"

The room suddenly felt hot. I was starting to perspire. I stood up and walked over to the guitar in the corner. It was a lot heavier than expected. I brought it over to her, and she reluctantly took it.

She rubbed her hand gently along the strings. "I don't play anymore."

"Why not? If it makes you happy, you should do—"

"It doesn't make me happy anymore." Her tone was frantic. "It just reminds me of a time when I was happy, that I can't get back. And that makes me sad. That's why I can't do it. I don't want to remember Ivy!"

"I understand. I—"

"But I miss it. I miss playing. I miss the feeling. I feel like I'm slowly dying without it."

After several minutes of just watching her caress the instrument, a thought popped into my head. It was a long-shot, and I didn't even know if it would make sense to her. "Maybe Ivy doesn't have to play. Maybe Aria could play for her. It can be separate from Ivy. Aria can start fresh, learn to play again. Do you remember who Aria is?"

It was a risk. Aria, after all, was an illusion. But I wondered if the musical alter ego was something she still kept tucked inside even when she was of clearer mind.

"Aria..." she simply whispered.

"Yes."

She continued to stare down at the guitar. My face broke out in a sweat because I was starting to feel trapped. I couldn't leave her in this state. I didn't know what was going to happen next.

I closed my eyes and let out a deep breath. The sound of a single strum of the guitar forced my eyes open, and my gaze landed on her fingers, which were positioned to start playing. They were shaking.

Placing my hand on her shoulder, I said, "Play something for me. Trembling hands can still play."

Ivy's bushy red ringlets fell over her forehead as she looked at me. Her half-covered eyes were still fixed on mine when she began to play a song. After a few seconds, I realized it was *Let it Be* by the Beatles.

When I started to hum along to the music to show her I recognized the melody, she smiled at me for the first time. That caught me off guard. A teardrop ran down my cheek. If someone had told me that this moment would be one that would make me cry, I wouldn't have believed it.

Slightly bending her head back, she closed her eyes and continued to play.

It was hypnotic, haunting and beautiful. How fitting that she'd chosen a song about acceptance, leaving problems behind and moving on with life. Just as she had to accept her life as it was, I had to move on from my hang ups about her. Ivy was so much more than I ever imagined, a passionate and talented soul imprisoned by her own mind. And as for Jake, I'd always known I'd married a good man. But this whole experience made me realize I'd married a fucking saint.

You think you know something, but you have no idea.

When the song finished, I stood up, leaving her sitting on the bed.

"That was amazing."

With the guitar still in hand, she suddenly looked agitated. "Please leave."

I nodded. "Okay."

I walked toward the door and took one last look around.

She called out to me, "Wait."

I turned around.

"Will you come back?" she asked.

If there was one thing I knew with absolute certainty, it was that Ivy would never see me again. We couldn't be friends or anything else to each other for that matter. But Jake was a part of me. So, in a sense, a part of me would always be with her.

My mouth spread into a sympathetic smile. "It was nice meeting you," I said, continuing to walk toward the door.

"Hey."

I did an about face. "Yeah?"

"Anyone ever tell you that you look like those twins from TV?"

"No. I haven't heard that before," I lied.

"Well, just so you know, you do."

I shook my head in amusement. "Thanks."

As Ivy graced me with a second rare smile, I let that be my last memory of her before closing the door behind me.

Just let it be.

TWENTY-ONE

NINA

Leaving a cloud of exhaust in its wake, Jake's black Cobra Mustang sped past the diner. I'd been staring out the window and heard the engine revving before I even noticed it was him whizzing by. He must have been a wreck, circling around for a parking spot on the snowy downtown streets while he wondered what the hell had happened between me and Ivy.

Over the phone, I'd dropped the bomb on him that I'd gone to see her. Jake was speechless. His reaction was one of absolute shock, as if that were the last thing he ever expected me to say. He hung up right after he told me to stay put, that he'd come to me.

Now, I sat alone in a booth watching the door as my heart raced. Any minute, he'd walk in, and I would have to explain myself.

Bells chimed as the door opened, letting a brisk wind inside.

He took my breath away.

Looking painfully gorgeous wearing a black down parka and a gray knit cap, Jake slowly approached my booth. Chills ran through me when his eyes landed on mine. His expression was intense but impossible to read.

Instead of taking a seat across the table, he moved in next to me, took my face in his hands and placed his lips firmly on my forehead. So relieved that he didn't seem mad, I shut my eyes and drowned myself in his intoxicating smell. There was nothing else in the world like the combination of his cologne, skin and the pheromones always unleashed when we touched.

He kissed the top of my head over and over. When he pushed back, his eyes were glistening. "Are you okay?"

"Yes," I said, nodding repeatedly. "More than okay. I'm so sorry."

He gently brushed his thumb against my lips. "Whatever happened, you don't owe me an apology."

I exhaled to compose myself. "They thought I was a volunteer. I never told her who I was. I hadn't planned on going to see her when I left this morning. It was an impulsive decision, but—"

"You had to know. I get it, baby. You don't need to explain why. If it were me instead of you, I could have never waited as long as you did. Curiosity would have killed me."

"I just needed to see for myself."

He placed his hand on my knee under the table. "I get it."

A waitress interrupted us. "Can I get you something, sir?"

Jake didn't take his eyes off me when he answered, "Just a coffee."

"I'll take a pot of green tea."

Over the next thirty minutes and two cups of tea, I leaned into him and relayed the entire group home experience from meeting Leo (whom Jake apparently sometimes hung out with when Ivy slept) to my whole encounter with Ivy.

"Seeing what you've had to deal with is eye opening. I will never be one hundred percent comfortable with it, but seriously, where would she be if you hadn't looked out for her all these years? You've single-handedly saved her, Jake."

"Maybe. But don't you get it?"

"What?"

"From the day you first walked into my life, you've been saving *me*. I was already on my last leg of sanity when we met. My ability to sustain that life with nothing else to live for would have never lasted. So much passion, so much love was trapped inside of me with no one to give it to. If I hadn't met you, if I couldn't have released all of that, it would've turned toxic. Having you and A.J. to come home to every day, the way you love me, it recharges me, gives me a reason to live. I'm certain I'd be dead without it. I thought I might be losing you today."

"Never. All those years ago, I promised I'd never leave you. Even when I convinced myself it was the right thing to do, I couldn't stay away. You're my everything."

Our legs were locked together under the table. The warmth of being near him made me realize how much I'd missed him.

Jake drew me into his arms. "Do you have any idea how much I love you? It doesn't compare to how I've ever felt toward anyone else. I'm talking about the once in a lifetime soul deep love, the kind you told Ryan you felt for me when he tried to steal you away from me after A.J. was born."

My jaw dropped. I'd specifically never told him about that because it seriously made me afraid for Ryan's life.

"How did you find out? I—"

Jake put his finger over my mouth and smiled. "Shh. It's okay. I understand why you didn't tell me. I would have gone after him, and we didn't need any more stress back then. I'll tell you the story of Ryan's and my phone call another time. Not gonna waste time on it tonight. We're good, Nina. We've never been fucking better. I don't want to talk about anything upsetting anymore. All I want is to take you home, get you under a hot shower and suck on every inch of your body before I bury myself deep inside you. That is all I fucking want right now."

Oblivious to the people around us, we fell into a deep kiss.

"I want that, too. How are we gonna manage that with houseguests?"

"We'll have to figure out a way."

Nearly jumping out of my skin, I wanted so badly to tell him about the baby, but doing it at the diner just didn't seem appropriate.

He slid his cup and saucer across the table and spoke into my ear, "Let's get out of here. I want to take you home."

As we made our way toward the exit, Jake walked closely behind me, pressing his hard body against my back while his arms were wrapped around my waist. My nipples were hard as steel from the contact. The hormones that were triggering my crying earlier were now simply making me horny as hell.

Two women eating together looked enviously at us as we walked by. They likely wished my hot husband were rubbing up on them instead of me. He looked particularly smokin' tonight, too with the sides of his hair sticking out from under his beanie. A long time ago, I realized that being with Jake meant getting used to women checking him out.

The bells on the door dinged as we stepped out into the snowy air. It wasn't a blizzard like the previous night, but the white stuff was starting to stick.

"Where are you parked?"

"There were no spots on the road, so I had to park in the small lot behind the diner. It's for employees only. Hopefully, they didn't ticket me."

He led me down a hill to the rear of the building. Jake's Mustang sat in the back of the lot next to a dumpster. The aluminum rims gleamed in the darkness.

It was desolate and quiet compared to the noise of the street.

He walked around to the passenger side and opened the door for me. "Get in, baby."

I was glad this day was over. My body buzzed just thinking about what he'd do to me later. The best type of sex with Jake was the make-up kind after we'd worked through a rough patch. It was always the most intense.

He stuck the key in the ignition and turned on the engine but stayed parked. "They're all waiting to see you to make sure you're okay. I sort of rushed out of the apartment like a bat out of hell. I don't really feel like going home to a full house."

"You just said *bat* and *full house* in the same sentence. You realize that, right?"

"Old habits die hard."

I laughed. "I don't want to go back there, either."

Jake turned the knob to blast the heat. Flurries stuck to the windshield, obstructing the view.

"You know what this reminds me of?" he asked. "That first year we met, before you had to go upstate for Christmas when we stayed out in the snow after coming home from our Chicago trip. Remember?"

"Yeah. How could I forget?"

"I was so in love with you that night, but I couldn't tell you." He reached over for my hand. "You know what I spent today doing? Recalling the entire story of how we got together to Mitch and Skylar. Mitch never realized a lot of the shit we went through. I swear, going over everything made me fall in love with you all over again. At the same time, I was petrified because I didn't know what happened with you today. Yet, there I was, reminiscing and more certain than ever that my life would be nothing without you."

"Today was enlightening for both of us. But that was the first and last time you'll ever see me walk out on you like that."

"You can walk out anytime you need to as long as you come back to me. Sometimes, you need to step away to realize you can't really walk away from something that's a part of you."

"We've had our ups and downs, Jake. But every single time we go through something, I feel even closer to you after."

"Adversity only strengthens the kind of love we have. When you're with the person you're meant to be with, that's what happens. Ultimately, every experience, even horrible stuff, binds us tighter. It's all a test. The ones who let it tear them apart find out they were never really in love at all."

"We're damn lucky."

"What it really comes down to is a much simpler concept, actually."

"What's that?"

He wiggled his brows. "Less fighting, more fucking."

"Is that your motto?"

"I think it's gonna have to be now."

I shivered.

"You cold, baby?"

My teeth chattered. "A little."

His mouth curved into a crooked smile. "You want me to warm you up?"

Everything was still, except for the sound of the car running.

My lips parted as my visible breath met his in the cold air.

"Yeah, I do."

His gaze travelled slowly downward and up again. The look on his face was a bit devious, and his eyes turned deliciously dark.

I knew that look.

That was the exact look he gave me when he was about to fuck me, no matter the time nor place. It was why he hadn't moved the car yet. My entire body quivered in anticipation once it hit me where this was going. I felt myself getting wet as he continued to give me the *look*.

He licked slowly across his bottom lip. Jesus. *Nine years*. Nine years, and that tongue ring still drove me wild.

The muscles in between my legs tightened, and more wetness pooled there. These hormones had me in a frenzy.

"Take off your boots."

I slipped the Uggs off, leaving my black leggings.

"What if someone sees us?"

Jake unbuckled his belt. "Honestly, I don't really give a shit. I hope they enjoy the show. I need you now. We can try to be discreet."

He unzipped his jeans, and his beautiful thick shaft stood at full attention.

Wetting my lips, I said, "That doesn't look very discreet to me." I couldn't help leaning over, slowly and teasingly licking his wet crown. I loved his taste.

He pushed back against the headrest and hissed, "Stop. Seriously...stop."

I listened, sensing he'd lose it if I didn't.

He slid his seat back as far as it would go and tugged at my leggings. "Take those off and come sit on me."

I pulled them off, tossing them inside out and climbed on top off him. Keeping my knees bent, I wrapped my legs around his waist. I unzipped his jacket and slipped my hands under his shirt. The skin beneath was surprisingly warm as I rubbed over his solid chest. He made an unintelligible sound as I started to nibble on his neck. Then, he grabbed my chin and pulled me toward him into a ravenous kiss, swirling his tongue ring along the inside of my mouth while he moaned down my throat.

He wouldn't enter me yet. I was so frustratingly turned on, soaking wet and pulsating with need as he squeezed my hips while I grinded against his slick length. His balls felt hot underneath my ass. The need to have him inside of me was intolerable.

The heat of his breath warmed my entire body as our lips stayed locked.

When he broke the kiss, his breathing was ragged. "I don't think you've ever been this wet for me. You're more than ready, aren't you?"

Unable to wait any longer, I positioned myself over him and bore down hard as he sunk into me.

"Fuck, Nina. Ahhh," he moaned with his eyes shut tightly. Positioning his hands firmly around my ass, he moved my body over his cock as he buried himself as deeply inside of me as he could go. "This was exactly what I needed," he growled. "God, your pussy is so wet. What's up with you tonight? I wish I could fuck you forever like this. It feels...so...amazing."

"I'm really sensitive. This feels almost too good. Is that possible?"

"Fuck, no. No such thing," he said, thrusting into me harder.

I loved the deep connection of locking eyes with his as we fucked. When Jake looked up at me as I rode him, it felt like I'd gotten completely lost in him. It seemed like he was staring deep into my soul when he said, "This. This right here. Makes it all worth it. I love you, my angel."

"I love you."

He dug his fingers into my hair and fisted it. "I'm gonna come so hard right now, Nina."

"Give me everything. I'm coming, too."

Jake groaned so loudly, I could have sworn the windows of the Mustang shook.

We were still gasping for air, coming down from our high. Wrapping his hand around the back of my neck, he continued to look at me like I was the only thing that mattered to him.

I knew that was the moment.

I smiled down at him as my heart leapt for joy. "I'm pregnant."

His eyes widened. "What?"

My mouth was shaky as I repeated, "I'm pregnant."

Still inside of me, he straightened up a bit. "I...I saw the empty box in the trash. I assumed you were upset because it was negative. Oh my God. You're..." He covered his mouth with both hands. "Holy shit."

"My hormones have been making me crazy. If anything, that was the reason I left. I took the test shortly before you told me you weren't coming home. I had been waiting for you to get back so I could tell you."

His eyes were watering. "This is really happening?"

"Yes. It's real. We're gonna have a baby."

"You've just made me the happiest man in the world." Jake held me close, burying his face in my chest. "I'll never forget this moment. What started as one of the scariest days of my life ended up being one of the best."

We waited a couple of weeks to tell our son about the pregnancy. A.J. jumped up and down in excitement when we broke the news to him that he was going to be a big brother. He'd stopped asking for a sibling a couple of years back when I explained to him that God decides when to give someone a child, and that Momma and Daddy had no control over it.

A few weeks after we told him about the baby, we were sitting around the table for lunch one Sunday afternoon when our son hit us with an interrogation we weren't ready for.

I'd been making him a plate when his first question startled me. "You said God put the baby in your stomach?"

"That's right."

"So, does that mean God put a baby into Mr. Heath next door?"

Jake spit out his drink then answered, "No. Mr. Heath just drinks too much beer."

"Oh."

"Only women can have babies in their bellies," I said.

"Why? I don't get it. Why does God only give them to women?"

"That's a good question."

"Aidan from school said you lied to me about how babies are made."

Jake's fork dropped. Looking like he was going to lose it, he downed his water to keep from cracking up.

"What exactly did Aidan tell you?" I asked.

"He told me Daddy plants a seed in you and waters it. And that makes a baby. Kind of like a Chia pet."

"Oh."

Jake's shoulders shook in silent laughter.

A perplexed look washed across A.J.'s face. "But how does he do it? Plant the seed. I don't get it. That sounds kind of difficult."

Thoroughly amused, my husband's face lit up. "It's a lot of hard work, son."

A.J. looked back and forth between the two of us, his spiked Mohawk sticking up in the air. "So, Daddy does all the work?"

Jake shrugged his shoulders. "I don't mind."

Crumpling a napkin, I threw it at him jokingly.

"When did you do it?" A.J. asked.

My face must have been a deep shade of pink. I was at a total loss for words and just let Jake take over the conversation, which turned out to be a mistake.

"I've planted and watered several hundred, actually. Technically, we should have a massive crop."

"Can I watch next time you plant one?"

My eyes were bugging out as I threw my fork down. "Okay. I think we're done with this conversation. After lunch, Daddy is going to take you for a walk to the bookstore. They have a book there that will explain exactly how babies are made."

Jake flashed me a shit-eating grin. Even when I wanted to kill him, I loved him so much.

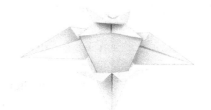

TWENTY-TWO

JAKE
SEVEN MONTHS LATER

It was hard as a rock, looking ready to burst and always moved when it got excited.

There was nothing better than time alone with Nina's gigantic belly while she slept. It was like a beach ball wrapped in silk.

Dim sunlight peeked through the heavy sliding curtains in our room. We were at a hotel in New Hampshire on a babymoon and were scheduled to head back to Boston early this evening.

Nina was sleeping soundly through the noise of the rickety air conditioner. She was eight months along now. We'd decided to let the gender of our baby be a surprise. I was sure it was a girl. Nina and A.J. thought it was a boy. It didn't matter to me as long as it was healthy.

My sister had taken A.J. for the weekend so that Nina and I could have one night away before the big arrival next month. Since the pregnancy with A.J. had been problematic, resulting in a C-section, Nina's doctors scheduled her for another one this time around just to be on the safe side.

"Hello, my little alien," I whispered against Nina's belly as the baby did what looked like slow breakdancing. It was impossible to resist softly kissing the taut skin whenever it moved. It was just the two of us up now, after all, while Nina snored.

"You're a morning person like Daddy, eh? Well, your brother and Mommy like to sleep in. So, when you come out, maybe we can watch the sunrise together sometime. Would you like that?" I ran my lips along the smooth skin of her stomach again. "It's probably pretty dark in there right now, huh?"

"Hmmm." Nina stirred before rolling over toward me and asked in a sleepy voice, "Who are you talking to?"

"The little alien. We hang out sometimes when you're sleeping."

"Who?"

"Our kid. She was showing me her moves."

Nina flashed a joyful smile. "*She*, huh?" Her mood seemed to quickly shift. "Oh my God."

"What?"

"Jake, I'm so wet."

"Giddy up."

"No!" she said, jumping up and patting the sheets. "Not that kind of wet. Feel."

The sheets were damp, the spot right under her completely soaked.

"Shit."

"I think my water broke! Oh no. No, no, no. This is not good."

I frantically searched for my phone. "Can we call your doctor?"

"She's just gonna tell me to go to the hospital. I don't even know where the nearest one is to us right now."

I opened Google and started searching for hospitals close to the lake region where we were staying. We were far from a major city, which was unsettling. "Saint Andrews is the nearest one. It's five miles away."

The words were spilling out of her mouth so fast. I could hardly understand her. "This isn't supposed to happen. My body is not supposed to go into natural labor. I'm scared because I'm more prone to uterine rupture because of the prior C-section. What if we don't get there in time and something happens to the baby?"

"Is there a chance you're not actually in labor?"

"I think once the water breaks, that means it's happening."

"We'll get you there, baby. Don't worry. Everything is gonna be fine."

Now, if I could only convince myself of that.

Nina scrambled to throw some of her things into the suitcase then said, "I'm gonna take a quick shower. It might be a while before I can do that again."

"Yell if you need me. I'll pack the rest of our shit in the meantime."

About ten minutes later, when Nina returned from the bathroom, she was leaning back into her hands, grasping the bottom of her hips. "I think the contractions are starting now. They seem to be coming from the back. I never had them with A.J., so I don't know what they even feel like, but I'm getting these sharp pains."

Fuck.

"We'd better go."

The loud click of the heavy suite door locking behind us echoed through the hallway. Our suitcase rolling along the carpet of the desolate hotel seemed like the only sign of life. It was still early and a Sunday. We were probably the only people awake in the entire building aside from the front desk staff downstairs. Our room was located on the tenth floor. I pushed the down button and prayed that the elevator came quickly. The busy floral pattern on the rug made me dizzy as I looked down in an attempt to calm myself. I couldn't let Nina see how freaked out this situation was making me.

Rubbing her back, I tried to soothe her. "Don't worry about anything. I'm with you. We're gonna get through this. We'll get to the hospital in no time."

She nervously nodded and let out a long breath but said nothing.

The wait seemed to be taking forever. When the doors slid open, I placed my hand on the middle of her back and gently led her into the elevator.

Nina's back was pressed against my chest as we started to descend. Using my palms to gently massage her belly, I whispered into ear, "Everything is gonna be fine."

Almost as soon as the words came out of my mouth, the elevator made a jerking movement that caused us to lose balance before slamming against the wall. The car was no longer moving. The door was still shut tight.

What's happening?

No.

No.

No.

"Jake! Are you kidding? Don't pull this on me now, please!"

"It wasn't me. I swear," I said, frantically pushing all of the buttons repeatedly.

"My eyes were closed. I didn't see. I assumed you pushed the stop button as a joke. Oh my God! Please...no. This can't be happening!"

She had every reason to suspect that I'd made the elevator stop on purpose. In the past, I'd intentionally done that twice, first during our fear excursion way back when and then again when I proposed to her. But joking about something like that under these circumstances would have been pretty sick and not funny at all.

"I wouldn't do that to you, baby. Unfortunately, this looks to be the first time we've actually ever gotten legitimately stuck in one."

Inhaling and exhaling loudly, she said, "That's a pretty horrible irony right about now."

Pressing the emergency call button with one hand, I looked up the number for the front desk with the other, having to dial it several times because my nervous fingers kept screwing up the numbers.

The phone kept ringing and went to a general voice mailbox. No response from my pressing the button ad nauseum, either.

Are you fucking kidding me?

Slamming my hand against the wall, I yelled, "How the fuck could there be no response?"

Nina held onto her back with both hands as if they were keeping her from falling to the ground in pain. "Oh my God. This is so bad, so very bad."

"Don't panic, baby. What are you feeling right now?"

"The pains...they're getting closer together."

Banging on the door frantically, I yelled at the top of my lungs, "Can anyone hear us? We're stuck. Help!"

Bang. Bang. Bang. Bang.

After several minutes, it seemed useless.

"I'm calling 9-1-1," I said.

Clutching her stomach and practicing her breathing, she slowly slid down onto the floor.

The emergency line picked up. "What's the address caller?"

"Old Ridgewood Estates off Washington Highway."

"Please confirm your telephone number."

"617-596-9968."

"And what is the nature of your emergency?"

"We need help. My wife is in labor, and we're stuck in the hotel elevator. She's feeling a lot of pressure."

"Does building maintenance know?"

"No one is responding to our calls."

"Okay, we're sending a crew over right away, but if you think she's having the baby, I'm gonna transfer you to someone who can help guide you through in case the paramedics don't get there in time. Stay on the line."

What was actually happening here was starting to sink in. "Jesus Christ."

Kneeling down next to Nina, I let out a deep breath before rubbing her back as I waited on hold. "It'll be okay, baby. We're gonna get out of here."

Then, came static followed by a woman's voice. "Hello, sir. Can you tell me how old your wife is?"

"Thirty-one."

"How many weeks pregnant?"

"Uh...thirty-seven."

"What is she feeling right now?"

"Baby, describe what you're feeling."

"Just...a lot of pressure, especially around my ass. It feels like something's going to come out of there. I'm scared."

"It feels like the baby's gonna come out of her ass."

"Sir, you don't have to worry. That's never actually happened before." She laughed. "She's just having back labor. How far apart are her contractions?"

"How far apart, Nina?"

She blew out a long breath and shook her head, looking too pained to even answer. "I don't know exactly. Less than a minute, maybe."

The air felt stuffy. Nina was sweating and lifted the shirt off of her head.

"Sounds like she's definitely in labor now," the woman said. "Does she have any complications?"

"This was supposed to be a C-section because she had one prior with our son."

"Do you have any soft materials that you can place on the ground for her?"

"Yeah. We have our suitcase here with us. It's full of clothes."

"Place some shirts or whatever you have underneath her to make her comfortable. Make sure you put some aside for the baby. If the baby is delivered, it's going to be important to keep him warm and dry."

"Alright."

Keeping the black suitcase vertical, I unzipped it halfway, taking out all of the shirts we had packed and throwing them on the ground.

"Okay, tell her to just keep breathing. Have her pant in a rhythm of three quick breaths in and one long blow out. This could help delay the birth. I also want you to have her lie on her left side. Her face should be near the floor, and her bottom in the air. Can you do that?"

Her face near the floor. Her bottom in the air. There was a good chance that position got us into this predicament.

"Sir?"

"Yeah..."

"Everything is going to be okay. Your wife's name is Nina? What is your name?"

"I'm Jake. Jake Green."

"Mr. Green, I'm Bonnie. We're gonna get through this together. You're doing a great job."

I looked down at Nina struggling against the brown paneling of the wall. Panic was building inside of me fast, and for the first time in my life, I probably understood what Nina used to feel like before hyperventilating. A long, shaky breath escaped me. "Thank you for helping us."

"Continue to keep her on her side. That might help ease the urge to push."

"Nina, baby. Make sure you stay on your side."

The minutes that followed felt like a dream. Things were quiet for a while, a massive calm before the storm. Up until that point, I hadn't even realized that there was elevator music. A slow ballad playing on the overhead speaker mixed with the rhythm of Nina's formulaic breathing were the only sounds as I held my wife's hand and just prayed.

"If you can, have her massage the space between her vagina and anus. This will help improve elasticity and decrease tearing."

"Say what?"

Before I could even begin to explain that bizarre suggestion, Nina screamed, "Ow, ow, ow! It's getting worse!"

"Help!" I barked into the phone. "The pains are getting worse."

With every wailing sound coming out of her, sharp pains shot through me.

"Okay, have her continue to breathe," Bonnie said.

"I feel something there now, like a big lump!" Nina yelled.

"Make sure her pants are down," Bonnie said calmly.

How the fuck could she be so calm?

I helped Nina pull her leggings off and repositioned two shirts under her. I put the phone on speaker.

"It feels like a lump?" I asked, spreading her legs apart. Something *was* there.

It was the head.

"Oh my God. It's the head."

"Sir, okay. Bring her bottom nearer to the floor and place the palm of your hand against her vagina. Apply firm but gentle pressure. This will keep the baby from coming out too fast and prevent her from tearing."

Firm but gentle pressure.

Firm but gentle pressure.

Nina squirmed as she held her belly. "It's coming!"

I looked down. "Holy shit! The heads out. The heads out!"

Bonnie's staticky words resonated throughout the small space as she raised her voice. "Okay, you're gonna want to support the baby's head and shoulders. Be careful. The baby's body will be very wet and could easily slip out of your hands."

My entire body tightened to gear up as I opened my arms and prepared to pull my child into the world.

Nina gave one final push. "Oh my God, Oh my God, Oh my God!"

Within seconds, the baby was in my arms. Celine Dion's *The Power of Love* started playing above on the elevator speaker. It was the most surreal moment of my life.

Gasping for air, I said, "I've got it. It's out."

"It's completely out?" Bonnie asked.

Tears filled my eyes, and my lips shook. "Yeah."

The baby's cry was strong. I looked down between its tiny legs.

"It's a girl. Oh my God. It's a girl! Baby, we have a daughter."

"Really? A girl?"

Bonnie's voice interrupted our moment. "Grab a shirt and gently wipe the baby's nose and mouth."

I looked around me.

Shirt.

Shirt.

Shirt.

Cradling the baby, I grabbed one of Nina's tops from the pile and did as Bonnie instructed. "Okay."

"Now, wrap the baby in another clean shirt. Make sure the head is covered. This is to prevent hypothermia. Whatever you do, do not pull on the cord."

"Alright."

I carefully wrapped our daughter in one of my flannel button downs.

"Make sure your wife is warm."

"Baby, are you okay?"

Nina groaned and nodded her head.

"Listen carefully, Mr. Green. Can your wife hold the baby? Have her place the baby on her stomach."

Nina reached out her hands, and I slowly transferred the baby onto her stomach.

"Mr. Green? You're doing great. The afterbirth will probably deliver soon."

"The after what? It's not over?"

"No. Have her hold the baby against her skin and place something over them both. This will help keep everyone calm until they can get you out of there."

I grabbed my coat and draped it over them.

"You'll stay on the phone with us?"

"Of course. You may want to grab a bag if you have one from your suitcase to put the placenta in. The baby will still be attached to it until the paramedics get there. So, you'll put it inside a bag somewhere close to Nina."

Nina muttered, "We have large Ziploc bags that the toiletries are in. Grab one of those."

"Ziplocs! Thank God for small miracles."

We spent the next ten minutes or so huddled together, cradling our baby before Nina said, "I'm feeling like I have to push again."

I hopped up. "She has to push again."

Bonnie immediately responded, "Okay, that's the placenta. Have her move into an upright position."

After a few pushes, the placenta came out.

Holding what looked like a piece of raw meat, I asked, "What do I do again?"

"Just put it in the bag and keep it next to you."

A pool of red surrounded the area underneath Nina.

"There's blood everywhere."

"That's normal."

"This doesn't look normal."

"The paramedics are almost there. I'm told the fire department is on site working with hotel maintenance right now. They should have you out of there shortly. Try to remain calm."

An indeterminate amount of time passed. Nina was starting to sound disoriented. "Jake, I don't feel good. Something's really wrong. You need to take the baby."

My daughter's legs and arms flailed through the plaid flannel shirt wrapped around her tiny body as Nina handed her to me. I felt like I was about to have a heart attack.

Panic-stricken, I yelled into the phone, "She's still bleeding. She's losing a lot of fucking blood. You need to tell them to hurry! Please!"

"Does it look like more than a pint? Listen, Mr. Green, you need to massage her lower abdomen immediately."

Suddenly, her head slumped over.

"No! Nina!" I cried.

Holding our baby in one arm, I repeatedly tapped Nina's cheeks with my other hand. "Baby, please. Stay with me. Nina. Please."

"What's happening, sir?"

"She's passed out. She's unconscious." My vision was blinded by the tears in my eyes. My lips were trembling as I spoke, unable to catch my breath, "Nina, wake up. Wake up. Please!"

It felt like the middle of a nightmare, my baby's deafening cry a reminder that this was very real and not something I was going to wake up from. Bonnie's voice became jumbled in the midst of my panic.

Then, came a jolt followed by sudden and steady movement downward.

As Nina continued to remain unconscious, looking like she was bleeding to death, the descent felt more like a downward spiral into the depths of hell.

The doors slid open, and even though light streamed in, darkness surrounded me.

The darkness of men rushing in.

The darkness of someone taking my crying infant away.

The darkness of Nina being put onto a stretcher with an oxygen mask over her face.

The darkness of their voices. *"She's hemorrhaging."*

It was all happening at lightning speed, the fate of everything that mattered to me hanging in the balance in the hands of total strangers.

Nina's words from years past haunted me.

There is nothing that could make me leave you.

You brought me back to life.

Yet, I was helpless to save her now.

How I'd gotten from the hotel into that ambulance and to the hospital was a mystery to me. Those twenty or so minutes were a blurry montage of terrifying sounds, voices and flashing lights as Nina lay semi-conscious and bleeding while paramedics tended to her and the baby.

Once at Saint Andrews, I tried to barge my way into the operating room, but they wouldn't let me inside. Medical staff in masks pushed me away from everything that mattered to me. Too afraid to take any focus off of the job they needed to do, I backed down and stayed in the waiting room as they instructed.

Now, as I sat with my head in my hands, I didn't know if she was dead or alive. They'd taken our daughter to the nursery, but my shock paralyzed me, making me unable to move from my spot long enough to go visit her.

Nina had to be okay. Not only for me but for our son and daughter.

A flash of her beautiful smile from when she first woke up this morning hit me. Life had changed in an instant.

It wasn't possible to imagine life without her. Before today, I thought I understood how strong my love for her was. Faced with the threat of losing her forever, the depth of that love was truly realized. Because even with my healthy baby girl and son at home, the future was blank without Nina. I didn't just love her. To me, she *was* love, *was* life.

My life started the day she entered it. It would end the day she left it. There was no gap between where I began and she ended. We were one.

I'd always accepted whatever hand I'd been dealt, especially with Ivy. I never blamed God or anyone else for the tragedies in my life. But if something happened to Nina, I knew I would never recover. I wouldn't be able to forgive Him. And that terrified me, what that would mean for my kids if their father was just an empty shell for the rest of their lives.

For the first time in my life, I was truly scared.

"Mr. Green?"

My head flew upward as I stood up to meet the doctor's face which held an indecipherable expression. My heart was struggling to keep up with the fear driving it to beat faster than what it could sustain.

"Your wife is stable."

Stable

Alive.

Every muscle in my body relaxed at once as the breaths I'd been holding for what seemed like an eternity released out of me.

Thank you.

Thank you.

Thank you.

"As you know, there was an excessive amount of bleeding from the hemorrhaging. We were able to compress the arteries supplying blood to the uterus without having to do a hysterectomy. There shouldn't be any long-term implications on fertility. She is very lucky to be alive given the circumstances you were found in."

"She's conscious now?"

"Yes. The fainting happened because of a sudden drop in blood pressure as a result of the bleeding."

"Can I see her?"

"Yes. But she should get some rest soon after. We had to give her oxytocin to help the uterus contract in order to stop the bleeding that ensued after the placental delivery, so she'll be tired from the drug not to mention the ordeal.

We'll be keeping her here a couple of extra days over the norm for observation."

"Thank you, doctor. God, thank you so much. You saved her life. I could never repay you. Never."

"No need for thanks. It's what I do." He smiled. "I'm told your daughter is doing just fine, too. You're a lucky man, Mr. Green." He gave me a single pat on the shoulder and said, "Follow me."

Eagerly following the path to Nina's room, I said a silent prayer to the man upstairs for coming through when I needed Him most.

Her hair was splayed across the pillow, and her eyes were closed. An IV was connected to her arm. My poor baby was exhausted.

Exhausted but alive.

I wanted to be strong. She'd been through enough without seeing me break down. But the moment my face landed in the crook of her neck, I came apart. Smelling the scent of her skin, listening to the breaths I wasn't sure I'd ever get to hear again, my body shook. An endless flow of tears poured from my eyes and onto her hospital gown.

"Jake..."

"Shh. Yes, baby. I'm here. You don't have to say anything."

"Is the baby okay?"

"Baby's great."

"Why are you crying?"

"Because I love you."

"I don't remember much after I blacked out. Am I gonna be okay?"

"Yes. They stopped the bleeding and fixed it."

"Can I still have babies?"

"Yes. That's what the doctor said." I held her tighter. "You mean, you would want another one after all this?"

"Only with you." Teardrops were streaming down her cheeks. "You were amazing. You delivered our baby!"

"Nina...you were the amazing one, so brave. We have a daughter. I couldn't even truly appreciate her because I was so terrified to lose you."

"Where is she?"

"She's in the nursery. I haven't checked on her because I couldn't move from outside the operating room until I knew you were okay."

"I want to see her."

"I'll go check if they can bring her to us."

The door opened just as I was getting up. A nurse carried our baby girl who was swaddled in a blanket. She was wearing a pink hat and had white mittens covering her hands.

Nina cradled the baby to her chest. Our daughter immediately started to search with her mouth for sustenance, her little head twisting back and forth over Nina's breast as she tried to locate the goods.

"Look at her!" Nina laughed. "She knows who her Mama is. She's not wasting any time."

"She's like her Daddy that way."

The nurse coughed and smiled awkwardly. "Are you planning to breastfeed?"

"Yes."

"The baby had a little formula. But if you like, we can try seeing if she'll feed right now."

Nina lowered the hospital gown, revealing her swollen breast. Amazingly, our daughter latched on almost immediately. Couldn't say I blamed her one bit.

"I'll leave you alone with your daughter," the nurse said before exiting the room.

Nina lifted the pink hat. "She looks like you, Jake. She's got the same dark hair as A.J. I guess I have weak genes."

"You just can't escape me. Now, I'm multiplying inside you." I ran my thumb along the baby's soft fuzzy hair as she continued to devour Nina's nipple like there was no tomorrow. The suckling sound was freaking adorable. "My little alien. You wreaked havoc today."

"Is that what you want to name her? Aliena?"

"That would be fitting. But I think we should come up with something else."

"Actually, I kind of had a name in mind," she said.

"What is it?"

"Kennedy."

"Kennedy Green. I like the sound of that. The two of us."

"Yes. Exactly."

"It's perfect, baby. Perfect." Tears were returning to my eyes. She had a name. I was finally able to absorb the magnitude of my daughter's entry into the world now that Nina was safe. "You like that, Kennedy?"

"She doesn't care what her name is right now. She's too busy eating."

"I can relate. You make me forget my name all the time when I'm feasting on you."

"It will be a little while before that happens again. I have to heal."

I groaned, "Don't remind me."

She lifted her brow. "We can be creative."

"Oh yeah?"

"I think your delivering our baby warrants a pretty damn epic blow job when we get home."

"I'm gonna be pushing for an early release then."

"Seriously, Jake. You were incredible in that elevator."

"We do elevators well, baby, don't we?"

The following day, Nina was extremely sore, but thankfully, all of her vitals were checking out normally. She was taking a nap while I held the baby in the seat next to the bed.

Earlier in the day, I'd gone out to purchase a car seat for the long ride back to Boston. We were counting the minutes until we could take Kennedy home to meet her big brother. We'd told our families not to bother travelling up to New Hampshire, to save their energy instead for when we got back. Nina needed her rest now anyway. Her mother was planning to stay with us for a couple of weeks, so we'd have plenty of help.

There was a light knock at the door. A woman walked in with some paperwork.

"Hi, Mr. Green," she whispered. "Your wife filled in the information for the birth certificate earlier today. You weren't in here at the time. She wasn't sure of exactly how you wanted your occupation listed. Would you mind adding it in for us?"

"Of course." I kissed Kennedy's head as she lay cradled in my right arm. "It's official, little alien. I'm your Daddy on paper, too."

I moved Nina's plastic water jug to make room on the small table for the piece of paper and took a pen from the woman.

"You're a lefty." She smiled.

"Yup. My son, too."

Filled with pride, I looked down at my daughter's first name on the form. Nina and I hadn't discussed a middle name. I wasn't even sure if we were going to give Kennedy one. So, when I noticed that Nina had filled that line in, it took me by surprise. But what really shocked me was the name she chose. She'd told me the story, so I knew it wasn't a coincidence. It was a beautiful sentiment meant to give us some closure. More than that, it spoke volumes about the kind of person my wife was. It was a bigger level of acceptance than she'd ever gifted me with before. It touched me so deeply that the pen was shaking in my hand.

Kennedy Aria Green.

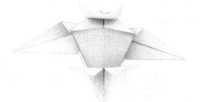

TWENTY-THREE

NINA

Four weeks later, our house had turned into a virtual zoo. Somehow, in the midst of the baby coming home, A.J. had convinced us to get a dog. We ended up adopting a black pug. We came up with the name Luna because it's the Spanish word for moon.

So, we had a newborn baby, a pug yelping at all hours, and now Skylar and Mitch were arriving for a weekend visit to meet Kennedy for the first time. They were bringing their entire family: three kids and their aging blue-fronted Amazon parrot, Seamus. A.J. had gotten on the phone earlier this week and begged them to bring the talking bird who always provided hours of entertainment.

On his way home from visiting Ivy, Jake was out stopping for beer and wine. So, I was alone with the kids when our friends arrived. The noise that emerged from behind the door was evident before the doorbell even rang.

I lifted myself off the couch with Kennedy attached to my breast before throwing a blanket over her head to hide myself. Luna raced me to the door as her tiny scurrying paws scratched against the hardwood floors.

I opened the door. It was quite a vision to behold: Skylar, Mitch, three kids and a caged parrot.

"Pick a lane, ballbag!"

"Ugh...what did the bird just say?" I asked, stepping out of the way to let them enter.

Skylar sighed. "Sorry. We have no way of controlling what things stick with him. Mitch got a little bit of road rage on I-95, and Seamus just won't let it go."

The bird squawked. *"Pick a lane, ballbag!"*

"Well, that's just great for the kids," I said, sarcastically.

Skylar kissed me on the cheek. "Welcome to our lives, Sissy. How's your fiery vagina, by the way?"

"Only you would ask me such a question right off the bat. It's actually a lot better. Thanks for asking."

"Let me at her." She lifted the blanket to get a peek of Kennedy, who was still suckling on my breast. "She looks just like Jake."

"I know."

Mitch was holding their one-year-old son. "Do you know your Wi-Fi password? Henry needs the internet."

"Sure. It's written down next to the cordless phone in the kitchen."

Mitch and Skylar's older son, Henry, had autism and was mostly non-verbal. He kept to himself the majority of the time while fixated on electronic devices. Henry had already taken his spot on the couch with his iPad.

Their daughter, Lara, who was around A.J.'s age, went in search of my son.

A.J. appeared, holding his tablet. "Hey, Lara. You wanna play terraria in my room?"

"Sure." Lara's long auburn hair swung as she followed him down the hall.

Mitch lifted a sippy cup to Mitch Jr.'s mouth. "If your son is anything like his father, I think we're gonna have to put a stop to the hanging out in A.J.'s room in about five to seven years."

"We'll deal with that when it comes." I laughed.

"That's gross. They're practically like brother and sister," Skylar said.

Mitch put his arm around her. "That's not gonna matter to them when their hormones start taking over. Remember how we felt at that age? You were sort of like my sister back then, and I wanted to do very bad things to you."

I interjected, "Well, I'm his mother, and I have to agree. A.J. is just like Jake, and if that's the case, we could be in trouble."

The door slammed shut, and Jake appeared. "Did someone call my name? Trouble?"

"We were talking about how similar you and A.J. are and how they might want to lock Lara up in about seven years."

"Oh, without a fucking doubt," Jake said, taking off his coat.

Mitch sat down with the baby next to Henry. "I have to say, having a daughter gets scarier with each year."

"Lara's starting to get boobs already." Skylar shook her head. "It ain't even funny."

Jake walked over and kissed me before lifting the blanket to peek in on Kennedy. "If this little thing ends up being anatomically anything like her mother, I better start a gun collection."

Skylar took Mitch Jr. from her husband and joined them on the couch. "I was just saying how Kennedy is like your mini-me, Jake."

"What can I say? Let's just hope she'll at least have Nina's sweet personality."

"Pick a lane, ballbag!"

Jake whipped his head to the left where the bird sat in his cage in the corner of the room. "You brought Seamus?"

Laughing, I said, "Yes, I told them to bring him, figuring it's a zoo around here lately anyway. We might as well add him to the mix."

Jake snapped his finger and turned to Mitch. "You know what I just bought?"

"What?"

"That stuff to make your favorite drink, Bitch."

"What drink is that?"

"What do you call it again? Crying Climax?"

"Weeping Orgasm."

"Well, we're making it later. How about a beer for now?"

Jake took two bottles out of the paper bag he'd brought in and handed one to Mitch.

Mitch twisted the cap off, took a swig and said, "So, Jake, you'll have to tell us the full story of the elevator birth. I can't even imagine."

"Man, you haven't lived until you've pulled your child out of the woman you love with a Celine Dion song playing in the background."

Mitch held up his palm. "I'm pretty sure I'm okay with foregoing that rite of passage."

We all got a good laugh out of that one. I looked around the room. The dog was now licking Jake's face. The bird was shouting obscenities from his cage in the corner. Squeals of laughter from A.J. and Lara could be heard coming from down the hall. Henry was listening to frightening YouTube videos of television jingles playing in slow motion. My best friend, Skylar, was cancer-free, and we were holding the miracle babies we both thought we'd never have. *This was life.* Life was good and so precious.

The health and well-being of the people I loved most were all that really mattered. Driven by our egos, we spend so much time worrying about the little stuff while letting what's really important pass us by.

A week after our friends' visit, I was lying in bed when Jake's voice streamed through the baby monitor on my nightstand. He was in the other room changing Kennedy, talking to her as he always did and probably didn't realize that every word that came out of his mouth was being transmitted to me in our bedroom.

"Don't tell her about our little surprise, okay?"

What was he talking about?

"Speaking of surprises, damn girl! Momma must have known you were due when she sent me in here. That wasn't very nice of her. How do I always get stuck with these? Huh?"

She must have had a massive dump. *Whoops.*

"Well, you're lucky you're cute. I'm gonna call Popeye, though, and tell him my baby is harboring some of his spinach in her diaper. Call the authorities."

Kennedy cooed.

"Yeah...you think that's funny?"

I covered my mouth in laughter then closed my eyes, listening to the sounds of the diaper crinkling and Jake's smooching her.

"Ow. You like to pull on my lip ring, huh? I know. That's your favorite thing to do."

More smooching.

"All clean."

More smooching.

"I love you to the moon, little alien."

The sound of the door closing in her room prompted me to straighten up in bed to deter from my eavesdropping.

Jake walked in. He was shirtless and smelled so good after his shower. His tanned skin was amazingly smooth. He'd recently added two star tattoos on the right side of his chest. They represented each of our two children, the stars to his moon.

Jake sighed as he joined me under the crisp sheets. "It feels so good to be in bed."

"Long day?"

"Yeah...work was a cluster fuck. But kissing my little alien goodnight and getting to end the day right here is what gets me through."

We were waiting six weeks per the doctor's suggestion before having sex again. We still had one week to go, and I knew the wait was killing him. Even though I felt ready physically, we'd decided to follow the doctor's orders.

Pressing my ass into him, I encouraged him to spoon me. Exhausted, we both nodded off within minutes.

Sometime in the middle of the night, what seemed like a bad dream woke me up. It wasn't your typical nightmare, though. It was an actual recollection of things I thought had been erased from my memory. I could suddenly clearly remember all of the terrifying moments from the day Kennedy was born: waking up in the ambulance, the fear that I was bleeding to death, the fear that I'd never see Jake or my babies again. Up until tonight, I'd suffered amnesia when it came to the events right after the delivery. I remembered the baby coming out of me then Jake at my hospital bedside in tears, but everything in between had been a blur.

Sweat was pouring off of me. The realization of how close I'd come to possibly dying hit me.

Jake turned on the lamp. "Nina?"

"Huh?"

"Are you okay?"

"No."

"What happened?"

"I remember waking up in the ambulance now. I thought I was dying. The thought of never seeing you again...you know what's crazy? I was thinking about you more than even our children. Somehow, I knew *they'd* be alright because they'd have you. But I didn't think you'd be okay without me. And I didn't want to leave this Earth without you. Does that make sense? I knew you'd be there for them because you had to be, but I didn't think you'd really be okay."

He held me tight. "You're right."

"This might sound strange, but I feel like we've been together before this life and like we'll be together again. It's as if we're—"

"Truly connected. I know. When they made me stay out of the operating room and I had to wait not knowing whether you were okay, I came to that same conclusion. I felt dead until the doctor came out and told me you were alive."

"That must have been so scary for you."

"Try not to think about that. Just be with me now. We have to trust that even when our time here is over, the powers that led us to each other will bring us together again. In the meantime, don't waste another second worrying about what could have happened that day. Okay?"

"This moment...that's all there ever is."

"I'm glad you remember some of what I've taught you over the years."

I reached over to kiss him on the cheek, but he abruptly turned his face toward me. His mouth devoured my lips in a ravenous kiss. My body melted into his. It had been too long. My hand started to slide down to his crotch.

"Whoa, whoa, whoa. I thought we were following the doctor's orders," he said over my lips. "I've been very good, but if you touch me like that, I can't be responsible for what happens next."

"This *is* what the doctor ordered tonight."

"Fuck. It's been five weeks." He placed his hand firmly on my ass and pulled me into him. "You're not gonna hear any argument from me."

"I know how hard for you this wait has been."

"Hard for *you*. Yes. You got that shit right." He sucked on my bottom lip before slowly releasing it. "Let's not talk anymore."

"Less fighting, more fucking. See? I remember that, too."

He laughed as he kissed down my neck and said, "That one might just be the wisest thing I ever came up with."

As he started to lift up my nightgown, I snapped, "Turn the lamp off."

"No."

"Yes."

"No way. I want to see every inch of you while we fuck. Your body is amazing like this. You know how I feel about it." He palmed my breasts. "There's even more of what I love. I want to enjoy it."

"We're not doing it with the lights on."

Ignoring me, he said, "How about I start?"

He got up and slowly took his pants off, kicking them away. His body was rock solid, jacked, and his skin was flawless. Jake only got better with age. Meanwhile, I felt fat, and knew the insecurity would stick with me until every ounce of the baby weight came off.

He still had his underwear on when he kneeled over me. "Like what you see?"

"Mm-hmm."

"Keep your eyes on me, but don't touch me," he said gruffly.

I went along with it.

My eyes travelled from his strong jaw, down the length of chest to his six-pack. A thin happy trail of hair formed a sexy line down the middle of his V muscle.

His voice was low. "What do you want, Nina?"

"I want you to take these off." When I tugged on his underwear, he grabbed my hand and moved it off him.

Giving me a sexy smirk, he slid his tongue across his bottom lip. "No touching."

"Okay."

The tip of his cock stuck out from the top of his boxer briefs. He was fully hard.

"So, you want me to take these off, huh?"

"Yes."

"The thing is, you wanted to shut the light off. Then, you won't be able to see me, either. Don't you want to see me?"

My mouth was agape. "Yes."

"I want to see you, too. Let me see you first."

I reluctantly slipped my nightgown over my head but left my nursing bra on.

"Take it off."

I unsnapped it from the front and threw my bra on the ground.

"Good girl. Now, your panties."

I slid my boy shorts down my legs and tossed them aside.

A month and a half felt like an eternity. It was a really long time for us to go without contact. We'd barely touched each other since the baby because it would have been too much of a tease if we weren't going to be able to have sex.

"Do you have any idea how much this body turns me on, Nina? Look at me. Look what you're doing to me." His cock stretched the fitted cotton of his boxers to capacity. A wet spot from his arousal dampened the material.

He went on, "When we fuck, I need to feel every inch of that naked body against me."

The sneaky bastard still wasn't touching me. This was his way of getting me so hot and bothered that I no longer cared about the way I looked, no longer gave a shit about anything but what I needed from him.

His eyes were dilated as he looked down at me and began to jerk himself off hard and slow. This was Jake's modus operandi: denying me for fun until I was practically begging him for it. He got off on it and honestly, so did I. The stimulation of watching him masturbate to me was making me so wet and caused my full breasts to tingle. A little milk leaked out. He swiped some of it before sucking it slowly off his thumb.

What my body looked like was starting to matter less and less. Clearly, from the look on his face, he was very turned on. How he was looking *at me* was quickly becoming more important than my hang ups about what I looked like.

Jake bent his head back in ecstasy. I couldn't take watching him pleasuring himself anymore. I grabbed his hand and stopped him from stroking his cock. Spreading my legs open wide, I begged, "Please."

His mouth spread into a wry smile as he lowered himself and finally entered me. Letting out a throaty moan as he buried himself deep inside, he fucked me slowly until he saw he wasn't hurting me. Then, he picked up the pace and eventually our entangled naked bodies were rocking the bed. Our fingers were locked as we stared into each other's eyes until we came together.

We lay awake for a while, our hands still intertwined. I admired the tattoo on my ring finger bearing his name. He had one of my name on his finger, too. The permanent markings were the perfect symbolism for what we were: bound for life.

He took my hand to his mouth and kissed it. "I liked what you said earlier, that we might have known each other before and that we'd be together again someday."

"Yeah." I smiled. "Make sure you keep an eye out for me in the next life, Green."

"Baby, I'd recognize you anywhere."

The moonlight glowed onto Jake's face as he slept through the sound of Kennedy's voice coming in through the monitor. My hardened breasts tingled as milk trickled out of my nipples with every cry. It was time for her 4 a.m. feeding.

Rubbing my eyes and yawning, I reluctantly lifted myself out of the warm bed and headed down the hall.

"Shh, sweetie, it's okay. I'm here. I'm—" My words abruptly stopped once I noticed it.

Wow.

Wow.

Wow.

I covered my mouth in surprise before lifting Kennedy to my breast, needing her to stop crying so that I could just marvel at it in peace and quiet.

Just...wow.

Over a dozen pink origami bats hung in rows from a mobile high above her crib. I reached out and lightly touched one of them. The paper that each had been made from was much thicker than the construction kind he used to use.

When had he found the time to do this?

"So, *this* was the surprise, huh?" I whispered down to her, kissing her little chest that smelled like Dreft baby detergent.

Sitting in the padded rocker, I put my feet up on the ottoman and just stared at the mobile in awe until Kennedy finished feeding.

When I finally looked away from it, I noticed a lone black bat sitting atop the changing table.

With Kennedy still in my arm, I walked over to it and unfolded the paper.

It's been a long time,
Since you've heard me rhyme.
But I've been watching you.
And all you've been through.
I came back to let you know,
You'll forever be my hero.

You've done good, kid.

Love always, Mr. Bat

My lips curved into a wide smile as I clutched the bat to my chest. I placed Kennedy back in the crib and looked up at the mobile. Noticing for the first time that there was a plastic knob at the top, I began to wind it.

Twinkle Twinkle Little Star started playing as the bats slowly turned round and round. Kennedy's wide eyes were transfixed on them as she cooed, kicking her little legs and flashing what looked awfully like a smile.

Footsteps crept up behind me. Strong tattooed arms wrapped around my torso and rocked me slowly to the music.

Complete and utter peace.

It may have taken my entire life, but I was finally learning to live in the moment. This one may have been the best of all.

OTHER BOOKS BY
PENELOPE WARD

Moody
The Assignment
The Aristocrat
The Crush
The Anti-Boyfriend
The Day He Came Back
Neighbor Dearest
Just One Year
When August Ends
Love Online
Gentleman Nine
Drunk Dial
Mack Daddy
Stepbrother Dearest
RoomHate
Sins of Sevin
Jake Undone (Jake #1)
My Skylar (Jake #2)
Jake Understood (Jake #3)
Gemini

OTHER BOOKS BY
PENELOPE WARD & VI KEELAND

Well Played
Park Avenue Player

Stuck-Up Suit
Cocky Bastard
Not Pretending Anymore
Happily Letter After
My Favorite Souvenir
Dirty Letters
Hate Notes
Rebel Heir
Rebel Heart
Mister Moneybags
British Bedmate
Playboy Pilot

AcKNOWLEDGEMENTS

First and foremost, thank you to my loving parents for continuing to be my biggest fans.

To my husband: Thank you for your love, patience and humor and for finally seeing this as more than a hobby! You take on a lot of extra responsibilities so I can continue to write.

To Vi: I am so happy to have found the other half of my brain! Thank you for your invaluable friendship, support and chats.

To Allison, who believed in me from the beginning: You manifested all of this!

To my besties, Angela, Tarah and Sonia: love you all so much!

To Julie: You are the best writer I know and an even better friend.

To Erika G.: It's an E thing.

To Luna: Thank you for your passion, the beautiful teasers that help motivate me and for loving Jake!

To my editor, Kim: Thank you for your undivided attention to all of my books, chapter by chapter.

To my facebook fan group, Penelope's Peeps and to Queen Amy for running the ship: I adore you all!

To Aussie Lisa: We'll always have George. You live way too far from me.

To Mia A.: How did I ever write before I had you to sprint and procrastinate with?

To Allison E.: The song *Demons* is in here because of you. Your love of Jake helped push me to write this book.

To all the book bloggers/promoters who help and support me: You are THE reason for my success. I'm afraid to list everyone here because I will undoubtedly forget someone unintentionally. You know who you are and do not hesitate to contact me if I can return the favor.

To Elaine of Allusion Book Formatting and Publishing – Thank you for being the best proofreader and formatter a girl could ask for.

To Letitia of RBA Designs: Thank you for another stellar book cover.

To my readers: Nothing makes me happier than knowing I've provided you with an escape from the daily stresses of life. That same escape was why I started writing. There is no greater joy in this business than to hear from you directly and to know that something I wrote touched you in some way.

Last but not least, to my daughter and son: Mommy loves you. You are my motivation and inspiration!